# Something UNEXPECTED

SPLIT ROCK RANCH

RORY MAXWELL

Published by Rory Maxwell Writes

www.rorymaxwellwrites.com



Cover Design and Interior Layout: Rory Maxwell

Editing: Alicia Z. Ramos

Proofreading: Charity VanHuss

# Contents

For Sylvia, my first fan, without whose undying support this book would not have been possible.

# PROLOGUE

NICK

NICKY URGED PEPPER FASTER along the old trail, bent low to avoid the branches whipping by. The compact mare snorted with exertion every time her hooves hit the packed dirt, the familiar rhythm nearly enough to drown out Nicky's racing thoughts. The cool morning air—so different from home—stung his flushed cheeks. It made his eyes burn and well with moisture until the world was nothing but a blur. The wet streaks on his face were just because of the wind. He wasn't crying.

Pepper dodged something on the trail, and Nicky gasped. His fingers dug, white-knuckled, into the saddle horn as he nearly lost his seat. Still, he didn't ask her to slow. He had to go fast. He needed to outrun his aunt's words, outrun her wet, red eyes and crumpled expression.

Outrun the news that his mom was—

Nicky loosened his grip to dash at his eyes, fighting the tightness choking his lungs. No. It wasn't true. It couldn't be. His mom was coming to get him. They were going to have a Mom-and-Nicky week before they had to drive back to New

York and Dad. Her bright, smiling face would greet him. She would hug him tight and exclaim over how tall he was getting. He was sure he'd grown a lot in the last month. Aunt Maggie said all the boys in their family had a big growth spurt around thirteen, and Nicky was right on track. He wanted his mom to see him. She was tiny, and she'd be so surprised that he was taller than her now.

He dug his heels into Pepper's sides, and the quarter horse sprang forward with a jolt. A sob caught in his throat, and he didn't see the stream until it was too late.

Pepper, well-trained animal that she was, launched herself across without hesitation. Totally unprepared for the motion, Nicky found himself airborne, the blurry world tumbling past. He braced himself for a sudden stop as the ground rushed up, but instead, he splashed down into icy water.

The world went quiet. Water filled his ears, blocking out everything but the fast thud of his heart. The cold was shocking, and for a moment he was frozen, staring up at the sunlight glinting off the surface of the creek. Then his lungs heaved for air, and he launched himself upright, breaking the surface with a gasp.

"Ugh," he groaned and struggled to his feet, shoving his dark, wet curls out of his eyes as he took stock. He rotated his wrists and ankles carefully. Nothing seemed to be broken. He was lucky, he guessed. The stream was deep where he landed. A few yards in either direction and he would have come down in the rocky shallows instead, and that would have hurt. As it was, he was more stunned than anything. He didn't think he'd even scraped the bottom.

Splashing out of the water, he tried to get his bearings. "Pepper?" he called, scanning the trail for movement. God, he hoped she was okay. She was nearly twenty and hadn't ever been a jumper.

The forest was quiet apart from the babbling creek and the chirps of early morning birds. He figured the fact that Pepper hadn't stopped was a good sign. At least she hadn't fallen when he did.

Suddenly exhausted, he sank down on the sandy bank, his wet jeans stiff and uncomfortable as they bunched against the backs of his knees. He tugged off one boot, then the other, pouring the water from them and propping them upside down against a rock. It was gonna suck if he had to walk all the way back in those. He hugged his knees to his chest and dropped his forehead to rest on them. The breeze picked up, rustling the leaves overhead, and he shivered. A red-tailed hawk cried. His mom's favorite. Nicky's breath caught painfully in his throat.

They *had been* her favorite.

His heart cracked, grief crashing over him as he finally broke down, muffling his sobs in his sodden jeans.

"Oh, honey. Are you hurt?"

Nicky stirred at the sound of his aunt's tired voice. He wasn't sure how long he'd been sitting there. Long enough that his clothes had started to dry. His nose was clogged and his head was pounding, but the burning tears had slowed to a trickle. He shook his head in response to her question.

"Okay. Up you get, then." Strong, calloused hands gripped him under the elbows and lifted him to his feet. She might be small, but Aunt Maggie was strong from working with thousand-pound animals her whole life.

Nicky kept his head down and tried to turn away, wiping at his wet cheeks.

Wiry arms pulled him into a hug tight enough that it was almost painful. "Hey," his aunt said, her voice firm. "You don't have to hide it. You're allowed to be sad. I'm going to miss her too. So much." She pressed her palm to the back of his head, holding him close.

Nicky sniffled and hid his face against the sharp edge of her collarbone, wishing he could smell the comforting scent of horses, hay, and leather, but he was too stuffed up from crying. "It hurts," he managed to choke out.

"I know. I know it does, Nicky." The nickname made him flinch. Only his mom and Aunt Maggie called him that. She shifted her hold, steadying him as he put his boots back on before leading him toward Diego, who was ground tied a few yards away. Nicky hadn't even heard her ride up. Seeing the other horse made him remember his own.

"Pepper?" he asked.

"She made it back to the barn just fine. Scared the dickens out of me when she came out of the woods without you, though." She gave him a squeeze.

Nicky let out a relieved breath. "I fell in the creek. I'm glad she's okay."

"Well, she could definitely use a good rubdown and some treats when we get back. She had a rough morning."

The corner of Nicky's mouth tried to curl up, but he couldn't quite manage a smile. Maggie urged him up into the saddle, then swung up behind him. It had been a few years since he'd had to ride double with a grown-up, and it felt awkward until her arm came around his waist and squeezed him tight.

"Ready?"

Nicky shut his eyes, because he wasn't ready at all, but nodded. It wasn't like he could hide out in the woods for the rest of his life.

"It's gonna be okay, honey. I know everything feels awful right now, but I promise it won't hurt this much forever."

Nicky's lower lip wobbled, and his eyes burned again. That didn't sound right. There was a gaping hole inside him where his mom should be, and nothing was ever going to fill it back up.

"I know you don't believe me, and that's okay. Just remember that I'm gonna be here for you, no matter what."

Nicky let out a shaky breath and relaxed into the movement of the horse under them and his aunt's comforting arms around him.

*Pick up the fucking phone, Nick.*

Nick took his eyes off the road just long enough to read the text. Yeah, no. Xavier was the last person—well, second to last—he wanted to deal with right now. The drive was bad enough without his ex-husband in his ear, judging his life choices. He let the call that followed go to voicemail. He'd call Xavier back when he actually had something to say to him.

The device started vibrating again almost immediately. With a growl, Nick pushed the button to silence it. Except he hit it too hard, and the phone slipped from its holder and tumbled down into the footwell, where the buzzing of incoming text messages continued.

Goddammit.

After a late start out of the city and bad weather turning the interstate into a parking lot, Nick had given up and spent the night in a shitty motel just south of Richmond, deeply regretting his decision not to fly into Greensboro and rent a car from there. Unable to sleep, he'd gotten back on the road early. Five hours and another rainstorm later, he was finally nearing his destination. At least the rain had tapered off once he hit Boone. The skies had cleared, but the mountain roads were a mess with remnants of the storm. Luckily, the weather seemed to have kept most people home, a fact he was grateful for as he swerved left to avoid a broken branch in the road. The last thing he needed was to get stuck out here in the middle of bumfuck nowhere. The roads weren't even traveled enough to rate a painted yellow line, just too-narrow, unmarked blacktop.

That probably wasn't fair. Split Rock, North Carolina, the closest town to his destination, had a population of just over four thousand according to the Welcome sign he'd passed a few miles back. And he knew they did well with tourists in this part of the state. The Blue Ridge Mountains were beautiful by anyone's standards. Still, as far as Nick was concerned, nothing with a population under a hundred thousand could be considered civilization.

"In five hundred feet, turn right onto Split Rock Road," the GPS's mechanical voice intoned.

Fucking finally.

Most of the turn onto the side road was underwater. As Nick was determining the best path around it, he glanced up to see a box truck barreling over the rise. The driver laid on their horn, as if Nick had anywhere to go. The asshole was in the middle of the road, not even trying to keep to his own side. Only quick reflexes and a car that was built to be responsive allowed Nick to swerve before he was hit head on.

Nick swore as he went into the massive puddle too fast and at a bad angle, sending up a sheet of water. The steering wheel was nearly ripped from his hands as he bounced through what felt like several craters—punctuated by the horrible scraping sound of metal on asphalt—before coming to a shuddering stop.

His heart thudded in his ears as he stared at the fence inches from his headlights and the peaceful grassy field beyond it. Fucking fuck. He dragged in a breath that shook more than he would ever admit and took stock, determining quickly that he wasn't injured, then forced his hands to unclench from the steering wheel. He pushed the button to turn off the engine and listened to the click of hot, settling metal in the sudden quiet. A glance told him the truck was gone. It hadn't even slowed down.

Fucker.

Now what?

"You have arrived at your destination," the GPS announced.

Damn it all to hell. Could this day get any worse? He let out a breath, steadier this time, and levered himself out of the car to take in the damage.

Avoiding the truck had forced him through the giant, rain-filled pothole. Its depth was mostly hidden by the water, but it was bad enough to have flattened both front tires, twisting one of them to a worrying angle. The only positive was that he'd ended up off the road and out of the way of any other reckless drivers. Nick let loose with a volley of curses and spun away from the damaged car, then nearly lost his footing on the slick ground and had to grab the door to stay upright. Regaining his balance, he wanted to kick something, but experience reminded him that wouldn't do anything but leave him with a throbbing foot in addition to a long walk.

See? he told the mental version of his ex. Thirty-four years old, and he'd finally learned some impulse control.

Directly across from him was a large sign—hand-painted but professionally done—that read "Welcome to Split Rock Ranch," and next to it, a wide gravel driveway bordered by lush green grass. The white farmhouse he remembered from his childhood was just visible past a low rise and a bend in the road. He didn't recall the driveway being so long, but his memories of those distant summers were hazy at best.

Sticking his keys into his pocket, he slammed the car door with a little more force than necessary and slid on his sunglasses. A half dozen careful, squelching steps got him off the soggy shoulder and back onto the blacktop. Hopefully, someone at the ranch would know where he could get a tow. He grimaced at the chances of any local shop stocking parts for an Audi. He carried a spare tire in the too-small trunk, of course, but no one on earth drove around with two. And he didn't want to think about what the accident had done to his rims—or the axle, for that matter.

The spring sun was warm on the shoulders of his leather jacket, and steam rose from the damp earth as he trekked toward the house. The scent of hay and animals that wafted on the gentle breeze was a sucker punch of nostalgia. They said scent was the strongest trigger for memory. How many summers had he spent here growing up? Four? Five? It had come to an end when his mom died, and Nick hadn't been back once in the twenty years since.

It looked the same. The two-story farmhouse with its cream-painted siding, dark metal roof, and deep front porch hadn't aged a day. Nick climbed the front steps, noting that a few of the boards looked new and freshly painted. Off to one side was a small seating area. On the other, an old porch swing rocked gently in the breeze coming off the mountains. Before Nick knew what he was doing, he had walked over to run his hand along the back, the raised wood grain rough and familiar under his fingers. It conjured memories of cool summer evenings with a throw pillow under his head and one foot on the ground to keep the lazy motion going while he read his way through the books Maggie kept for him on the lowest shelf. She'd had all his favorites, like *The Black Stallion* and *Man O'War*. He could almost hear her laughing as she teased him about reading in the dark.

He stepped back abruptly and returned to the front door. He had a job to do and didn't have time for a stroll down memory lane. The screen was shut, but the door behind it was open. Nick knocked firmly, then, after a moment, rang the bell, listening to the chime echo through the house.

For a moment it was silent and dark inside. Then he heard the click of claws on hardwood, and an older border collie trotted into view. When it reached the door, it sat and looked up at Nick, tail swishing against the floor, tongue lolling from its mouth in a happy smile. It was gray around its eyes and nose. Nick knew it couldn't be one of the dogs he remembered, not after twenty years, but it warmed his heart at the same time as it put an ache in his chest.

"Morning, bud." He crouched down and held a hand up to the screen for the dog to sniff. "Where's your mama, huh?"

The dog huffed in reply, stood with a shake, and ambled away.

Well, that answered exactly nothing, didn't it? What did he expect, asking the fucking dog? Nick waited a few more minutes, but despite the open door, it was obvious no one was home. He shook his head. Country life was bizarre. He couldn't imagine leaving his front door open in the city. His apartment would be empty of furniture and taken over by squatters within an hour.

With a resigned sigh, he headed for the dirt path leading down the hill to the barn's big double doors. The path had been carved into the grass from years of Maggie and her employees making this same trek. It was muddy from the rain, but his leather loafers were already a lost cause, and Nick was relatively sure the barn was where he would find people this time of day.

The large building looked newer than he remembered. Maggie must have had it renovated at some point—it was too familiar to have been rebuilt completely. It was still two stories tall, with cream siding to match the house and dark trim. Flower baskets hung on each side of the entrance. The path Nick was on hit the driveway just before a large, gravel parking area. To the left was a sand riding ring; to the right, the white fence that surrounded the bright green fields. He could see horses grazing a few hundred yards out, well before the start of the blue-tinged mountain range that framed the property.

Nick stepped through the open barn doors and into the dim aisle with some relief. The sun against his leather jacket had started to become uncomfortable. He removed his sunglasses, hooking them on his shirt collar. At the far end of the aisle, someone stood just inside an open stall door. Nick made his way over. "Hello," he called when he was still a handful of yards away.

The woman didn't look up, still raking wood shavings over the stall floor, so Nick repeated himself louder and waved a hand, hoping to catch her peripheral vision.

That earned him a startled gasp as she scrambled backward, the rake held defensively in front of her. "What the fuck?" she muttered, eyes darting past Nick to search the space behind him.

Nick winced as contrition warred with amusement at the over-the-top reaction. He held his hands up, palms open, schooling his face to be as open and friendly as possible. "I'm unarmed."

The woman blinked several times.

"I'm looking for Margo Lauder?" Nick tried again.

"What?" she asked, somewhere between wary and annoyed as she loosened her grip on the rake and tugged an earbud from one ear.

"I'm looking for Maggie," Nick repeated, trying not to let any hint of laughter sneak into his tone. He wasn't going to risk anything. That rake looked sharp.

The woman's grip on the rake loosened, and she lowered it to her side. Nick breathed out slowly. The last thing he needed was to get assaulted by a horse girl. Xavier would never let him hear the end of it. She was cute—now that she wasn't threatening him—in a farm-fresh kind of way, with big gray eyes, freckles scattered across her nose and cheeks, and brown hair gathered in two unraveling pigtail braids. She was dressed for barn work in jeans, work boots, an oversized flannel shirt, and heavy gloves.

"I'm not Maggie," she finally responded, frowning at a spot just over his left shoulder. "I'm Alice Beckett."

Nick wondered for a moment if she was being deliberately uncooperative but dismissed the idea. There was something about her blunt tone that pinged in his awareness. "Hi, Alice. I'm Nick. Do you know where I can find Maggie?"

She tilted her head and squinted, eyes darting to his face and then away again. "Is she expecting you?" she asked, her tone implying the answer had to be no. She wasn't wrong.

Nick held back a frustrated sigh. "I'm not sure." Not at all, was the truth. He'd sent an email before he left home, but he'd kept the details vague. It wasn't the kind of conversation he wanted to have digitally. Hell, it wasn't the kind of conversation he wanted to have at all, but that wasn't up to him. He was just the messenger.

A messenger who was caught between a rock and a hard place and was pretty sure no one around here was going to feel very forgiving once he delivered said message. He hoped none of them had an itchy trigger finger.

"Well," Alice said, "she's not here. I'll let her know you stopped by." She moved toward the stall door, then faltered when she realized Nick's much larger frame was blocking her escape route. Nick stepped out of her way, moving back to give her space. She edged out of the stall and looked past him toward the parking area, forehead creasing. "Did you… walk here?"

Nick sighed. Great. Not only was he about to become public enemy number one, but he was also going to have to figure out transportation. All for a trip he never wanted to make. This was just not his day. "Only from the driveway."

"Oh," Alice said, expression clearing. "That's good. The road is really bad because of the storm."

"I noticed. Unfortunately, it was after my car ended up in a pothole with two flats."

She shook her head. "I told Archer it was better not to drive through it. He can't afford new tires right now," she said, sounding vindicated. Nick raised an eyebrow, and it took a moment, but she seemed to refocus. "Right. You should call a tow truck." She pulled out her phone, removed her gloves, tapped rapidly at the screen, and then rattled off a phone number.

Nick reached for his own phone but came up empty. He growled a curse, remembering he'd left it buzzing on the floorboards. "My phone is still in the car."

Alice blinked at him several times, let out a put-upon sigh, and asked, "What's your number?"

Nick gave it to her, bemused by her take-charge manner.

"Okay. Archer will call a tow truck for you, 'cause I hate talking on the phone." She looked up at him, and her eyes narrowed. "I wasn't flirting with you, by the way. When I asked for your phone number. I'm not interested."

"I didn't think you were. And don't worry. My type runs more toward six-pack abs and a hint of stubble."

Alice cocked her head, one of her braids slipping over her shoulder. "Oh," she exclaimed after a pause. "You're gay."

Nick had to laugh. "I am. I was even married to a man for a while."

Alice nodded, the remaining tension leaving her shoulders. "That's good. Now I don't need to worry about you attempting to flirt with me."

Nick leaned back against the wall next to the stall door. "*Attempting* to flirt?" Nick smiled to let her know he was joking. "I'll have you know I'm great at flirting."

Alice shrugged. "You're probably not." She seemed to rethink what she'd said. "I'm not saying you're lying on purpose. Just that most people are really bad at it." She turned away and grabbed the wheelbarrow. "I guess you'll have to wait, since you don't have a car."

"Thanks." Nick followed as she moved to the next stall. "So, Archer's your boyfriend?"

Alice pulled a face so disgusted that Nick had to fight not to laugh. "No. He's my brother." She gave an exaggerated shudder.

"Nice of him to drive you to work."

"He has to. I don't drive, because it's way too stressful. People break the law all the time, and you never know which one is going to do it. And there aren't enough police around here to arrest them all. Just today, I saw someone roll through a stop sign." She shook her head like she couldn't believe some people.

"You should never visit New York, then. Most people there think traffic laws are more like... guidelines."

Alice narrowed her eyes at the stall floor. "That sounds like my version of hell." She started raking the shavings.

"How long have you worked here?"

She flicked her head, tossing a braid over her shoulder and glancing back at him, eyes narrowed. "Are you going to talk at me the whole time?"

Nick chuckled. "Only until you tell me to get lost." He wouldn't tell her, but he was enjoying their back-and-forth. So much of his life was about choosing the perfect words. Her straightforwardness was refreshing, and he liked the fact that she wasn't expecting him to flirt with her.

Alice sighed, long-suffering. "Thirteen years."

Nick whistled. She didn't look old enough to have been working that long. "And you like it?"

She glanced out the stall window at the horses grazing in the wide, green field, and her face broke into a smile of pure pleasure. He found himself smiling in response. "Yes. It's perfect for me."

Nick's smile faded, guilt stirring in his gut. Doing this was going to suck even more than he expected.

"He's fine," Micah repeated flatly, torn between relief and frustration.

"Perfectly fine," Keegan confirmed. "The X-rays came back clean. He even hopped off the table when we were done."

Micah glared at his husband's border collie, who looked back with big, guileless brown eyes, his—not broken—front paw held awkwardly off the ground. "You're such a drama queen, Milo."

Keegan chuckled and took a sip of his coffee, then grimaced and put it down again. Micah had watched him pour it an hour ago, so it was past cold. "You're not wrong. But I suggest you tell Ryan to watch where he puts his big feet, or the next time, Milo might not be so lucky."

Keegan was doing them a favor, so Micah refrained from making a "You know what they say about big hands and feet" joke to his husband's best friend. Even if it was true. "He does it again, and he can bring the little shit in while I help Izzy fix fences and check the trails."

Keegan hummed in agreement as he opened the door out to the waiting room. "That storm was wild. I ended up with two terrified bed partners. I thought I was going to have to sleep on the floor."

Micah snorted a laugh, imagining Keegan trying to share the bed with two very large and excitable German shepherds. "You know, this is why you're still single. The fur babies always get preferential treatment. No man wants to compete with that." He danced out of the way of the shove Keegan aimed at his shoulder.

"Keep it up, Avery, and I'll charge you full price after all."

Micah shot him a cheeky grin. "Sorry, Dr. Reid. I promise to have your favorite beer for family dinner?"

Keegan sighed and rolled his eyes. "Get out of here, brat. And tell your husband he owes me."

Out in the parking lot, Milo refused to jump into the truck, forcing Micah to lift forty-five pounds of squirming black-and-white dog with a grunt. Damn mutt was solid muscle. Micah threw hay bales around all day, but they didn't usually wiggle so much. He gave Milo a dirty look and closed the door.

His day had started out so well. There was nothing better than waking up to a lazy morning blow job followed by a mug of fresh coffee in bed and the news that his husband had already been out to feed the animals. Four hours later, he felt as if he should have just pulled the covers back over his head.

It wasn't all the dog's fault. Milo wasn't responsible for the storm that rolled through during the night and took down part of the far pasture fence. Ryan scrambling out of bed when Izzy pounded on the door to let them know about the damage and stepping on the dog's paw in the process wasn't his fault either. But the pitiful whimpering and refusal to put weight on the paw was definitely the little asshole's fault.

"I could have been out helping Ry and Izzy, but no. You're convinced you're maimed for life." He stroked the dog's silky head, getting a playful lick to the inside of his wrist in the process. "I think you just wanted to visit Keegan. We all know he's your favorite." It was a good thing that the vet liked Milo—and was also Ryan's best friend. Otherwise, the X-rays would have put a serious dent in their monthly budget.

He slowed at the turn that would take him either into town or back to the ranch. He had a few errands to run, but he'd left Alice alone, and she wasn't a fan of the tourists who occasionally drove in hoping to pet some horses. Though the state of the road this morning would dissuade all but the most determined.

Fishing his phone out of the cup holder, he dialed Ryan and put it on speaker. It rang through to voicemail, like he expected, which meant he and Izzy were still out.

*You've reached Ryan Avery. Leave a message, and I'll get back to you as soon as I can.*

Even after three years of marriage, hearing Ryan call himself "Avery" still gave Micah a thrill. He'd only been in love with the man since he was old enough to recognize that he was more into boys than girls. And now Ryan was his forever.

"Hey, babe. Just wanted to let you know your dog's a dramatic asshole, and I'm stopping in town to pick up Keegan's beer and the barbecue he likes. We owe him big-time. Again."

He pulled into the parking lot that serviced the grocery store, the feed store, and the gas station. Mac Finnegan, the feed store owner, was sweeping the front walkway and nodded in his direction. Micah waved in reply.

"I hope the trails aren't too bad. When you get back, we need to deal with the fucking pothole again." He threw the truck into park and let his head thump against the headrest. "It's totally washed out. I thought I was gonna have to pull an Oregon Trail and ford the damn thing." The pothole was right at the end of their driveway. It was technically a county road, but the county was understaffed, and it could be weeks before they got out to fix it. He and Ryan could pack it with gravel in the meantime and hopefully save their customers some tire damage. "Anyway, we can talk about it later. I hope you and Izzy are having a better morning than me. Love you, see you soon." He smacked an obnoxious kiss into the phone that he knew would make Ryan roll his eyes and try not to smile. The man loved him, even when he was being ridiculous.

He hopped down from the truck, followed by Milo, who suddenly had full use of both front paws. Micah sighed and threw up his hands. "Just wait until your father gets home," he told the dog before heading toward the store.

Milo trotted happily next to him until he saw Mac. Then he looked up at Micah with big, pleading eyes and whined. Micah sighed. "It's not like you've earned it, but go ahead." Milo gave a happy whuff and raced off toward the shop owner.

"Morning, sir," Micah called with a wave. "I'll just be a minute."

Mac waved back and paused in his sweeping to dig a treat out of his apron for Milo, who sat, wiggling happily, at his feet.

Micah grabbed a basket at the door and tried not to stall, not wanting the dog to bother the old man for too long. He grabbed Keegan's beer and an IPA for Ryan, then stopped in the meat department.

"Morning, Micah," Mrs. Ellis called as she slung what looked like half a pig onto the carving counter. "How's your dad?"

Micah grinned. "Morning, Mrs. Ellis. He's good. Still hates the Tar Heels but watches every game."

Mrs. Ellis, who had worked in the store as long as he could remember, nodded in understanding. "You tell him Mr. Ellis wants him over for dinner next week. It's been too long, and I could use a night off from pretending I care about baseball." She got the carcass in place and turned to him. "Now, what can I get you? A center cut for Dr. Reid's brisket?" Her lips curled up, and her eyes twinkled.

Micah's jaw dropped. "How did you..."

"Jean was in here half an hour ago. She saw your truck parked in front of the vet's office. How's the puppy?"

"He's a drama queen and perfectly fine, apparently." Micah rolled his eyes despite his amusement. You'd think after living in this town for every one of his twenty-five years—apart from the three he spent in college—he'd be used to the gossip pipeline. But they still managed to surprise him. "And yes, you guessed right. Can we get enough for six this time?"

Mrs. Ellis moved to the meat case and pulled on a fresh pair of gloves. "Is Maggie's surgery this week?"

"It's tomorrow," Micah replied. "Archer drove her to the city this morning for her pre-op appointment."

Mrs. Ellis gave a nod as she deftly portioned out Micah's order. "Well, we're all thinking about her and praying it goes well. You boys let us know if you need anything, because heaven knows Maggie won't say a word."

Micah laughed and agreed. Maggie was fiercely independent. It was honestly surprising that anyone in town knew she was having surgery.

"Your dad have the night off Sunday?" Mrs. Ellis asked.

"He's supposed to. If he doesn't make it, I'll take dinner over to him." His dad had a busy schedule down at the station, and he was the kind of guy that switched shifts with his officers when they needed him to. He said it was something his father-in-law, Micah's granddad, had done, and that was the kind of sheriff he wanted to be as well. Micah was proud of how much everyone there loved him, and it was worth the occasional changed plans if someone needed to stay home with their kid or take their wife to a doctor's appointment.

Micah waved goodbye to Mrs. Ellis and promised to pass her regards along to Maggie, and his husband, and his dad. He finished up his shopping—they didn't need much other than food for family dinner—and headed for the checkout. He made it out of the store without getting pulled into any more conversations and crossed the parking lot to retrieve his dog.

Mac was nowhere to be seen, so Micah dropped his bags off in the truck and ducked into Finnegan's Feed and General Store to track Milo down. He found him lounging on a dog bed behind the front counter with a massive marrow bone propped up between his front paws. Mac's grandson, Corey, was looking on, bemused, from his spot at the register.

"I see how it is," Micah said to Milo, making Corey startle. "You're just a whore for treats."

Corey grinned, then ducked his head to hide the expression.

Milo froze with his mouth half open around the bone, fangs poking out from under his lips, and raised his eyes to Micah.

Micah snorted and shook his head, then turned to Corey. "Sorry, I got held up talking to Mrs. Ellis. I didn't mean for you to have to puppysit."

Corey glanced up from under his fringe of dark hair. "It was no problem. Milo's a good boy." As always, it was hard not to stare at his eyes. They were a striking green, except the left iris was split, the lower half pale blue. Ryan said it was called "partial heterochromia." Micah just thought it was cool.

"Still, I appreciate it," Micah said.

Corey's pale cheeks went pink. "I, um—"

Micah didn't get to hear what Corey had to say, as Mac chose that moment to walk out of their stockroom, tying on his apron. "Good morning, young Avery," he said, his voice warm and inviting as always. "What can we get for you today?"

Micah had to grin. Mac had been bemused to hear that Ryan Astor was taking the Avery name and instantly dubbed him "Mr. Avery." "Just getting my dog, and apparently the bone he's claimed." He gestured to the treat that Milo was once again gnawing on.

Mac waved him off. "A gift for our favorite customers." He turned to Corey. "Has the rest of Mr. Avery's order come in?"

Corey shook his head. "Not until next week."

Mac nodded like he knew that already. "I'll send Corey by when it gets here. Apologies again for the delay."

The phone rang, and Mac headed off to answer it. Micah frowned. He didn't think they were expecting another order.

"A few things were out of stock the other day. Mr.— Your husb— I—I mean..." Corey flushed red and shut his eyes. "Mr. Avery said it was fine and to bring them by when they come in."

Micah repressed a laugh. "You can call him Ryan. He prefers it." Corey's striking eyes opened and flicked up to Micah's face. "Though, personally, I like 'your husband.' It really rolls off the tongue." He gave Corey a wink and got a shy smile in return. "And I hope you're still calling me Micah. I'm only three years older than you, Corey."

Corey lifted a hand and rubbed the back of his neck. "Yeah. Of course."

He was cute, and Micah had noticed when a little rainbow flag sticker appeared in the corner of the shop door around the same time Corey came back from college. Micah wondered if he was seeing anyone. Maybe they could set him up with Keegan? He'd seen the way Corey watched the vet when they were both at the ranch at the same time.

He grabbed a couple more of the rawhide bones for the dogs and gestured for Corey to ring him up—it didn't feel right to leave the store empty-handed. As he headed toward the door with Milo happily trotting next to him, bone in tow, Corey called out, "It's Finn."

Micah paused and looked back in question.

"I go by 'Finn.' Corey was too..." He licked his lips nervously. "It's just that it's kind of a kid's name."

Micah tilted his head, then glanced in the direction Mac had disappeared.

"Granddad still calls me Corey—he's not so good with change—but my friends all call me Finn." He scrubbed his palms against the sides of his thighs and sucked his lower lip into his mouth, then seemed to notice what he was doing and released it again.

Micah gave him a warm smile. "Got it. I'll let Ryan know. Thanks, Finn."

He got a brilliant grin in return that turned the kid from cute to gorgeous. Micah was definitely gonna let Keegan know, too, just in case.

# SOMETHING UNEXPECTED

The switch from the off-season to the tourist season was always kind of a mindfuck. Their little mountain town had changed a lot since Micah was a kid. Back when his mom was alive, they couldn't walk down the street without stopping multiple times to say hello to someone they knew. Everyone was warm and always up for a visit—something Micah had both loved and hated as an impatient elementary schooler. Sometimes you just wanted to get to the ice cream shop without waiting while Mom chatted with a friend's mother, who wanted to know all the latest gossip.

And sometimes you went on ahead without asking and got in the most trouble of your life when you got lost on the way and Dad and all his coworkers had to come looking for you. Micah didn't get any ice cream for a week after that.

Sometime in his early teens, things had started to get busier, with tourists flooding town on the weekends and eventually building summer homes on what used to be empty lots. It was great for the town's economy, and Maggie's business had picked up enough that she needed to hire a ranch manager to run the day-to-day. Which was when Ryan came along.

Micah had been a lot less interested in anything happening in town after that. As an adult he could appreciate the changes more. The town council had worked hard to balance tourism with the small-town feel that everyone loved, and Micah liked to think they'd been successful.

The drawback was the traffic. It was Art in the Park week, a twice-yearly gathering of regional artists selling their craft, and he was literally inching along as cars with out-of-state tags searched for parking on the flower-basket-lined main street. Milo rested his head on the car windowsill and heaved a sigh.

"I know, buddy," Micah said, reaching out to give him a pat. "Remind me not to come into town on event weeks, would you?"

The road eventually opened up, and Micah was able to maneuver his truck through the last of the traffic and escape the crush of people.

His cell rang just as he was turning onto the main road out of town, and Archer's face flashed on the screen. Micah was hit with a bolt of worry. Had something gotten off track with Maggie's surgery? They'd been waiting months for the specialist who was doing her hip replacement. It was supposed to be as straightforward as these things got: a day or so to recover in the hospital, and she'd be released on Monday or Tuesday. It was too early for something to have gone wrong, wasn't it? He hurriedly shut the window and turned down the music, sending the call to Bluetooth. The car was old, but Ryan had insisted on upgrading things, so Micah wasn't driving with the phone in his hand. "Arch?" he answered, trying to keep the anxiety out of his voice.

"Hey, man." Archer's tone would have read as normal to anyone else. Micah knew him too well, though.

"What is it? Did the doctor—"

"No, no," Archer promised quickly. "It's all good. Allie just texted me."

Micah had sagged in relief but now straightened again. Alice could manage most things on her own, but not all of them, and she was the only one at the barn this morning. "Everything okay?" He pressed his foot harder against the gas pedal, taking the road out of town a little faster than he normally would. It was just like Alice to text Archer, hours away, instead of Micah who was right in town.

"Everything's fine, but it sounds like some guy wrecked his car at the end of the driveway, and now he's waiting to talk to Maggie."

Micah frowned. He'd known that pothole was going to cause problems. Hopefully, whoever it was wasn't blaming Maggie for the accident. "Some guy?" he repeated. "No other details? Did she tell him Maggie won't be back until next week?"

He could practically hear Archer's eye roll. "You know how she is."

Alice tended toward blunt, and her texts were short and to the point. "Wonderful. Well, I'm on my way back now."

"Good." Archer sounded relieved. He didn't like his twin stressed out, and dealing with strangers wasn't something Alice enjoyed. "Maggie just went into her pre-op appointment. I'll let you guys know when she's done."

Micah pushed away his worry. Maggie had assured him everything would be fine, and the doctor at Duke was one of the best in the country. “Don’t worry,” he told Archer. “I can handle whoever it is. They probably just need a tow.”

Archer agreed, and Micah said goodbye to focus on the road. Hopefully, Alice had everything under control.

NICK BALANCED ONE KNEE on the driver's seat and reached into the footwell, fishing around for his phone. He'd seen it bounce when it fell, but who knew where the hell it ended up after that. He twisted, trying to feel under the seat, his other hand braced on the center console. His fingers grazed the hard edge of the case, just out of reach.

"Come out here, you little piece of shit," he snarled, stretching a little farther.

"Oof," a man said from behind him. "I'd hide from you, too, with that kind of language."

Nick jumped, and his hip hit the steering wheel, making the horn blare. The sound was startling enough that he jerked upright and smacked his head on the ceiling. "Ow. *Goddammit.*"

The man behind him let out his own curse. As Nick squeezed his eyes shut and waited for the flare of pain to subside, he heard footsteps squishing closer though the muddy grass. "Are you okay? Shit. I didn't mean to scare you. I thought you heard me drive up. My truck isn't exactly quiet."

Nick collapsed into the driver's seat, one hand pressed to the back of his head. "I was too busy cussing out my fucking phone."

Said phone chose that moment to start buzzing angrily again. Nick groaned and let his head fall against the seat. Whoever was calling—and there were really only two people it might be—could wait until his head stopped throbbing. He wasn't interested in talking to either of them anyway.

"Here," the man said, voice rich with concern. "I can grab it." Squelching footsteps circled the car, and a moment later the passenger door was pulled open. After a few grunts and some scrabbling, the man let out a triumphant "Aha!"

Nick looked over and met warm brown eyes, smiling at him from a face good-looking enough to catch even Xavier's attention. The man was crouched just outside the passenger door, holding Nick's wayward phone, his generous mouth curved in a grin, brown hair messy like it hadn't seen a brush that morning. He was younger than Nick had expected based on the timbre of his voice, maybe in his mid-twenties. His sharp jawline showed hints of stubble. Possibly he'd been running late, because his shirt was off by one button and looked like he must have grabbed it off the floor. Nick wouldn't be caught dead in something so wrinkled, but, he reminded himself, this was the country.

"Thank you," he finally said, taking the phone from the man's outstretched hand.

"No worries." The man tilted his head to the side. "You okay? Alice didn't mention if you were hurt when you hit the pot-hole." His gaze lifted to where Nick was still rubbing the back of his head.

"I'm fine," Nick said, letting his hand fall and examining the stranger anew now that it was clear he was somehow connected to the ranch. "And you mean 'were forced into the pothole.' I was perfectly happy to go around it, but a box truck had different plans."

The man winced. "Ugh. Yeah, some of the drivers out here are a menace. They think they own the roads." He held out his hand. "I'm Micah. I'm one of the horse trainers here."

Nick shook it, the warm, rough palm sliding against his own. *Big hands*, he noted, gripping a moment too long and watching Micah's eyes to see if his interest was returned. "Dominic Lauder, Nick to my friends. Your boss is my aunt."

Micah's eyes widened, as did his smile. "Oh my god. You're Nicky?" He squeezed Nick's hand in excitement. "What are you doing here? Does Maggie know? She's gonna be so happy to see you!"

Shit. Nick wasn't prepared for that response, or to explain himself to one of Maggie's employees. "I sent an email to let her know I was coming. She may not have seen it."

Micah frowned and rested his toned forearms on the sides of the doorframe. "She must have missed it. She and Archer, Alice's brother, already left for Durham."

Nick did his best to keep the flare of annoyance hidden. Durham was at least three hours away. Of course she was out of town when he was here on a time limit. He rubbed a hand over his face and ignored the increased throbbing in his temples. "Could you give me her cell number? I only have the house phone, and she doesn't seem to answer that anymore."

"We got rid of it when we renovated. But you can't call right now anyway. Archer said she's in her pre-op appointment."

Nick stilled. "Pre-op?"

Micah's head tilted in confusion. "For her surgery?"

"What?"

"That's not why you're here?"

Nick's stomach sank. "No. I had no idea. What surgery?" And why hadn't Phillip given him a heads-up? Maybe it was something minor that wasn't worth mentioning. But if so, why was she all the way in Durham? There were closer hospitals.

"She's finally having her hip replaced."

Nick tried not to let his surprise show. The timing had to be an unfortunate coincidence. His father might be a demanding asshole, and he tended to lack empathy for anyone other than himself, but he wouldn't set this up and send Nick all the way down here when Maggie wasn't even in town.

"It's been planned for months. You really didn't know?" Micah sounded unsure and shifted back on his heels.

Nick thought fast. No need to raise suspicions with his aunt's employees. Not when Nick didn't have answers to any potential questions—not answers he was able to share, anyhow. "She probably just didn't want me to worry."

It was a weak excuse, but Micah seemed to accept it, giving a huff of amusement. "That sounds like her. Still, she'll be thrilled that you're here."

Nick swallowed his first response, which was swift, sarcastic denial, and gave Micah his most charming smile. "I'll be glad to see her." That part was true, at least. His aunt had always been his favorite relative, and he'd let too much time pass. If only his visit were under better circumstances.

Micah stood and brushed his hands down the front of his jeans, giving Nick a nice view of muscular thighs. "Let's get your stuff, and I'll call Joey to tow your car to the shop." He shut the door and started squelching his way back around to the driver's side, talking the whole time. "Do you have a place to stay? You should stay with us. We have plenty of room."

Nick had a refusal on his lips as he swung his legs out of the car. There was no way he was staying with Micah and whoever else "us" was. If he was staying anywhere, it would be with Maggie. But really, that was a terrible idea. He should just book a hotel—

As he stood, the leather sole of his shoe slipped on the wet, muddy grass, and he lost his balance. He bit back a yelp and flailed for the doorframe, but missed.

Oh, fuck his luck.

Before he could do more than skid sideways, strong hands grabbed his biceps and helped him catch himself against the side of the car. He blinked down at Micah, his heart racing. Damn, the man was *strong*. He was compact, and a handful of inches shorter than Nick, but his grip was solid.

"You good?" Micah asked as he peered up at Nick, his brown eyes mirroring the humor trying to twist his lips.

Nick huffed, hoping it hid his sudden embarrassment. He was definitely wearing the wrong shoes for this. "Yeah. Thanks." He slid his phone into his pocket for safekeeping as Micah let him go.

Micah stepped back at the same time that Nick shifted and again found no traction. He sucked in a sharp breath as the movement sent him right into Micah, who stumbled.

With no way to stop it, they tumbled to the ground, Nick landing on top of Micah, who hit with a laughing "oof," though catching Nick's weight had to be painful. Nick tried to push himself up, wetness soaking into his knees. "Goddammit," he bit out, glancing around for a way out of this mess.

Micah was still laughing, sprawled on his back in the mud. Nick stalled, caught by the way the sun turned Micah's eyes amber and his wide grin showed off his generous mouth and perfect teeth. He was gorgeous in a way that Nick—who was more familiar with polished, celebrity beauty standards—wasn't used to. He had good bone structure, sure, and Nick had felt just how toned the body beneath him was, but there was something about the way his features came alive with good humor that made Nick look again. And then keep looking.

Micah flopped his arms out to the sides, spread before Nick like an offering, his chest still rising and falling as his laughter ebbed.

Nick frowned. "Aren't you getting soaked?"

Micah shrugged. "Yep. But it's too late to do anything about it now. And I'm stuck until you get off me."

Nick didn't want to get off him. In fact, he wanted to get closer. To trace that smiling mouth with his thumb and see if Micah's plush lips were as soft as they looked. Then he reminded himself that picking up pretty young things wasn't why he was here, and that sobering thought got him moving. "Apologies," he murmured, carefully getting back to his feet with only a little more sliding. He thought about offering Micah a hand up but was waved off.

"Save yourself. I'm already a goner."

Nick chuckled but agreed and managed to pick his way across the grass and back to the more secure footing of the road.

Micah rolled to his hands and knees, giving Nick a great view of his ass, then climbed to his feet, leaving one dirty handprint on Nick's fender as he steadied himself. The back of his shirt was wet enough to cling, showing off the defined vee from broad shoulders to narrow hips. Nick swallowed and almost missed Micah asking him if he needed anything from the car.

He only had a small suitcase and a laptop bag, both of which Micah retrieved. "There's a garage in town we can have it towed to," he told Nick. "They deal with a lot of fancy tourists' cars. I'm sure they can get it fixed up in no time." He stepped carefully over to the road and set down Nick's suitcase, handing over the laptop bag. His boots were thick with mud but looked a lot more resilient than Nick's loafers, which were basically destroyed. Having rescued Nick's things, Micah pulled out his phone and made a call before Nick could protest. It was just as well, Nick figured as he brushed at the dirt and grass clinging to the palms of his hands, then attempted the same with the knees of his pants. He didn't have a better solution, and his car wasn't drivable. If this mechanic couldn't fix it, he could have it towed to someone who could—probably in the nearest city.

In the meantime, Nick needed to find a place to spend the night that wasn't with the much-too-tempting Micah. He retrieved his phone from his pocket and started looking for a hotel the tow truck driver could drop him at.

A minute later, Micah got off the phone. "He'll be here in an hour or so. He's got to deal with the traffic in town. He said he'd come up to the house to get your keys if you don't want to leave them here." He grabbed Nick's suitcase and started toward a vintage, baby blue pickup that Nick hadn't noticed before.

Nick closed his hand over Micah's on the suitcase handle. "I can wait here. It's fine."

Micah frowned, his brow creasing in confusion. "Why?"

Nick blinked. "I don't want to intrude. I'll just have the driver drop me at a hotel."

Micah rolled his eyes. "You think Maggie would ever let us hear the end of it if you stayed in town when there's a perfectly good guest room here?"

That made Nick huff a soft laugh. No. No, she wouldn't.

Maybe it would work out. He'd have a few days before she got back, and by then he might have something approaching a plan.

"Besides, with Art in the Park week starting, I doubt you'd find a room within fifty miles." Reaching the truck, Micah lifted Nick's suitcase into the bed with ease. When he pulled open the driver's door, a black-and-white blur flew out and beelined for Nick. "Damn it, Milo," Micah snapped. "Stop!"

The blur skidded to a halt at Nick's feet and dropped flat to the ground, revealing itself to be another border collie, this one younger than the one up at the house. It gave Nick a tongue-lolling, doggy grin, its tail wagging so hard its whole back end was moving.

Micah trudged back to Nick with a sigh. "Sorry," he said. "I promise he's better trained than that. He just loves new people and hasn't had a chance to get his energy out yet this morning."

Nick crouched down to let the dog sniff his hand, then stroked his head. "Milo?"

"Yeah. He's Ryan's. He was a birthday present last year."

Milo pushed himself back to his feet when he saw Micah and lifted one front paw off the ground, hind end still wiggling.

"Oh, no you don't," Micah said pointedly. "I saw you. No going back on it now."

Milo gave a short bark, and Micah pointed to the truck. "In the back. I'm done babying you."

Milo shook himself, then bounded over to hop up into the back of the pickup.

Micah chuckled and explained their morning at the vet. Ryan's dog sounded like a lovable disaster. Micah led the way to the truck, and Nick fell into step next to him before realizing he'd been distracted from the debate about where he was going to stay.

"Honestly, are you sure staying in Maggie's guest room isn't a problem? I would feel better asking her first."

Micah just waited with raised eyebrows until Nick gave in and climbed into the cab. "First of all, it's totally fine. And second, you're not staying with Maggie. You're staying with me and Ryan."

Nick didn't get to voice his protest before Micah continued.

"Maggie doesn't live in the farmhouse anymore. When her hip got bad and she couldn't do stairs, we fixed up that old cottage off the back. It only has one bedroom. Ryan and I moved into the house, and Izzy took the spot in the apartment over the barn. So it's technically our guest room you're staying in, which means no one to ask permission from."

Nick took that in, trying to remain neutral. He wasn't sure if staying with Maggie's employees made things more complicated or less. "Not even your roommate?"

"My...? Oh." Micah laughed and flashed his left hand in Nick's direction. Then he frowned at it. "Shit. I forgot my ring." His eyes flicked to Nick, then back to the road, a blush darkening his cheeks. "Ryan's my husband."

Oh. Damn. Now that he was looking, Nick could see the faint band of paler skin where a wedding ring would normally sit. He pushed down the sudden flare of disappointment. It wasn't like it mattered. He'd already told himself the pretty horse trainer was off-limits. Still, it was a shame. He would have made a nice distraction while Nick was dealing with his responsibilities here. "And he won't mind a surprise houseguest?"

"Nah," Micah said. "We have friends in and out all the time. It won't be a problem. You can stay as long as you want."

Maybe this kind of thing wasn't a problem out in the country. Nick struggled to picture it.

As they traveled the long driveway, Micah pointed out things that might have changed in the years since Nick had last been at the ranch: the different fields assigned to their main herd of trail horses, the mares and foals they were breeding, and the smaller paddocks for the horses that belonged to outside clients that Micah trained for.

The whole operation was larger and better organized than Nick remembered. He didn't know what he'd thought he'd find when he got here, but this well-run business wasn't it.

Closer to the farmhouse there were two riding rings, a round pen, and the large, refurbished barn. Split Rock Ranch had fifty horses on site at the moment, he learned, though they only owned forty-five of them, and ten of those were foals and young horses that would eventually be sold. Ryan was the ranch manager, and Micah's official title was head trainer, though it sounded like he doubled as an all-around assistant to Ryan.

Nick found himself impressed with the work that went into the business. As a kid, he'd only been aware of the lessons Maggie taught and the foals she raised. Micah said they typically had five to eight trail rides going out per day on the weekends—though they'd cut back this week, with one of their lead riders away helping Maggie with her surgery appointments.

Micah drove with one arm hanging out the window and the other braced against the wheel. Nick found his eyes focusing on Micah's forearms, which were tan and lean with ropey muscle and a dusting of fair, sun-bleached hair. Nick had never thought himself much of a forearm man, but in this case, he was making an exception. Something about the rolled-up sleeves was working for him. Who knew?

"After last night's storm, Ryan and Izzy are out checking the trails and making repairs to some of the fences. Luckily, we don't have any rides scheduled until this afternoon," Micah said as he parked in front of the farmhouse and hopped out, grabbing Nick's suitcase again before Nick even had his door open.

Milo leapt from the back of the truck and bounded up the steps to the front door, waiting impatiently as Micah and Nick followed. They left their muddy shoes on a mat outside. Nick briefly mourned his designer loafers and tried to remember if he'd packed anything that would hold up to all this mud. He was sure the answer was no. He was supposed to be comfortably checked into a hotel by now.

"I'm gonna get cleaned up," Micah said with a gesture to his wet and muddy clothes. "Then I'll start lunch. Make yourself at home. There are drinks in the fridge, and Ry and Izzy should be back soon." He took Nick's bags with him, promising to put them in the guest room, and disappeared up the stairs.

Nick took the opportunity to look around, taking in the changes. He loved how they'd opened up the first floor of the house by expanding the doorways. It wasn't open concept, but it made the rooms feel bigger than he remembered. The furniture was different—which made sense, not only because twenty years had passed since he was last there, but with new residents as well. Micah and his husband had good taste. The leather couch was flanked by two large chairs, the seating arranged around the big stone fireplace that was the same as Nick remembered. The TV hanging over the fireplace was new, but again, flat-screens weren't a thing back in the day. All the furniture was overstuffed and looked perfect for sinking into after a long day of hard work. It couldn't be more different from the mid-century modern furnishings in his condo at home.

As Nick headed for the kitchen—which looked to now include part of the old dining room—the older border collie he'd seen earlier trotted in and plopped itself down in his path. He bent down to give it a pat, and its tail thumped against the wood floor eagerly. "Hey there, bud," he murmured, giving it a good scratch behind the ears. A quick flip of its collar showed its name to be Rascal. Appropriate, from what Nick remembered of the breed and what he'd seen of Milo. They were full of energy.

When Micah returned, Nick had made it into the kitchen and settled at the counter with something that tasted suspiciously like his aunt's famous lemonade. Micah had changed his clothes and run a brush through his messy brown hair. He cleaned up well, and the bolt of attraction Nick had felt before hadn't been a passing thing. Micah was gorgeous. He was also wearing his wedding ring. That was enough to remind Nick to get his libido under control. No need to make things awkward.

"The house looks great. Seems like you've put a lot of time into it," he said, biting back the comment he wanted to make about the way Micah's jeans fit him.

Micah flashed him a bright grin and went to pull sandwich fixings from the fridge. He set the ingredients on the island across from Nick and started assembling the food. "We made a deal with Maggie when we moved in two years ago. She refuses to charge us rent, so we've been working on fixing things up for her instead."

"Well, it looks great." Micah and his husband were obviously doing a lot for Maggie—making improvements to the house was only part of it. It sounded like they had been better family to Maggie than he had. Nick ran his hand over the wide stone countertop. "You can't be all work and no play, though. What do you do for fun?"

"Sometimes we go riding," Micah replied without a hint of irony.

Nick was trying to school his expression into something that wasn't dismayed when Micah burst out laughing.

"Oh, man. Your face." He shook his head, mirth shining in his eyes. "We do normal stuff. Hit up one of the bars in town, see movies. Sometimes I can even get Ryan to go dancing with me." His expression turned dreamy and a little lovesick. "He swore our wedding was the last time, but I can get him out on the dance floor if I tease him enough." He gave Nick a playful smile that Nick returned wryly.

Nick knew that he'd never stood a chance with the pretty horse trainer, but seeing how in love the guy was with his husband took some of the sting away. "He's the jealous type, is he?" Nick teased.

Micah shot Nick a conspiratorial look and leaned in like he was sharing a secret. "He pretends to be, 'cause he knows I like it when he gets all possessive." Micah waggled his eyebrows, making Nick release an honest chuckle. "But it's an act. He knows he's it for me, just like I am for him."

Nick forced a smile, even as his chest ached with phantom pain. He couldn't imagine having that kind of bond with someone. His marriage to Xavier certainly hadn't been anything like that. "Sounds like a pretty special guy."

Micah's smile was soft as he looked down at his wedding band. "He's the best. I couldn't ask for a better partner. He made my dreams come true."

For a moment, Nick despised everyone in his family: his father for the choices he'd made, his aunt for putting herself in this position, and himself for being involved at all. Micah and his husband didn't deserve what was coming. Neither did Alice. They were good people.

And Nick was a fox sneaking into the henhouse.

MAGGIE'S NEPHEW WASN'T WHAT Micah expected. After years of hearing about him, Micah had thought Nicky Lauder would be less... slick. None of the old pictures Maggie had from when Nicky—or Nick, as he went by now—was a kid did justice to the man he'd become. On Maggie's hall table there was a framed shot of tiny Nicky riding one of Maggie's old ponies. In the photo, Nicky's mom, a pretty, dark-haired woman, stood next to him holding the reins.

These days, Nick was tall, maybe even taller than Ryan, with styled brown hair and a dark five o'clock shadow, despite the fact that it was only lunchtime. His clothes screamed, "My monthly salary is twice your yearly income," from his fancy shades all the way down to his now ruined leather loafers. Micah felt a little bad about that, but really, who wore nice shoes to a ranch in the spring? *Nicky* might have known better, but the little boy with dirt on his cheeks and scuffs on his boots was apparently long gone. Grown-up Nick was someone else. A handsome someone else, Micah had to admit. After all, he was married—but he wasn't dead.

He would have to have been six feet under not to notice the rock-hard biceps under his hands or the firm chest pressed to his own when they went sprawling in the wet grass. Micah had been lucky Nick was so distracted, or he might have noticed Micah's highly inappropriate blushing at their too-intimate position. The last thing he wanted was for Nick to think Micah was interested in something he wasn't. He was blissfully married and ridiculously in love with his husband. His body just got a little confused: usually, being in that position meant sexy times in the near future. He'd shaken it off quickly, and thankfully, Nick hadn't clued in. The last thing Micah wanted was to make things awkward with Maggie's nephew. Especially since he was their guest now.

Micah wondered if he should call Archer and give him a heads-up about Nick's arrival, but he decided not to. Knowing Maggie, she'd rush home as soon as she was out of surgery, when the doctor wanted her to stay in the city for a few days until he could clear her for the drive back.

No, the call would have to wait. They'd have some time while Nick's car was being repaired. If Maggie wasn't back by the time it was ready, they'd have to convince him to stay longer. Maggie would love that. It would be a great coming-home surprise.

Micah was just finishing up the lunch prep and chatting with Nick about the long drive from New York City, where he currently lived, when he heard footsteps on the porch and his husband's voice. He grinned and left Nick in the kitchen as he jogged to meet Ryan and Izzy at the door. "Hey. How'd the repairs go? Were the trails a mess?"

Izzy came in first and ruffled Micah's hair. "Everything's good. How was your lazy morning?" He only got away with the hair ruffling because at six foot three he was really freaking tall, and also because he was one of Micah's closest friends.

"Ugh," Micah responded, ducking away. "I'll show you lazy." He gave Izzy's arm a shove and grumbled, "Asshole."

Izzy laughed and slipped by him, making room for Ryan to step through the door. Micah's husband immediately grabbed him around the waist and drew him into a deep, searching kiss.

Micah melted, one hand gripping Ryan's strong shoulder, the other coming up to stroke his cheek and neatly trimmed beard, loving the feel of it under his fingers. He kissed back for all he was worth, losing himself in Ryan's taste and the rich, masculine scent that surrounded him.

"Mmm," Ryan said as they separated. "Didn't get enough of you this morning, what with everything going on. That's much better."

Micah grinned into his sky-blue eyes, his heart fluttering happily. "That all you needed?" he teased. Because *Micah* had gotten a good-morning blow job—even though that felt like days ago—but they'd had to scramble out of bed before he could reciprocate.

Ryan cupped his cheek and stroked it with his thumb. "You know the answer to that."

Micah leaned up on his toes to smack another kiss to Ryan's lips. "Flirt."

"Right back atcha." Ryan kissed him again, then said, "So, we have a visitor?"

Micah let him go, even though he would have been happy to make out in the doorway all afternoon. "You got my message, then. He's in the kitchen. Come on." He grabbed Ryan's hand and led the way.

Izzy was at the fridge, filling glasses with Maggie's lemonade. Nick turned on his barstool, then stood when he saw Ryan and Micah.

"Since I just met Izzy, I assume you're Ryan," he said. "Nick Lauder." He held out his hand, and Ryan stepped forward to take it. Nick's eyes flicked down and then up again, checking Ryan out so subtly that Micah wouldn't have noticed if he hadn't been watching for it. Micah fought to hold back a vindicated grin. It was a long-standing debate between them. Ryan didn't notice the effect he had on others. He would say Nick was just surprised by the age difference between him and Micah, but Micah knew better. He'd seen the appreciation, quickly hidden, in Nick's gaze. Yeah, Micah's husband was smoking hot, and he loved pointing out when other people noticed. It made Ryan's ears darken in the cutest way.

"Nice to meet you. Sorry to hear about your car."

Nick's answering smile was more of a grimace. "Micah here was kind enough to help me get it towed and offer me your guest room while they figure out whether it can be fixed locally."

Ryan raised an eyebrow at Micah, making him second-guess his decision. "What? We have plenty of space."

Ryan shook his head. "Did you forget about the bathroom?"

"Oh, shit." He totally had. He glanced at Nick, who returned the look with a concerned crease between his eyebrows. "We're in the middle of remodeling the guest bathroom. It's a mess right now. There isn't even a toilet." He dragged a hand over his face, feeling terrible. How distracted was he that he forgot about a whole-ass bathroom?

"It'll work out, baby," Ryan said, squeezing him close and dropping a kiss on his temple. "I'm sure Nick won't mind sharing ours for a few days."

Nick met Micah's eyes and shrugged. "As long as it's not an inconvenience."

Micah let out a relieved breath, glad he hadn't screwed that up too badly. "Of course not." He let Ryan go to the sink to wash up and rounded the island to help Izzy with lunch.

Nick glanced toward the front door. "No Alice?"

Micah shook his head. "Nah. She likes to eat later than the rest of us."

"And for the kitchen to be less chaotic," Izzy added as he reached over Micah's shoulder to snag a ham sandwich. Damn it. Izzy knew that was Micah's favorite. He grabbed for it and missed, ending up in a brief wrestling match, which he lost. Panting and tugging his T-shirt straight, he mock-growled at Izzy and settled for turkey instead. Turkey was healthier anyway.

"She likes her downtime to be quiet," Ryan added as he settled onto a stool next to Nick.

"And to have breaks from 'peopling,'" Micah agreed.

The four of them chatted while they ate. Nick turned out to be an entertaining storyteller, and they all made appropriate sounds of commiseration as he recounted his battle with the pothole. No one, not even Nick—who seemed to find a lot more humor in the situation in retrospect—could hold back their laughter when he described his realization that Ferragamo loafers weren't designed for muddy countryside.

Ryan filled Micah in on the trail repairs, and Micah told him the resolution to the dog drama from that morning.

Ryan sighed and shook his head. "We're damn lucky Keegan likes us."

Micah nodded. "I got his favorite beer at the store. And yours. Oh, by the way, Corey Finnegan told me he goes by 'Finn' now, and I think we should set him and Keegan up." Micah grinned at Ryan's eye roll. "What?"

"You know Keegan hates it when you do that."

Micah shrugged. "Sorry, not sorry? He's a great guy. And hot. And Corey—sorry, Finn—is so freaking adorable. I bet they'd be cute together, and I'm almost positive Finn's interested."

Izzy made a sound of disgust and shoved the last bite of sandwich into his mouth.

"Shut up, Izzy," Micah said. "No comments from the peanut gallery." Izzy refused to tell Micah what his problem was with Keegan, but the two of them had never gotten along. It was basically a fact of life at this point. Mention Keegan to Izzy and you'd get a scoff or a snarky comment. The other way around and Keegan tended to scowl and change the subject.

"All right," Izzy said agreeably. "I'm gonna head back to work, then." He grabbed the last sandwich and wrapped it in three paper towels, just the way Alice liked it, and slipped out, whistling for the dogs to follow him.

"Sorry about that," Micah told Nick. "Izzy..." He trailed off, not sure how to complete the sentence without making his friend sound like a jackass.

"He and Keegan clash," Ryan filled in. That was one way to put it.

"I think it's more complicated than that, but close enough." Micah hopped down from the island and started cleaning up the lunch mess.

Ryan stopped him with a hand on his shoulder. "Our guest looks like he might like a chance to relax. Did you put out clean towels for him?"

Micah gave him a confused look, then understood when Nick smothered a yawn. "Oh, shit. Sorry. I'm a terrible host."

Nick offered him a wry grin. "The trip's just catching up with me. It was a long drive, and the motel I ended up in last night had more springs than padding in the mattress." He pressed his thumb and index finger to his eyes for a moment, pinching like he was fighting a headache—or maybe just that grittiness that happened when you'd been staring at the road too long.

"Then it's definitely nap time," Micah said, grabbing Nick a glass of water and leading the way to the guest room. "Our room is right across the hall. Feel free to use the bathroom in there anytime."

Nick raised an eyebrow. "Anytime?" he echoed teasingly.

It took Micah a second to catch up. Then he flushed and gave Nick a dirty look. "If we're... busy, we'll lock the door," he said, eyes narrowed.

Nick chuckled and held his hands up in surrender. "Got it."

Micah rolled his eyes. "You're kind of an asshole, aren't you?" he accused, mostly joking.

"Oh, absolutely." Nick gave him a sharklike grin, but Micah could see the exhaustion behind the expression and wondered how much of that cockiness was a mask. How much of the little boy with the scuffed boots and dirt-stained cheeks was still hiding under all the glossy polish? Would Micah get to see more glimpses of him over the next few days?

He put those questions out of his mind as he made his way back downstairs. It wasn't his business what Nick was hiding, or why.

Micah found Ryan in the kitchen, finishing the lunch dishes. He walked over and slid his arms around his husband's trim waist, hugging him from behind.

Ryan shut off the water, dried his hands, and put one over Micah's, holding him in place. "So, Nicky Lauder finally came home."

Micah rested his cheek in the space between Ryan's shoulder blades. "He never exactly lived here, I don't think."

Ryan turned in his hold and looped his arms around Micah. "Did he say why he's in town?"

"He said—" Micah frowned. Now that he thought about it, Nick *hadn't* said. "I figured it was because of Maggie's surgery, but actually, he didn't know about that." Micah tried to remember if Nick had mentioned anything at all about his visit. He couldn't come up with an answer. "I forgot to ask. Oops?" He looked up at Ryan, who just shook his head, used to Micah barreling forward without all the details. He and Alice were two peas in a pod some days.

Ryan leaned down and dropped a kiss on his neck. "I'm sure we'll find out why he's here soon enough."

Micah hummed and tilted his head back, giving Ryan more room. In response, Ryan slid a hand into Micah's hair and kissed his way up his throat until he could claim his mouth, deep and hungry.

Micah moaned into it, his whole body coming alive as Ryan's tongue explored. God, his man could kiss. It never failed to set Micah on fire and make his toes curl in his socks. He reached down, skimming his palm over the bulge in Ryan's jeans.

Ryan hissed, his grip tightening on Micah's hair. "Baby," he warned.

Micah grinned. That didn't sound very convincing. "How much time do we have?"

"Not enough. Twenty minutes before I have someone coming to look at one of the mares for breeding."

Micah's grin turned dirtier. "Breeding, huh?"

Ryan gave him a narrow look and a smack on the ass that was sadly muted by his pants. He squirmed anyway, hoping for more.

"Sorry," Micah said—he definitely wasn't sorry. He got Ryan's pants open and dropped to his knees.

Ryan blew out a breath and leaned against back the cabinets, palms braced on the counter. "You sure you wanna do this right here, baby?"

Micah looked up, seeing the tension in Ryan's body, the way his pupils were dilated with want. "Worth it," he answered, then opened his mouth and swallowed Ryan down. The tip slid smoothly across his tongue, and the salty-bitter taste made Micah groan happily. He'd do this all day if Ryan would let him. Well, maybe not *all* day, 'cause then his jaw would hurt, but it was the thought that counted.

It wasn't often they could get away with a post-lunch quickie—and never in the kitchen—but Maggie was hours away in the city with Archer, and Alice and Izzy wouldn't come up to the house without a reason. Yeah, there was a guy sleeping upstairs, but the stairs squeaked. They'd hear him if he started to come down.

Micah took Ryan's cock deep and sucked firmly as he pulled back.

It was Ryan's turn to groan, though he tried to muffle it. He sank his fingers into Micah's hair and tugged just right. After four years together, Ryan knew exactly what Micah liked and was always happy to give it to him. Not only sex, but everything. From the little moments, like making his coffee in the morning, to the big ones, like taking on Micah's least favorite chores so he didn't have to do them. Ryan never stopped showing Micah he was paying attention, and Micah loved nothing more than doing the same for Ryan.

Micah's cock throbbed, and he fumbled to release it from his pants before he made a mess of them. Fuck, yes. That's what he'd missed when their morning got cut short. He reached up to grip the denim bunched at Ryan's thighs, encouraging him to go harder, to take what he wanted.

The sounds in the kitchen devolved into soft panting and bitten-off groans as Ryan held Micah's head and fucked into his mouth, over and over. Micah's cock twitched and pulsed between his thighs at the treatment. He loved this, loved it when Ryan took control and used Micah for his pleasure.

Ryan pulled out and smeared his cock across Micah's lips. "God, you're so fucking gorgeous like this." He thumbed Micah's cheek. "Love seeing you all dirty for me."

Micah smiled and opened his mouth wider, tongue chasing after Ryan's taste as he peered up at him. "Love it," he managed to get out, his voice rough from his abused throat. "Love you."

Ryan rewarded him with a slow, deep thrust. Micah groaned and swallowed him down eagerly, his body tingling with his approaching orgasm. Micah wasn't exaggerating—he loved Ryan's cock in his mouth almost as much as he loved it in his ass. Loved anything to do with sex and his ridiculously hot husband. Just sucking Ryan off was enough to push Micah to the edge.

The rhythm built as Ryan got closer, and Micah took it easily, swallowing around him until he felt Ryan's thighs tense and start to tremble under his palms, his cock swelling slightly in Micah's mouth. His eyes flicked up and met Ryan's, and Ryan gritted his teeth and came, hands tight in Micah's hair, cock buried deep in his throat.

Micah groaned as the taste flooded his mouth, and he reached down to grip his own erection. A few quick tugs sent him over the edge, his eyes rolling back, pleasure washing through him in waves.

He was still shaking with it when Ryan pulled free and crouched in front of him. "My good boy," he murmured, brushing kisses to Micah's trembling lips as he panted for air.

Micah hummed, the praise sinking in and making him feel warm all over. With his eyes still closed, he turned his head to chase Ryan's lips until he got a real kiss.

After a few minutes to get their brains back online, Ryan helped Micah to his feet. They shared another kiss, then Micah ducked around him to the sink. He'd had the wherewithal to cup his hand and collect the mess, so cleanup was easy enough. He washed his hands and face, then tucked himself back into his pants. He grinned when Ryan wrapped around him from behind and squeezed him tightly, a mirror of their positions from earlier.

"I'm a lucky, lucky man," Ryan said as he pressed a kiss to Micah's jaw.

Micah grinned and turned his head to kiss him back. "Damn right you are."

The rest of the afternoon flew by. He only realized the sun was lower in the sky when he saw Nick making his way down the hill from the house.

Even dressed in jeans and a V-neck, with his hair sleep-mussed, Nick still managed to look like he was headed to a photo shoot. Micah found himself wondering what Nick did for work, because from what he could see, it allowed him to spend a lot of time at the gym.

"Get some sleep?" Micah asked when Nick was in hearing distance.

Nick nodded. "Too much, probably. The mechanic calling woke me up." He ran a hand through his hair, which was starting to curl around his ears now that it had been slept on. Micah had the strange urge to mess it up further, to see what Nick looked like when he wasn't quite so put together. He bit the inside of his cheek to distract himself and get his focus back on when Nick was saying. "He thinks it'll be a week or so before he can get my car fixed. He has to order parts."

Micah made a face of sympathy, even though he was internally cheering. Nick sticking around for a week fit his plans nicely. "That sucks. Are you gonna have to miss work?"

Nick waved that off. "I can work remotely. But I'm not going to impose on you and Ryan for that long. Once the art festival is over, I'll find a place to stay in town."

Micah scrunched up his nose. That again. If Nick could work from here, there was no reason for him to leave. And if he stayed, Micah and Ryan could get to know Maggie's favorite family member. If Maggie were here, she would insist on it. Since she wasn't, the job fell to Micah. "No way. You're here already, and we have the space."

Nick still looked skeptical, so Micah pulled out the big guns.

"You keep talking about a hotel, and I'm going to tell Maggie."

That earned him a chuckle that was half groan. "Fuck," Nick said as he dragged a hand over his face. "Manipulative little shit." Micah smirked, pretty sure he'd won. Nick still looked troubled, but he gave in, "for now."

With that out of the way, Micah dragged him to the tack room to find him some boots. The leather loafers were beyond a lost cause. Luckily, an extra pair of Archer's work boots fit him well enough. While they were finishing up, Ryan came out of the office.

"I spoke with the town manager about getting a crew out to work on the road. It's gotten to the point where it's actively dangerous, and our patches aren't doing much good. He said he'd try to get someone to look at it."

Micah made a sound of disgust. "He'll *try*? It's his damn job," he huffed. "I miss Mr. Jones. He would have had it fixed right the first time."

"He's still getting a handle on the job. It's only been a few months since he took over," Ryan reminded him, though Micah knew his patience was wearing thin too. "If they aren't out soon, I'll top it off with some more gravel and try to make it a little safer in the meantime."

"Feel free to give the city my car repair bill and the number for my lawyer," Nick offered from where he was lacing up his borrowed boots. "I find threats quite effective when dealing with bureaucrats."

"I may do that." Ryan leaned against the tack room door. "Looking good, Nicky," he said in a tone that made Micah snicker.

Nick rolled his eyes as he straightened. "I wasn't planning to be in town long enough to need outdoor gear." He kicked his toes against the concrete floor, checking the fit. "Believe me, if I'd known I'd be trekking through muddy fields today, I would have packed differently." He seemed almost put out by the teasing. Still, what did he expect? He came to a ranch and didn't think he'd need boots?

"Well, you're staying with us now, so you better be ready to get nice and dirty," Micah said, then winced when he heard himself.

Ryan coughed to cover his laugh as Nick's eyebrows went up.

Crap. Micah's face flooded with heat. "That came out wrong," he insisted as Ryan shook his head in amusement and Nick's mouth curled into a smirk that made Micah want to squirm.

"Just say the word, sweetheart," Nick said, reaching out to give Micah a teasing pat on the cheek. "I'll show you how dirty I can get." He shot Ryan a wink as Micah groaned and shoved his arm away.

"Ugh." He took it back. Nick wasn't "kind of" an asshole, he was *definitely* an asshole. But for some reason Micah couldn't quite stop a grin from forming.

# FIVE

## NICK

NICK STRETCHED AND ROLLED over when his phone buzzed on the nightstand. He groped for it but missed and had to pry open his eyes. Not his nightstand. Not his bedroom. That was right, he was in the Blue Ridge Mountains, at Split Rock Ranch. No wonder it was so quiet. He couldn't remember the last time he'd slept without the hum of traffic outside his window. Maybe when he and Xavier went skiing in Crested Butte a few winters ago.

He finally managed to snag his phone, but it had gone silent. He dragged down on the screen enough to see the missed calls from both Xavier and his father before groaning and dropping the device on the mattress next to him. No. Not right now.

He has slept hard, and the clock told him it was later than he would usually wake up. Unsurprisingly, given their predawn wakeup time, Micah and Ryan weren't exactly night owls. After a relatively quiet dinner, the three of them—Izzy had driven Alice home, then gone out with friends—had settled on the deck with beers and gotten to know each other. Though Micah had grown up in town, he'd spent a few years in Boston for college. Ryan was from Florida originally but had spent his high school years at a boarding school in New England, then gone to college in Southern California. After a few years working for his father, he'd moved here, and the rest was history. Nick had a hard time wrapping his head around leaving the city for life in the middle of nowhere, but Ryan and Micah seemed to have found their place. And he had to admit there was something about watching the horses graze in the fields while the moon rose over the mountains that unknotted his shoulders and made him feel lighter than he had in months, if not years.

Still, after his nap the previous afternoon, Nick had struggled to sleep. In the end he'd gotten some work done before passing out around midnight to the sounds of the old house settling and an owl softly hooting in the distance.

Now the house was silent. With a groan, Nick rolled himself upright and hung his legs over the side of the bed. His bare toes just brushed the cool wood floor, and the high mattress reminded him of being a kid and waking up to the smell of pancakes and coffee, of Aunt Maggie and the dogs moving around downstairs.

Clad only in his boxers, Nick ducked across the hall to the en suite. He had used the half bath on the first floor the night before and hadn't really taken in Micah and Ryan's bedroom, but now he had a moment to appreciate it. They'd kept the style of the old farmhouse but updated it with clean-lined furniture and soft colors, and the result was warm and inviting. A chair next to the bathroom door had clothes draped over it, but the room was otherwise neat and organized.

The bathroom was large and spacious, newly remodeled with a walk-in shower and a long vanity complete with two sinks. Here, he could easily see the personalities of his hosts. One of the sinks had soap, a toothbrush, and toothpaste neatly arranged next to it. The other was more chaotic, with supplies scattered across the counter. If Nick had to guess, he'd say the chaotic one was Micah's, and the more orderly belonged to Ryan. He might be stereotyping a little, but he doubted it. Micah's energy didn't say neat-and-tidy the way Ryan's did.

After getting ready, Nick grabbed his borrowed boots and headed downstairs. A brief search proved the house to be empty.

Nick was just stepping onto the back deck when his phone rang again and his father's name flashed across the screen. He bit back a groan and answered. He knew it wasn't worth putting off any longer. "Phillip."

His father's voice came through the phone clear and strong. "How was the drive, son? I take it you made it to the ranch?"

It was hard to say if his father was actually concerned about his drive or if that was a reprimand for not calling as soon as he got in. But Nick was used to things like that with him. "No trouble. I got here yesterday around lunchtime."

"Good. Good," his father said absently. "And how did Maggie take the news?"

Nick forced himself not to tense. "I haven't been able to talk to her. She's out of town."

Phillip tutted, but his voice lacked surprise. "Unfortunate timing, but it can't be helped. We still need to move forward."

Nick bit the inside of his cheek to stop himself from making accusations. That Phillip had to have known Maggie was having surgery this weekend. That the timing was intentional. "Dad, are you sure there isn't some other way—" he started, but Phillip cut him off.

"Don't do this to me, Dominic. You know Melissa is giving us no choice."

"I know," Nick said, hating the "us" Phillip slipped in there and the use of his given name. Nick had no say, but he was being forced to take ownership of the results. Phillip had shown him the numbers, and Nick had worked them himself just to be sure. As much as he wanted things to be different, his hands were tied.

"Russell Miller will be there early next week. Let's get this piece of the process wrapped up quickly so we're ready for the next steps."

Nick shoved his hand through his hair, his gut churning. "And what about Aunt Maggie?"

"Don't worry. Nothing will be finalized before you get a chance to talk to her. You know I wouldn't do that." His father sounded offended at the idea. "We just can't sleep on this while we wait. It's going to be what's best for everyone."

"I understand." He took a steadying breath. He wished he didn't. But if there were some way to avoid this, his father would have suggested it. "I don't like it, but I do understand."

His father made a sound of disappointment, and this time his voice had an edge that made Nick wince. “You know this is as difficult for me as it is for you.”

Nick was sure it wasn’t, but he swallowed his protest. The last thing he wanted was to start a fight that would only make things more tense. “I know, Dad.”

His father *humph*ed in disapproval but didn’t push further.

Nick was out of wiggle room in this conversation. “I promise I’ll talk to her as soon as I can.”

“Good,” his father said, the tight tone leaving his voice. There was a sound in the background. “I need to run—your soon-to-be-ex stepmother and her lawyer are waiting—but call me once you’ve spoken to Russell.”

“Sure...” Nick trailed off when the phone beeped in his ear, his father having hung up.

Nick stuck the device back in his pocket, unclenched his jaw, and rolled his head from side to side, trying to loosen the muscles in his neck. He was going to end up with another migraine if he wasn’t careful.

He crossed the deck to the stairs that led down to the yard, passing a grill, a large table surrounded by benches, and a covered hot tub. He could easily picture the people who lived and worked here gathering in the evenings to eat, drink, and relax. He had vague memories of evening meals on the deck with his aunt and the other people who’d worked at the ranch, and nights around the fire pit farther down in the yard roasting marshmallows and telling stories.

He shoved the memories away. It wasn't the time to get sentimental. He had a job to do, and his father was counting on him. Nick worked hard to live up to Phillip's expectations, even when it was painful to do so.

Nick cut through the empty barn and exited at the far end of the aisle. In the shade of a large tree near the riding ring, the dogs were stretched out on the grass. There were two horses in the ring. One, led by Alice if he wasn't mistaken, was walking a pattern through some poles laid on the sandy ground. The other was being put through its paces by Micah.

The sun was warm against his neck and shoulders, so Nick moved to the shade next to the dogs and leaned his forearms on the top rail of the fence, content to watch for a while and enjoy the spring weather. How many summer days had he spent on the back of a pony, following that track in the dirt along the fence line?

"Bring back memories?"

Nick startled as the deep voice behind him echoed his thoughts. He turned his head as Ryan stepped up and leaned against the fence next to him, folding his arms in a mirror of how Nick was standing. Nick made a sound that he hoped conveyed agreement, distracted by how close the other man was. And how handsome. He was classic cowboy, from the weathered

Stetson down to his Wranglers and boots. Nick wasn't sure when his hormones had decided the rough, outdoorsman type was hot—maybe it was a feature of crossing the North Carolina state line—but he was pretty sure Micah had noticed his appreciation back up at the house. He swallowed to unstick his throat. "I definitely found my ass in the dirt in that ring a few times."

The corners of Ryan's eyes creased as he chuckled, somehow making them look even more blue. "Micah's also intimately familiar with it."

Nick raised an eyebrow. "But not you?"

Ryan shot him a quick glance. "Nah. I prefer to stay in the saddle."

The breeze picked up, rustling the leaves overhead as Nick laughed. "I'm sure," he tossed back. "Guess an old guy like you has to be careful about falls."

Ryan made an amused sound. "I'm only four years older than you, Nicky."

The nickname sent a strange warmth through Nick's chest that he did his best to ignore. The last thing he needed was a crush on Micah's husband, even if he was ticking all of Nick's boxes. Nick had always had a thing for older men.

Though four years wasn't that much older. That made Ryan thirty-eight. Maybe it was the beard, lightly dusted with gray, that gave Ryan the more mature vibe, or maybe it was just his general air of competence. Nick was a sucker for a guy who had it all together. Just look at who his best friend–slash–ex-husband was.

But as much as Ryan was apparently his type, Nick drew the line at people who were taken. Still, there were no rules against teasing.

"Four years, huh? What about your husband?" He glanced at Ryan and was surprised to see his ears go red as he reached up to tug on the brim of his hat. Nick had learned Micah had been coming out to the ranch for a long time before he started working there. He tried to do the math, but he wasn't sure how the numbers added up.

Ryan's lips twisted in a self-conscious grin. "He's a bit younger than you."

It was Nick's turn to tilt his head. He'd assumed Micah was somewhere in his late twenties. They'd been married three years. "Thirty?"

Ryan snorted. "Nope."

Nick's eyebrows went up, but he restrained himself, barely, not sure enough of Ryan's temperament to make a dirty joke.

Ryan sighed and pulled off his hat to rub a hand over his face. Then he shoved the hat back on his head and looked out at his husband on the far side of the ring with a warm gaze. "I can practically feel you vibrating from here. You can ask."

Nick's grin was sharp. "So, how old is baby boy?"

"Twenty-five," Ryan answered.

Shit. He must have been *young* when they started dating. "Robbing the cradle, were you, Daddy?"

Ryan snorted and shot Nick an annoyed look that didn't manage to mask the humor in his eyes. "He was fifteen when we met."

Nick's eyes widened. That was a lot younger than he'd expected.

With a chuckle at Nick's shock, Ryan turned so he was leaning back against the fence with his elbows propped on the top rail, his biceps straining against his shirtsleeves. Ranch work sure was good for the body. "He always says I tell it wrong. We were friends when he was a teenager. He was our little ranch mascot. Emphasis on little—the kid was scrawny. Then he grew up, and things changed." Ryan's smile was wistful. "Boy had me snared before I knew what was happening, and the rest is history."

That was sweet enough to cause cavities. Nick felt a flare of envy. Lucky bastards. He couldn't imagine having someone like that. He pushed the thought down. No point in dwelling on it now. "So, he pursued you?"

Ryan gave a nod and smiled, flashing his perfect white teeth at Nick. "And lucky for me, he was damn stubborn about it. It took us a while, but I caved in eventually. Best decision I ever made."

That tracked with everything Nick had seen of Micah so far. The guy was a steamroller when he wanted something. A lot like Nick was, actually. Except here he was totally out of his element and unsure what his next move should be. It was a strange feeling for someone who generally didn't take any prisoners. But these were good people, and Nick was lying to them—or at least omitting something important by not disclosing why he was there.

*My father is going to sell the ranch.*

Even thinking it made him feel sick. How was he supposed to tell them—tell Maggie? He swallowed down a surge of resentment—he was doing a lot of that lately. It wasn't his decision, yet here he was, about to be the bad guy.

No matter which way he looked at it, the situation was a shitshow. Melissa—or *Queen Narissa*, as Xavier mockingly referred to her after the evil stepmother from that princess rom-com—was his father's third wife. The pending divorce meant she was legally entitled to half their marital assets. Which, as of six years ago, included Split Rock Ranch.

When he'd found out his father had purchased the ranch from Maggie without a plan in place to protect it from his money-hungry wife, Nick had been furious and completely baffled. Maggie might have needed help keeping things afloat, but there were better solutions. Solutions his father, as the CEO of an investment firm, was fully aware of. Phillip, in typical fashion, refused to talk to Nick about his reasoning, saying only it had been what was best for everyone. Nick had had to grit his teeth and keep his mouth shut when he heard that bullshit. He didn't believe for a second that Maggie knew all her options when she agreed to the sale.

Not that any of that mattered now. It was too late. Melissa was demanding her share, and Phillip had no choice but to sell the ranch.

Ryan bumped Nick's arm, distracting him from his spiraling thoughts, and held out a bottle of water dripping with condensation. Nick took it, realizing his throat was bone-dry. He cracked it open and let the cool liquid soothe him as he focused past the ring to the fields that stretched toward the mountain. A handful of mares and foals were grazing nearby, and he could just see the roof of the springhouse. He tried to imagine this place as anything but his aunt's ranch and felt his jaw clench, the constant dull throbbing in his temples getting stronger.

From the corner of his eye, he caught a glimpse of Ryan watching him as he took a sip from his own water bottle. It made the back of Nick's neck prickle with awareness—whether good or bad, he wasn't sure.

"When was the last time you were on a horse?" Ryan asked.

Nick froze, having to consciously redirect his thoughts. God, it had been years. He'd been a decent rider as a kid, but he was long out of practice. Still, as Micah trotted past, the sound of hooves pounding on dirt, the creak of leather, and the huffs of the working animals took him right back. He could almost feel the motion of the big animal under him, the soothing sway of its back and the slide of supple leather through his hands. "I took lessons up through high school, but finding the time after college got difficult. Working for my father keeps me busy."

Ryan hummed and took another long pull of his water, his throat bobbing distractingly. Nick probably should have looked away, but he let himself enjoy the view instead. It had been way too long since he had eye candy as tempting as Ryan—or

Micah, for that matter. Too bad for him they were both unavailable—and unlikely to give him the time of day once they learned about the sale.

"We'll have to get you out while you're here. The trails are beautiful this time of year."

It took Nick a moment to get his head back in the conversation—god, he couldn't concentrate for shit today. Horses, right. He shifted uncomfortably and took another sip to hide it. He doubted Ryan's offer would stand for long, but he found himself agreeing anyway. He missed riding.

Ryan leaned over to tap their water bottles together in a mock toast. "Don't look so worried. Micah would kill me if I chased you off now."

That made Nick look over to meet Ryan's soft grin. The man was really unfairly attractive. Nick couldn't help but appreciate the way his shirt gaped open, more of the buttons undone than was strictly necessary. The gap revealed miles of tanned skin, defined muscle, and the hint of a small, bronzed nipple. Where Micah was compact, with beautifully defined bone structure and flawless skin, Ryan was stronger and more rugged. He definitely had that "daddy" vibe, whether from his looks or the confident way he carried himself. Not that Nick wanted a daddy. His actual father was more than enough to deal with.

Nick realized he'd been caught staring—if the humor in Ryan's eyes was anything to go by. He dragged his gaze away, out over the fields, and searched for something to say. "Feels strange to be back here," was all he could come up with.

Ryan hummed. "How long has it been?"

"Almost twenty years," Nick said. "After my mom passed, Phillip felt the trip was too much trouble. I did internships for his company instead. I missed it, though. Summers with Aunt Maggie were something special." Nick regretted the words even as they left his mouth. Ryan didn't need to hear his sob story.

"Was your mom sick?" Ryan asked.

Nick shook his head. "A car accident." He paused to swallow against the tightness in his throat. The last thing he was looking for was sympathy he didn't deserve.

He startled when Ryan's big hand closed over his forearm and gave a supportive squeeze. "That must have been tough."

Damn it. Nick's eyes flicked to his hand. "It was a long time ago," he ground out, keeping his arm carefully still until Ryan pulled back.

"Still. Sorry for your loss."

Nick shook his head, pushing away the ache. That part of his life wasn't something he liked to revisit. And he definitely didn't want to open up to Ryan about it when he was about to throw a wrench into the man's whole world.

Movement down by the barn had Nick looking up from his laptop, blinking spreadsheets and numbers out of his eyes. He had found a shady spot on the back deck, near the hot tub and with a great view of the mountains, to get some work done. He didn't really need to be doing it—technically his being at the ranch was work—but the distraction helped. Anything was better than sitting around waiting for the other shoe to drop.

Micah and Izzy were outside the barn. They were too far away for Nick to hear what they were saying, but Izzy gestured toward the driveway and Micah nodded. A moment later, Izzy hopped in his car and was gone. Micah ran a hand through his hair, then glanced at his watch, his frame tense. He pulled out his phone and dialed, then started pacing. Whoever he was trying to reach didn't answer, and he shoved the phone back into his pocket. Nick could see the worry coming off him in waves. Something was up, but it wasn't any of Nick's business.

He tried to go back to his spreadsheets. Izzy leaving meant only Micah and Alice were down at the barn. Ryan was out with a group on a trail ride. Nick had turned down the offer to join them, feeling the need for some distance after the emotions their earlier conversation had dragged to the surface.

Really, just being at the ranch was bringing up a lot of feelings he wasn't interested in examining. There were too many memories here, both good and bad.

Before he could spiral further into self-pity, he heard tires on gravel. A truck pulling a small trailer made its way up the driveway. It had to be the customers coming to collect the horse they'd purchased.

He glanced back to the barn and saw Micah on the phone again. He shoved his hand through his hair, and Nick managed to read "pick up" from his lips. He glanced toward the barn, his frame tense and anxious.

Nick told himself it was only curiosity as he set his laptop aside and made his way down the worn dirt path just as the horse trailer stopped outside the barn. He caught Micah's eyes in question, but Micah gave him a quick shake of his head and turned to greet the customers with a big, genuine smile.

So the customers weren't the problem. Nick stepped into the dimly lit main aisle of the barn, glancing around for whatever might be off. At first he didn't see anything. Then he picked up on movement in one of the far stalls that didn't seem to be a horse. As he made his way closer, he could hear low, frantic mumbling but wasn't able to make out the words.

"Alice?" he asked, unexpected concern tightening his throat.

The mumbling stopped abruptly, but the quick breaths didn't. Nick peeked around the stall door, then stepped carefully into the space. Alice was pacing back and forth across the length of the stall, twisting and tugging on her fingers as her chest heaved. She didn't look up—in fact, she didn't acknowledge Nick at all.

"Alice," Nick tried again, hoping to catch her attention without scaring her. "What's happening?"

Without answering, she turned for another trip across the stall, her feet digging furrows through the sawdust shavings.

She was clearly in distress. Possibly having a panic attack. One of Xavier's favorite clients had them from time to time, and Nick had witnessed a couple. He knew there were ways to help the person get through them, but he wasn't sure they would work for someone like Alice.

Alice stopped abruptly and crouched down, banging her fist against her thigh hard enough that Nick winced. Shit. He needed to do something. He didn't want her to hurt herself if he could help it. He stepped further into the stall.

"Hey, Alice?" he called softly. "Can you hear me?"

Alice shook her head rapidly, then nodded.

Well, that was vague, but he guessed it answered his question. "Do you want me to get Micah?" She was shaking her head again before he even finished, so he changed gears. "Or I could call your brother? Would it help to talk to Archer?"

"N-no," she forced out between too-quick breaths. "Don't-don't bother hi-hi-him."

"Okay, we won't call him," Nick said, keeping his voice calm and soothing. "How about I sit with you?" he asked. When she gave a short nod of assent, he slid down across from her with his back against the wall, hoping he wasn't crowding her as he draped his arms over his bent knees. "Is this okay?"

Alice gave a jerky shrug that wasn't a no, so Nick relaxed a little. She'd stopped beating up her thigh, at least, but her breathing was still ragged, and she wasn't making eye contact. Nick racked his brain for anything he remembered about panic attacks. Distracting the person was important. Getting them to focus on something other than the thing that was upsetting them.

All right. Distraction he could do.

"Did Maggie ever tell you about the time I tried to help her put the horses out?" he asked, keeping his voice as normal and conversational as possible despite the worry that was trying to make his muscles tense. God, he hoped bringing up Maggie didn't make things worse.

Alice's fingers stilled for a moment, then began plucking at a loose string on the hem of her jeans. Nick watched carefully, but she seemed to be listening, so he continued.

"The problem was, I was nine, and I thought it would be a whole lot faster if I just opened all the stalls at once. The horses knew where they were supposed to go, right?"

Alice gave a huff of what could have been amusement, and Nick shut his eyes briefly in relief.

"Well, obviously it didn't work out the way I planned..."

MICAH HAD NEVER NEEDED customers to leave as badly as he did this girl and her mom. Still, he had to be friendly and professional as he went over the final details with them. Meanwhile, he had no idea whether Alice was okay.

He'd seen the panic rising when she realized the trailer was arriving and she was still at the barn. This was totally outside of her comfort zone. Archer was always careful to take her home on the days her babies were being collected by their new owners. They gave her a chance to say goodbye in the morning, but it set off too many of her anxieties to be there when the horses were loaded up and driven away. Micah thought it probably had something to do with the twins' history. The details didn't really matter. What Micah knew was that Alice was upset, and he couldn't do anything about it.

The plan had been for Izzy to take her before the new owners arrived, but Izzy had some kind of last-minute emergency and had taken off before Micah even thought about getting Alice out of there. And the only other person she—and Archer—trusted enough was Keegan, who wasn't answering his goddamn phone. By the time the horse was loaded up and the new owners were on their way, Micah was keeping his own panic under control by a thread.

Nick had ducked into the barn a while ago and hadn't returned. Micah hoped that meant Alice was okay. At least relatively. Surely if she was having a meltdown or a panic attack, Nick would have come back to get him.

The second he was able, Micah jogged into the barn, his heart trying to beat its way out of his chest. He slowed when he heard a quiet voice coming from the last stall, and he peeked in.

Nick was sitting on one side of the stall, his back against the wall, legs stretched out in front of him and crossed at the ankle, hands folded in his lap.

Alice was next to him, leaning against the same wall, close enough that their shoulders were brushing. Micah blinked rapidly, not sure he could believe it. Alice wasn't a fan of being touched, or, for that matter, of anyone invading her personal space. Panic attacks only made it worse. But she seemed mostly relaxed, if a little twitchy, as Nick spoke. It took a few seconds for the words to filter past Micah's worry, and he found himself smiling when he realized Nick was telling her stories about his childhood on the ranch. Making a fool of himself seemed to be the theme as he told her about falling into a giant mud puddle while trying to ride his favorite pony bareback in the field with just a halter.

Alice's lips twitched up in a quick smile as Nick recounted getting mud *everywhere* and Maggie having him stand in the yard in his underwear so she could hose him down.

"I hope someone took pictures," Micah said as he slipped into the stall and sank down to sit cross-legged, facing them.

Nick rolled his eyes and gave him a brief smile. "I'm sure my mom did, but no way am I helping you look for them."

Micah laughed, warmth and gratitude flooding him. He also couldn't help but notice how handsome Nick was when he genuinely smiled. It made him look softer, more real. It was a side Micah hadn't expected. He kind of didn't want to ruin the moment, but they couldn't spend the rest of the day sitting on the stall floor. He turned to Alice. "How are you doing? Do you want me to take you home? I can, as soon as Ryan gets back."

Alice swallowed a few times and shook her head. Sometimes words were hard when she got upset, so he waited until she could gather them. "Nick said he'll take me."

"That's if I can borrow a car," Nick interjected. "We were just waiting for you to finish up so I could ask for your keys."

Micah agreed immediately, knowing Alice would want to be back in her own space so she could decompress. Panic attacks took a lot out of a person. He'd had a few after his mom died, and he remembered the bone-deep exhaustion that followed.

He got Nick the keys to his truck and walked them out to it, watching the way Nick stayed near Alice but didn't crowd her. It was a relief to know that he would get her home safely, since Micah couldn't leave the ranch unattended.

He stopped Nick with a hand on his arm. "Thank you."

Nick tipped his head in acknowledgment. "It's the least I could do. I know she doesn't drive."

"I mean for all of it. Not many people could or would do what you just did." Micah could count the number of people Alice trusted on one hand. That Nick, a virtual stranger, had been able to help her was something special.

Nick looked down at Micah for a minute. His eyes were green, Micah noted as they caught the light, and gentler than he expected. "Anytime," he finally said before pulling open the door of the cab and hopping up into the truck.

"Be careful with my baby," Micah said with mock seriousness.

"I'll try not to scratch any of the rust," Nick snarked.

Micah made a face. His truck might look a little rough after all these years, but despite being vintage, it was reliable.

Nick laughed at his expression, and Micah went warm with embarrassment. "I promise, I'll be careful."

Micah huffed and glanced around him to check on Alice. "Let us know if you need anything, okay, Allie?" he asked, using Archer's nickname for her. Alice gave him a nod and held up her phone to say she would text. Micah closed the driver's door and stepped back, letting them go. Then he turned back to the barn. There was a lot to get done, and with Alice gone and Izzy off who-knew-where, it was up to Micah to hold down the fort.

Micah kept the ranch in one piece, but his focus was shot for the rest of the afternoon. When Nick returned from dropping off Alice, he settled on the back deck with his laptop, and Micah kept finding himself glancing in that direction. Every time he pictured Nick and Alice sitting together in the stall, he felt a tug in his chest. He'd been so worried about her, but it seemed Nick had known exactly what to do. He couldn't remember Alice ever warming up to someone so quickly.

What was it about the guy? Micah had only known him twenty-four hours, and from what he'd seen, Nick was sharp, put together, but something about his perfect facade rang a little false for Micah's taste. On the other hand, he was also quick-witted, observant, and surprisingly soft when he needed to be.

Micah wasn't sure whether he wanted to banter with him or just shake him until he stopped hiding and let them see something real.

"Are you sure Alice sounded okay?" Micah asked as he finished toweling his hair and pulled on a clean T-shirt. It had been a long day, but he was still too keyed up to relax.

Ryan stepped up behind him and hugged him. "She's an adult. If she says she's fine, we need to respect that."

Micah sighed and sagged back into Ryan's arms. "Yeah, I know. But that doesn't stop me worrying. Especially when Archer isn't here." He rested his head against Ryan's shoulder and shut his eyes. "I'm worried about Maggie's surgery too. What if it doesn't go well?"

"It's gonna be fine, baby," Ryan said patiently, which was nice of him, considering how many times Micah had brought it up. "She has one of the best surgeons in the country. He's done this operation thousands of times."

Micah nodded and turned his face into Ryan's neck, breathing in the clean, familiar scent that never failed to make him feel both calmer and a little turned on. "I'm still gonna worry."

Ryan chuckled softly and kissed his jaw. "You wouldn't be you otherwise. Tell you what, we'll have a movie night to help take your mind off it. I'll even let you pick the movie."

Micah laughed and pressed a kiss to Ryan's mouth. Ryan almost always let him pick the movie. He agreed, though: a movie sounded good.

During their conversation, Micah had missed the sound of the shower cutting off, but he didn't miss the bathroom door opening in a cloud of steam. Nick stepped out, a towel wrapped around his hips, and Micah's breath caught.

Holy shit. He'd known that Nick was in good shape after basically getting pinned beneath the guy in the mud, but this was another level. He could be a freaking underwear model. His hair, which was still dripping, was surprisingly curly without any product to hold it in place. Water slid over the defined edge of his collarbone and down the curve of his pec, only to encounter the most perfect eight-pack Micah had ever seen.

Micah blinked a few times and tried to form words as Nick stepped forward and into the glow cast by the bedroom lamp. The light caught on his chest, glinting off metal. “Your nipples are pierced,” Micah blurted out.

That earned him a slow smile as Nick ran a hand through his wet hair, his bicep flexing with the motion. “Are they?” he teased.

“Wow.” Micah couldn’t tear his eyes away. His heart sped up, and he licked his lips as warmth settled low in his belly. He wanted—

“You’ve never seen nipple piercings before?” Nick teased.

Micah shook his head. “Only in porn,” he said, then caught himself a moment too late. Nick laughed at his dramatic wince.

Ryan chuckled, too, then said, “We’re headed down for a movie night, if you want to join us.” Micah was distracted from Nick’s response as one of Ryan’s big, strong hands slid to splay across his abs, his thumb tracing circles over the soft cotton of Micah’s T-shirt.

Micah shivered, breathlessly turned on. Oh, fuck. What the hell was his brain doing? He sucked in a trembling breath and tried to ignore his rebellious body as Ryan and Nick agreed to meet downstairs in ten minutes. *It was nothing,* he told himself firmly. Just the shock of having a half-naked porn star look-alike in his bedroom. That would mess with anyone.

The thing to do was to erase the last five minutes from his memory. Because there was no way—he was absolutely not attracted to anyone but his husband. Especially not Maggie's snarky asshole of a nephew.

"Baby?" Ryan murmured in his ear, giving him a squeeze to get his attention.

"S-sorry." Crap. That wasn't what he meant to say. His face was too warm, and he wanted to hide in Ryan's chest, but he was facing the wrong way. He met Ryan's eyes in the mirror over the dresser and couldn't help scrunching his nose up in apology.

Ryan just looked amused. "He looks like he was sculpted out of marble, huh?"

Micah groaned as he watched his cheeks and throat redden further. "I was gonna say 'porn star.'"

That made Ryan laugh. "Or that." He made Micah turn and tipped his face up for a kiss. "He's hot as fuck, baby. And if looking was a crime, they'd need to take us both down to the station." He pressed a second kiss to Micah's flushed cheek.

It took a minute for that to process, and then Micah relaxed with a shuddery sigh. Ryan wasn't annoyed with him, and Micah wasn't the only one who thought Nick should give up whatever career he had and get in front of a camera. He ducked his head and snickered into Ryan's chest, earning fingers in his ribs that only made him laugh harder.

"What's so funny?" his husband asked as dragged his fingers over the sensitive spot again.

Micah wasn't sure, other than the fact he was being tickled. He was probably just relieved. "I love you," he told Ryan instead.

Ryan shook his head and hugged him hard. "I love you too."

Micah was more in control of himself when they all met up in the living room. He was relieved to see Nick fully dressed in a T-shirt and dark gray sweats—and he carefully didn't check to see what might be visible through those sweats. Instead, he ducked into the kitchen to grab them beers and chips, then sprawled out on the couch with his head propped on the armrest and his feet in Ryan's lap. Nick had claimed one of the big armchairs and kicked his feet up on the ottoman.

Rascal was settled in her bed in the corner, but Milo wandered over to Nick and flopped on the floor next to him, his head in perfect scratching position. Nick obligingly lowered one hand to give him a pat.

"What are we watching?" Nick asked, taking a swig of beer, his throat bobbing as he swallowed.

"You can choose," Micah offered, waiting until he glanced over to toss him the remote. "We have Netflix and HBO." He snuggled down further, tugging the blanket off the back of the couch.

Nick flicked through movies for a few minutes before settling on a remake of an old Rat Pack film. Micah grinned when Ryan shifted but didn't say anything. Micah had been wanting to see this movie for ages, but Ryan complained that people shouldn't mess with classics. He couldn't say anything now; it was two against one. Micah rubbed his foot against Ryan's thigh in acknowledgment of his sacrifice and got a squeeze to his ankle in reply.

The movie ended up being good, but the day had been stressful and Micah felt himself fading around the three-quarter mark. It didn't help when Ryan started absently rubbing his feet and calves. He dozed and listened to the occasional murmured conversation between the two other men, the movie becoming background noise.

He wasn't sure how much time had passed when he felt his cozy blanket being tugged away. He grumbled in sleepy protest, and Ryan chuckled in reply. Then he was being urged to stand and walk. He blinked at the darkened room. The TV was playing some late-night soccer game on mute, its light revealing Nick asleep in his chair, his head back and Micah's stolen blanket over his lap.

"Not gonna wake him up?" Micah murmured to Ryan.

"I tried," Ryan replied, his voice a low, soothing rumble that made Micah want to curl into him. "He told me five more minutes. He's watching the game."

Micah snickered. Yeah. Definitely watching the game. Nick was out cold.

The dogs stayed on the first floor as Micah let Ryan steer him up the stairs. Rascal was Maggie's dog and usually slept at her house, and Milo seemed more interested in keeping her company than following them. After mindlessly brushing his teeth, Micah crawled into bed. He was asleep as soon as Ryan pulled him into his arms.

Micah was having an awesome dream. He was weightless, floating. A hard body was pressed against his back, holding him immobile, and an even harder cock rocked between his cheeks. Hands ghosted over his skin, leaving tingling trails in their wake. He moaned as the hands teased his nipples, the hollow of his hip, his quickly filling cock. They were everywhere, all at once. His lips parted on a sigh as his shorts were tugged past his hips and slick fingers dipped into his crease, teasing over his hole. He eagerly arched his back to allow them more access.

He realized he wasn't asleep anymore around the same time Ryan's lips pressed to his jaw and his growly voice purred in Micah's ear, "You done teasing, baby?" His fingers circled, setting off fireworks under Micah's skin. "Gonna let me in this tight little hole? Let me work you open and fill you up?"

"Oh, fuck yes," Micah whimpered. He wasn't sure what teasing he'd been doing, and he didn't care. His cock, already hard from his dream, throbbed in time with his quickening pulse.

He loved it when Ryan got like this, all deliciously dirty and demanding. It turned Micah into a desperate, whiny mess. It would be embarrassing if it weren't so mind-blowingly good.

Ryan pressed in with two fingers at once, and Micah gasped but was relaxed enough from sleep to take them easily. He groaned when Ryan shifted them just right to send little bolts of pleasure zinging up his spine.

"Please," he begged shamelessly, his mind fuzzy with lust. He wanted Ryan inside him right now. Needed it. "Please, please, please."

"Say it," Ryan said, his tone as impossible to ignore as the third finger he slid into Micah's body, stretching him until he shuddered, rocking his hips in time with Ryan's thrusts.

"Fuck me," Micah whined, fingers clawing at the sheets in an attempt to get some leverage. "I need it. Need you. Right now."

Ryan groaned and withdrew his fingers. Then he shifted so he was blanketing Micah, his erection dragging between Micah's cheeks.

Micah squirmed in encouragement and arched to get Ryan's cock closer to where he needed it. Finally. Finally, there was firm pressure against his hole as Ryan lined up and then pushed. He sank all the way inside in one smooth motion that made Micah cry out at the pleasurable burn.

A moment later, Ryan was draped over his back and pressing him down into the mattress, his mouth against Micah's ear. "Shh, baby. Unless you want our guest to hear me taking my boy apart." He followed the statement with a bite to Micah's earlobe that made him gasp and shudder.

Fuck. This was going to be impossible. Micah wasn't used to being quiet, and as Ryan started to thrust excruciatingly slowly, he knew this time was going to be even more difficult than usual.

His husband seemed determined to drive him wild, building his arousal until Micah was mindless with it. He could feel every inch of Ryan's cock dragging inside him, rubbing against all the places that made Micah whimper and try to force him faster. It was a mindfuck to have Ryan whispering filthy things in his ear while taking him so slowly Micah was shaking from it.

"Oh my god, Ry, please. More. I-I need. Fuck. More," he babbled, struggling against the grip Ryan had on his hip to prevent him from thrusting back.

"Patience," Ryan said, his voice way too calm and collected for Micah's liking. "I'll get you there, I promise." He kissed his way along Micah's throat before biting lightly at the spot below his ear.

Micah groaned and let his head fall to the pillow as pleasure rolled through him in gradually increasing waves. He couldn't be patient. It was overwhelming when his mind was fuzzy and half-asleep. He whimpered, shaking his head as one of Ryan's hands ran along his torso, tweaking his hard nipples and teasing the sensitive hollow of his hip and the soft spot high on his inner thigh. Micah reached for his aching cock, but Ryan batted his hand away. Micah made a frustrated sound that turned into a shout when Ryan sped up his thrusts, nailing Micah's prostate and whiting out his vision.

A hand clamped over his mouth, and Micah realized he was babbling, begging. "Shh, baby. Nicky's gonna hear you if you keep that up," Ryan said in Micah's ear, his strained voice finally giving away that he was just as affected as Micah was.

Micah groaned into Ryan's palm at the controlling hold—or maybe it was Ryan's words. Micah didn't want to get caught, but there was something about the threat of it that made him burn with embarrassment and arousal in equal measure.

Ryan cursed and picked up the pace again. "You like that idea? You want Nicky to hear me fucking you? Want him to know how good I'm making you feel?"

Micah's orgasm was barreling down on him, his breath coming in short gasps as his body tensed. He yelled into Ryan's palm as it crashed over him in surges that didn't stop until Ryan finally slowed and clutched him close, trembling through his own release.

Micah was still panting when Ryan released his mouth and turned his head to claim a kiss. Micah returned it eagerly, dizzy from the long buildup and how hard he'd come. Eventually their kisses slowed to brushes of lips, and then Ryan had to pull away and find something to clean them up with.

Micah shivered in his absence and burrowed into his side when he returned. Ryan wrapped strong arms around him and squeezed him close. "You okay, baby?" he asked, voice low and soothing as he slowly stroked a hand up and down Micah's back.

Micah hid his face in Ryan's chest. "That was super hot," he mumbled, feeling weirdly shy.

The way Ryan relaxed made Micah glad he'd said it. "Good," he replied, his hand skimming down to cup Micah's ass possessively. "I didn't plan it," he added.

"I—know," Micah said, a yawn cutting the words in half as he snuggled further into Ryan's arms. "But I wouldn't say no to more."

He was asleep before he heard Ryan's answer.

# SEVEN

## RYAN

WITH HIS HUSBAND WRAPPED safely in his arms, Ryan gazed toward their bedroom door and the hallway beyond. All was still now, but he was sure he'd seen movement minutes ago. Nicky had been watching them—or listening to them, at least. Ryan wasn't sure how long their houseguest had been out in the hallway, but it was long enough.

Maybe he should feel guilty for letting it happen. When he'd woken up to Micah sighing in his sleep and wiggling his perfect ass against Ryan's aching cock, he'd ignored everything else.

When he'd heard the stairs creak, Micah had already been gone, babbling and begging so sweetly that Ryan hadn't had the willpower to stop, cross the room, and close the door. So, when a shadow darkened the opening further, Ryan had been fully aware what was going on.

He probably should have warned Micah, but instead he'd shifted the blankets to give them a modicum of privacy and kept going, losing himself in Micah's pleasure.

He'd almost forgotten the eyes on them when he warned Micah about his volume, but he'd heard the quick intake of breath when he said Nicky's name. It probably made him a dirty bastard, but he wished he'd left a lamp on, something to let him see those intense green eyes as he made Micah fall apart with his words and his cock.

Now that Ryan had cleaned them both up and Micah was tucked to his chest and breathing softly in his sleep, the what-ifs kept circling. Supplying images of their houseguest, frozen in the hallway. What had Nicky been thinking? Had he enjoyed the view? Touched himself? What was he doing now, in his own room? Ryan swallowed a groan and buried his face in Micah's hair, inhaling the clean scent of his shampoo.

He took another deep breath and forced his thoughts to clear. Everything could be dealt with after some rest.

Nicky avoided them the next morning. It was late when he appeared, only to ask to borrow Micah's truck so he could run into town. Apparently, there was a "work thing" he needed to do.

Micah, who was notoriously possessive of his truck, agreed surprisingly easily, and Nicky headed off, once again dressed like he was going to a photo shoot. Ryan had to admit it looked good on him. Micah seemed to agree, because he teased Nicky about his fancy shoes but then checked out his ass as he climbed into the truck.

When he turned back to Ryan and saw that he'd been caught, he blushed furiously and tried hard to look busy coiling a hose.

Ryan searched for the jealousy he'd expect but found it lacked teeth. Sure, there was a little voice whispering that these thoughts weren't acceptable, but it sounded enough like his long-estranged father than Ryan made the executive decision to tell it to fuck off. Nicky was gorgeous. He oozed sex appeal and confidence in equal measure. It was no surprise that Micah had noticed. Hell, Ryan had noticed, and according to his friends, he was oblivious these days when it came to attractive men. They teased him about being so wrapped around Micah's finger that he'd let Remy Dalton walk by without a second glance.

Ryan didn't bother to argue. They weren't wrong. Why would he care about some Hollywood heartthrob when he had the man of his dreams in his bed every night? It might have taken them a while to get there, but Ryan wouldn't change their story for anything.

For some reason, his single-minded focus didn't apply to Nicky. Maybe it was the way Micah had reacted to the man that made Ryan take notice. Or maybe it was Nicky himself. At any rate, he couldn't find it in himself to be upset about it. He liked Nicky, and Micah clearly did too. Ryan was sure that, if they weren't there yet, they were well on their way to being friends.

Was Micah interested in something more than that? Was Ryan? The question had no easy answer, so he set it aside. For now, he would watch, and listen. If there was a spark, even for just a bit of flirty fun for the three of them, Ryan would take it as it came.

After finishing up his morning paperwork—his least favorite part of the job—Ryan noticed the barn was too quiet. He tracked down his wayward husband and two employees in the tack room. Micah and Alice were sitting on saddle racks while Izzy told them some story that had them both giggling. Ryan was happy to see Alice feeling better. Often it took her a few days to recover from a bad panic attack, but this time she seemed to have bounced back.

He leaned against the doorway, watching as Izzy did an impression of Keegan turning down a date in favor of going home to see his dogs. Micah and Alice apparently found it hilarious, and Ryan had to admit Izzy had his best friend's mannerisms to a T. Still, it was up to him to be the grown-up when the "kids" got going. It was even worse when Archer was there. He and Micah somehow managed to forget they were in their twenties and regressed to the rowdy teens they'd been when Ryan met them.

He cleared his throat to derail Izzy's joke, and the three of them jumped, looking sheepish when they realized they'd been caught.

Well, Micah looked sheepish. And a little coy. His brat was probably going to angle for a "punishment" later. Only long practice kept Ryan from reacting outwardly to the thrill of desire that caused.

Alice just switched gears, gave Ryan a nod, and hopped up to get back to work cleaning tack.

Ryan kept his eye on Izzy, who smirked as he gathered supplies for the horses he was supposed to be preparing for their next trail ride. Speaking of a brat angling for a punishment…

"Working hard in here?" Ryan asked, raising an eyebrow. He wasn't particularly bothered by them taking a break, but they couldn't afford to slack off when they were already short-staffed for the weekend.

"Hardly working," Micah quipped back with a playful grin. Oh, yes. His boy was definitely looking for a spanking.

Ryan ignored him and turned back to Izzy. "We just had two more sign on to the one o'clock ride." He glanced at the other two. "If you could help out, I'd appreciate it. I'd like to get done on time today."

Micah and Alice nodded, and the three of them got to work, grooming and tacking horses like the well-oiled machine they were after all these years. They were finishing up when Micah made his way back over to Ryan.

"Archer called so we could talk to Maggie before she went into pre-op." He bit his lip and moved in so Ryan could wrap an arm around him. Fuck. He shut his eyes for a moment. She'd better make it through okay. Ryan wasn't sure what any of them would do without her. He might be the boss, but Maggie was the backbone of the ranch. She kept them all going, and, despite the distraction of Nicky, the last few days had been strange without her.

Now he understood why they'd all been gathered in the tack room. He hugged Micah tighter and looked up at Alice and Izzy, who were watching them. "She's going to be fine. The procedure is quick, and she'll be home before we know it."

Alice tugged on her fingers anxiously but nodded. Izzy wouldn't meet Ryan's eyes, but some of the tension left his shoulders.

Ryan jerked as teeth nipped at his neck, then tugged Micah back by the hair to glare at him. Micah just gave him a cheeky grin that made Ryan need to kiss him, then give him the smack on the ass that he'd been angling for.

Micah squeaked and laughed it off, but Ryan could see the way his pupils dilated with want. They'd have to save that for later.

He urged his employees back to work and joined them, getting the horses ready for the group ride that was going out in the next hour. He'd been scheduled to lead it, but he decided to send Micah instead. His boy needed the distraction, and nothing—apart from sex—calmed him down like being out on the trail.

Alice would distract herself with the foals for the next few hours. And Izzy... well, it was hard to say what he would do, but if Ryan noticed him struggling, he would figure out a way to help.

Izzy was complicated. He and Ryan were friendly, but they'd never been particularly open with each other. Izzy kept his emotions close to the vest. Ryan wasn't sure what made Izzy happy, other than horses—though he didn't ride them—and hookups. It worried Ryan sometimes, but unless Izzy asked for advice or it affected his work, Ryan didn't think it was any of his business.

The guests for the ride came in, and Ryan, Micah, and Izzy helped them get set up and out on time. Micah had huffed a little about being sent out where he wouldn't be able to check his phone for a call from Archer, but he agreed easily enough.

Once things settled down, Ryan noticed Nicky had returned from town. Ryan could see him moving around through the kitchen window that faced the barn, and he paused to watch. Nicky seemed to be unloading groceries. At least, that was Ryan's best guess. That was nice of him, but unnecessary.

Nicky was another contradiction, and like Izzy, he was hiding something. Ryan noticed it in the moments when he went quiet and distant. When he wasn't focused, his eyes were tired, and he moved like there was a heavy weight on his shoulders. It was a feeling Ryan recognized from his own years of trying to live up to other people's expectations and ignoring his own needs. Seeing it in Nicky, a virtual stranger, bothered him more than it should.

He hoped that a few days on the ranch, and reconnecting with his aunt, would go a long way toward healing whatever was hurting the other man.

Once Maggie was back, she'd drag the problem out of him. Maggie was good at that.

Archer called again when Maggie went into surgery. He didn't have much to report, but Ryan let him ramble anyway, recognizing that he needed someone to talk to. As much as Izzy and Nicky stumped him, Archer had become a close friend over the years.

Archer had been nineteen and home from his first year of college when Ryan started working at Split Rock Ranch. They'd formed a solid friendship that centered first around the ranch and then grew to include other interests. Archer was the only one who would willingly watch sports with him, for example. Micah didn't mind a game from time to time, but he'd rather be doing other things.

They also had a running joke that they were the only two within ten miles with any interest in women. Ryan was bi, and Archer was the only non-queer person on the ranch—with the possible exception of Maggie. Micah and Izzy were proudly gay, and Alice said she had enough labels but figured she was somewhere on the ace spectrum.

Even at nineteen, Archer had been mature. He'd started working at the ranch to support Alice, who had struggled much more as a teenager than she did now. Archer was a protector, and he had taken responsibility for his twin, driving her to and from the ranch and working alongside her to help her find success. It meant he had put his own dreams on hold, but Ryan had never heard a word of complaint from him or gotten the idea that he wasn't happy with the way things were. It was just unfortunate to see someone with so much talent not take advantage of it.

Archer was a phenomenal artist. He'd been in school for it when things took a turn at home, and he'd dropped out, putting his sister's needs before his own. Ryan, Micah, and Maggie had all encouraged him to go back, but it had been almost ten years now, and he'd gone from saying he wasn't ready to changing the subject entirely when it came up.

Ryan eventually got off the phone, exacting a promise from Archer that he would call back if he needed anything and would let them know as soon as Maggie was in the recovery room.

At some point they were going to need to tell Maggie that her nephew was in town, but Ryan agreed with Micah that they needed to wait at least a few days or Maggie, stubborn woman that she was, would ignore her doctors and rush back to see him. Ryan was going to put that off as long as he could. He didn't think it would be difficult to keep Nicky at the ranch in the meantime.

Ryan was on the phone in the office, dealing with one of their suppliers, when Micah returned with his group. He'd just hung up when Micah slipped into the room and shut the door, locking it with a click.

"What's up, baby?" Ryan asked. "How did the ride go?"

"All good," Micah responded as he beelined for Ryan.

Ryan pushed his chair back from the desk to make room as Micah crawled into his lap, knees tucked on either side of his hips. He pressed himself in close and buried his face in Ryan's throat. Ryan could feel him sucking in deep, calming breaths. "What's wrong?" he murmured, stroking a hand up and down Micah's back until he shuddered and slumped.

Micah shook his head without lifting it. "Just need this," he murmured, lips against Ryan's skin.

Ryan wrapped his arms around him and held him, lips pressed to his temple. Micah wasn't one to keep what was bothering him bottled up for long. If Ryan waited, he always opened up.

"I'm anxious about Maggie's surgery. Something's going on with Izzy that he won't tell me about." Micah reached up and picked at one of the buttons on Ryan's shirt before adding, "And then there's Nick."

There it was. Ryan had suspected this was coming. He knew Micah better than he'd ever known anyone, and it was easy to see something had changed. Still, he wanted to hear him talk it out. "What about Nicky?"

Micah groaned and mashed his face into Ryan's shoulder in a way that had to be uncomfortable.

"Did he do something?" Ryan tried.

Micah shook his head without lifting it. "No. I mean yeah, but it's just *him*. He's all fancy, and slick, and sarcastic. It's driving me up the wall."

Ryan had to chuckle at that, and he got jabbed in the ribs in retaliation. "Baby, you like those things. You like *him*."

"No, I don't," Micah said, his voice muffled again.

Ryan shook his head and eased Micah back until their eyes could meet. His husband's cheeks were flushed, and he was chewing on his bottom lip. "Would it help if I told you I like him too?"

Micah looked away, his blush darkening further. "It's not like that," he muttered, fingers twisting in the front of Ryan's shirt until Ryan covered them with one hand.

"You have a crush."

He cursed himself as Micah's eyes welled with tears.

"Oh, baby," Ryan said, lifting a hand to brush his thumb over damp lashes. "It's okay."

"It's not," Micah shot back, his voice harsh with emotion. "I shouldn't feel like this. I'm married to you. I love *you*."

Ryan gathered him into a hard, deep kiss, and he kept it up until Micah relaxed with a sigh and kissed him back. After a minute Ryan pulled away enough to say, "I know I'm supposed to be jealous, but that would make me a hypocrite."

That made Micah sit up and blink at him, his face unguarded with shock and something that Ryan thought looked like hope. "What does that mean?" Micah asked before biting his lip, his eyes wide and unsure, his hands clinging to Ryan's shirt.

Ryan gave a rough chuckle, hoping this was the right call. "It means I'm interested too."

Micah's face broke open with relief, and Ryan felt like he could breathe again. "Oh," was all he managed to get out before he ducked his head and started to snicker.

Ryan found himself grinning in response. "You think me having a crush on our guest is funny?" he teased.

Micah pressed his lips together and nodded, eyes sparkling.

Ryan leaned up to kiss the tip of his cute nose. God, he loved this man. "The bigger question is, what are we going to do about it?"

Micah blinked rapidly, his nerves making a reappearance. "Um. Nothing?" he said, sounding unsure again.

Ryan nodded slowly, watching his eyes. "That's definitely an option."

"What—" Micah licked his lips. "What are our other options?"

Ryan relaxed back in the old office chair, bringing Micah to settle comfortably against his chest as he tried to decide the best way to phrase his thoughts so as not to freak Micah out. "You know I've had multiple partners in the past. Both relationships and hookups."

"Yeah," Micah agreed. "That never bothered me."

Ryan snorted. "Baby, I've seen your OnlyFans subscriptions."

Micah snickered, and Ryan knew he was blushing again. "Yeah, well..." he started. "It's sexy as fuck. In theory."

"Would you ever want to find out if it's sexy in reality?"

Micah twitched and sucked in a breath. "With—with Nick?"

"With Nick, or someone else we find that we're interested in."

Micah looked down, his lashes hiding his eyes so Ryan had to wait for an answer instead of reading it on his face. "What if I don't want to?"

"Then we won't. Micah." Ryan hooked a thumb under his husband's chin and lifted his face again. "It's you and me, forever. I'm not interested in anything that you're not a part of."

That earned him a warm but somewhat wobbly smile. "Same," Micah said, tilting his head so Ryan's palm cupped his cheek. They stayed like that for a few minutes while Micah turned his thoughts around in his head, Ryan's thumb smoothing over Micah's cheekbone and down to trace his gorgeous mouth. He knew what that mouth could do, and his dirty mind kept supplying images of what Micah's plush lips would look like on another man's body. On Nicky's body. Because, to be honest, he wouldn't be nearly as interested if the potential third were anyone else.

"I think," Micah said, "I think I want to wait and see what happens. Maybe Nick wouldn't even want to." Micah tensed up as that thought took root. "That would be really embarrassing."

Ryan didn't think that would be an issue, but he let it go. This needed to be at Micah's pace. "All right. We can wait and see." He pressed his lips to Micah's temple, breathing in his familiar scent and hoping he hadn't made a big mistake.

# EIGHT

NICK

NICK LOOKED UP AT the hesitant knock on his bedroom door and quickly slid the paperwork for the real estate developer back into his suitcase. The screen door had slammed a few minutes ago, the sound bringing back a rush of memories. How many times had he heard that door slam as Maggie left the house to tend to the horses? How many evenings had that been the signal that dinner would be ready soon? How many more before it was the last time?

There was another, slightly louder, knock. "Nick? You awake?" It was Micah.

"Yeah," he replied, flipping his suitcase closed. "Come in."

The door opened, and Micah stuck his head in. He was sweaty and pink-cheeked, with dirt smeared across one cheekbone. It gave him a roguish, playful look that was only enhanced by his grin when he met Nick's eyes. "We just heard from Archer," Micah announced. "Maggie's surgery went great, and they expect she'll be released from the hospital Monday morning."

"That's fantastic news." Nick was surprised by how much relief he felt. He hadn't thought he was worried, but hearing that Maggie's surgery was a success took a huge weight off him. Of course, the knowledge that her—all these people's—time at the ranch was running out put that weight right back again.

"Right?" Micah said, his eyes shiny with emotion. "The doctor wants her to rest and to come in for a follow-up before she leaves, so she and Archer are staying with a friend in Durham for a few days, but she should be back by the middle of the week." He looked briefly embarrassed. "Um. We didn't exactly tell her you were here, 'cause she'd probably tell the doctor to go screw himself and come straight back to see you."

Nick couldn't hide his wince as guilt sucker punched him. Fuck. Maggie was going to be devastated when he told her what Phillip was doing. He kept running through his speech in his head, but it didn't help. He only hoped that he could find a way to break the news gently.

"We're going out tonight to celebrate. You should come with us," Micah continued, bouncing on his toes. "We may be a small town, but we have one of the best gay bars in a hundred miles."

Nick met Micah's big brown eyes, and any resistance he might have had to the idea melted away. He challenged anyone to say no to that pleading look. It got right into his chest and gave a tug that had Nick agreeing before he could think better of it. "What time?" he asked.

"After dinner."

"Sounds good," he agreed. "I could use a night out."

Micah shot him another sunny smile. “I’m gonna hop in the shower, unless you need the bathroom first.”

Nick declined. When he heard the shower cut on a minute later, an image of Micah wet and naked under the spray flashed through his mind. With more detail than he should really have, thanks to his accidental voyeurism the night before.

He’d been so intent on not disturbing them as he made his way up the dark, creaky stairs and down the hallway that he hadn’t registered the sounds coming from the bedroom until it was too late.

There had been just enough moonlight to make their skin glow, throwing them into sharp relief. Nick was both grateful for and resentful of the sheets that had strategically blocked his view. Still, the curve of Micah’s back where Ryan had him pressed to the mattress, the bunch of Ryan’s muscles as he rocked into his husband, were more than enough to send fire racing through Nick’s veins. And then he’d heard their sounds. Micah’s pleading whimpers and desperate begging. Ryan’s murmured praise and grunts of pleasure. Then Ryan said Nick’s name, and it hit him like a shot of adrenaline. He had to grip the doorframe as his knees caved, and he was pretty sure he gasped. He was even more sure that Ryan heard him, though he didn’t stop, or even slow.

By the time Micah came, Nick was barely in control. His cock was rock hard and throbbing, and it took every ounce of his willpower not to relieve the pressure. Ryan had glanced to the door then, and Nick was sure he’d been caught, but Ryan didn’t say anything, just dipped his head and pressed a kiss to Micah's shoulder blade.

For a moment, Nick had imagined he could feel those soft lips and prickly beard against his skin as Ryan's weight pressed him into the mattress—or maybe it was Micah's firm body and round ass spread beneath him that he wanted...

Nick had fled to his room as quietly as he could.

This morning he'd done his best to act normal, but he'd caught a few glances from Ryan. Micah, at least, seemed totally oblivious. Nick wasn't sure he'd have agreed to go clubbing with them so easily otherwise.

That was a lie. Micah's puppy eyes were lethal.

Going out with them tonight was a fantastic idea, or it was going to be a disaster. Either he'd find a quick, anonymous hookup to get his mind off things, or he'd spend the night pining for his very hot, and very unavailable, hosts.

He was so fucking screwed.

Nick drained the last of his beer and relaxed back against the leather booth. The bar Ryan and Micah had invited him to was larger than he'd expected for this little mountain town. The dance floor was packed with a surprising number of same-sex couples. Nick caught a glimpse of Micah and Izzy in the middle of things, bouncing and weaving to the fast beat of the music.

He almost wanted to join them. It had been years since he got out on the dance floor. He'd probably still been married to Xavier at the time.

The bar itself ran the length of the building, with liquor shelves on the back wall and a variety of taps, both familiar and ones he assumed were local, along the front. Above that were neon signs that cast a rainbow of light on the three bartenders who moved with grace as they served the Saturday night crowd. Between the bar and the dance floor were a dozen or so high-top tables, all filled with people wearing everything from denim and flannel to skintight dresses and stilettos. It was an impressive crowd for relatively early in the evening.

Ryan slid in across from him and handed him a new bottle, clinking the necks together before taking a swig. Nick was more cautious, not recognizing the label. He was pleasantly surprised by the smooth Belgian tripel. He took a larger sip and caught Ryan watching him.

"One of my favorites." Ryan nodded to the bottle, and Nick took note of the brand absently.

"You have good taste," Nick said, raising his voice as the volume of the music increased with a new song.

Ryan shifted to the U end of the booth and leaned closer, his knee bumping Nick's thigh. "I'm glad someone appreciates it. Micah wouldn't know a good beer if it bit him on the ass."

Nick laughed, eyeing the colorful cocktails Micah and Izzy had left on the table, condensation now soaking the bar napkins. Micah had chugged half of his drink before he hit the dance floor. "Guess he has to have at least one flaw," Nick teased.

Ryan chuckled and turned to settle into the corner of the booth, one arm stretched along the back, his knees wide, leg pulled up and resting against the cushion. Nick had to take another swig of his beer to stop his eyes from being drawn into inappropriate territory.

Ryan and his husband cleaned up well. Really well. Ryan was in a dark, fitted tee and jeans that molded perfectly to his tight abs and long legs. Micah was in jeans as well, the sleeves of his soft gray Henley pushed up to show off the muscles of his forearms. They were both hot as fuck. The hungry looks that followed them through the bar were in agreement.

"All right, next question," Ryan said, continuing their conversation from before he went for another round of drinks. "Wildest night."

Nick snorted. "My ex and I accidentally went to an orgy." They'd started on this topic after Nick joked about the disappointment on the nearby men's faces when they realized Ryan and Micah were together. A few drinks later, they were sharing more than Nick was used to, but he was enjoying the hell out of it.

Ryan's eyebrows went up. "Accidentally?"

Nick laughed. "It was before we were married. One of his clients invited us to this party and somehow 'forgot' to include some important details. I still think the guy just wanted in Xavi's pants."

Ryan shook his head. "What did you do?"

"Oh, we stayed. Xavi was still building his business and didn't want to insult the guy. And neither of us is a prude. But it gets better." Nick took a swig of his drink. "It was a puppy-play orgy."

Ryan coughed and had to put his drink down to wipe a hand over his mouth. "What?"

"Yeah. The guy overheard Xavier calling me a 'good boy'—as a joke—and made a few too many assumptions. So, we show up at the party, and it ends up being a mansion full of puppies and their leather daddies going wild."

"And you stayed?" Ryan sounded both impressed and intrigued.

"Hey, I'm not one to kink-shame." Nick gave Ryan a lazy smirk. "And some of those puppies were hot as fuck. Their daddies too."

Ryan clinked their bottles together. "All right, you win that round. Your turn."

Nick hummed thoughtfully. They'd already covered their first crushes, a girl in elementary school for Ryan and a boy at summer camp for Nick, and longest relationships: Micah and Xavier respectively. "Most disastrous hookup."

Ryan flashed his perfect teeth, his eyes dancing with humor in a way that made Nick want to lean closer. Nick set his beer on the table and told himself to slow down before he got himself in trouble. "I was in grad school. I went home with a guy I met at a club and was balls deep when the smoke alarm in the apartment went off and someone started screaming. I ran into the living room naked, condom still on, and found the guy's roommate flailing around and clutching his wrist. He'd put a frozen pizza in the oven and passed out on the couch. When the smoke alarm went off, he grabbed the pizza with his bare hand and burned the hell out of himself. I spent the rest of the night dealing with firefighters and EMTs, then sitting in the ER with the two of them."

Nick couldn't stop laughing at the image of Ryan trying to manage that situation while naked. "Did your hookup at least make it up to you?"

Ryan snorted and shook his head. "Turns out he was in love with the roommate, and the adrenaline made everything come tumbling out. I did get invited to their wedding."

Nick reached out and squeezed Ryan's shoulder playfully, taking a moment to enjoy the firm muscle under his palm. "Well, I'm sorry for your blue balls."

Micah popped back up next to their table before Ryan had a chance to reply. "Hey," he said breathlessly, shoving his fingers through hair damp with sweat. His skin was flushed, his shirt clinging to him. Micah grabbed his drink and drained it, licking his lips as he abandoned the glass on the table again.

Fuck, he was gorgeous. Nick swallowed. He couldn't drag his eyes away. He realized a second too late that he was still squeezing Ryan's shoulder and let him go abruptly.

"Hey, baby," Ryan replied, his voice a deep rumble that made Nick's pants too snug. He needed to get himself under control.

Or find someone on the dance floor to relieve some tension with.

"I'm roasting," Micah said to Ryan. "Why did you let me wear sleeves?" He tugged the front of his shirt.

Ryan's mouth curled into a small grin, but he didn't answer. He didn't need to when Micah peeled the shirt from his body, revealing toned muscles, a smooth chest, and broad shoulders with a complex tattoo curling over one and stopping just at the base of his neck. The view was so much better when he wasn't mostly obstructed by sheets and shadows. Nick's mouth watered. He could pick out mountains and horses in the tattoo design, but the rest of the detail was lost in the flashing lights.

Micah dropped the shirt onto his seat. "Dance with me," he told Ryan, who shook his head and gestured to a server approaching with a tray of shots.

Micah's eyes lit up, and he waved for Izzy, who appeared at his side a moment later. The tall blond was attractive as well, with sharp cheekbones and angelic curls, and from some of the glances Nick had received, he was probably willing. But Nick couldn't get into it. If he was being honest, he couldn't drag his attention away from Ryan and Micah long enough for anyone else to matter. He was screwed, and not in the way he wanted to be.

As the shots were set in front of them, Micah gave an excited wiggle that made Nick laugh.

Ryan slid each of them two shots and took one for himself. Nick raised an eyebrow. "Someone has to make sure we get home," was Ryan's explanation.

Nick lifted the glass of amber liquid to his lips and got a strong whiff of cinnamon. Ryan grinned and leaned over to speak in his ear. "Micah's not a fan of whiskey. We compromise with Fireball."

Nick suppressed his shiver and tapped his glass dutifully to the others'.

"To new friends," Micah toasted, dark eyes glittering in the lights from the dance floor.

"And new strangers," Izzy added with a sharp grin before he downed his shots back-to-back and disappeared into the crowd. The guy was something, that was for sure.

The liquid burned Nick's throat, but not unpleasantly. He set the glass down just in time for Micah to crawl up on the bench next to him and lean across precariously. Nick's hand came up automatically to grip his hip and steady him.

"I want a kiss," Micah told Ryan, who shifted closer in response, his warm thigh pressing into Nick's as their lips met inches from his face. Nick's breath caught, cock thickening. Ryan slid a hand into Micah's hair, cradling his head as he moved to deepen the kiss. Even over the music, Nick was sure he heard Micah groan, and he sucked in a quick breath, trying to be still.

The couple finally broke apart, leaving Micah on his knees next to Nick. Micah rested a hand on Nick's shoulder for balance as he grabbed the second shot off the table and downed it, eyes locked with Ryan's the whole time. "Fuck, that's good," he said, licking his lips. Then, in a move that made Nick's heart skip a beat, he dipped down and smacked a kiss to Nick's cheek. Then his lips brushed Nick's ear. "Come dance with me," he said, voice smooth and so close it made goose bumps rise on Nick's skin. "Let's make Ryan jealous." Nick shivered at the heat coming off Micah's body and realized too late that he was still clutching Micah's hip, fingers pressed to soft, worn denim and firm muscle.

Micah laughed and pulled away, giving Nick a meaningful look before slipping back into the crowd.

Nick was helpless to resist. He remembered Micah's comment a few days ago about teasing his husband to get him out on the dance floor. He might be a little more buzzed than he'd thought, but if it meant getting to put his hands on Micah, Nick was absolutely on board. He turned his head to gauge Ryan's reaction and found the man watching him with a half smile. Nick hesitated, wondering if he was about to cross a line he couldn't come back from.

Ryan read the indecision on his face and shifted closer. His hand dropped to rest on Nick's thigh, warmth soaking through his pants, and gave a squeeze. "Have fun."

That was the permission Nick needed.

He downed his second shot, then wove through the bodies on the dance floor until he spotted Micah, his head back, eyes closed as he moved to the heavy beat. When Nick stopped in front of him, his eyes opened and a grin flashed across his face. Though it was hard to tell in the shifting lights, Nick would swear his cheeks flushed as well.

Nick reached out, slow enough for Micah to refuse, and hooked his fingers through the belt loops of Micah's tight jeans. Micah swayed closer when he tugged, and Nick's heart sped up at the nervous excitement in Micah's eyes.

It was easy to pull Micah into his space and slide his hands to the small of his back, keeping him there as they moved together. Micah's skin was hot and damp against Nick's palms, and it was a real effort not to let his hands wander.

Micah leaned in, pressing his chest to Nick's. The movement put his mouth against Nick's ear. "This okay?" he asked over the music.

Despite the sweat he'd worked up on the dance floor, Micah smelled fantastic. Citrus and spice mixed with something deep and masculine. Nick wasn't sure if it was cologne or hair product, but he was a fan. He turned his head, his lips brushing the shell of Micah's ear as he breathed him in. "You want to get your husband riled up, I think we're going to need to do better than 'okay.'"

He could feel the shiver that went through Micah. He skimmed one hand up Micah's back, the other moving to catch his hip and tug Micah into the motion of the beat. Micah's chest was rising and falling against his as he lifted his arms and looped them around Nick's neck.

The moving bodies on the floor parted just long enough for Nick to spot Ryan back at the table. He was sitting with his knees spread, his arms stretched along the seat back behind him, the neck of a beer dangling from his fingers. His expression was unreadable from that distance, even as he locked eyes with Nick. As he lifted his drink for a slow sip, his other hand dropped down to the noticeable bulge in his jeans. Nick wet his lips as Ryan gripped that bulge and casually adjusted himself, his eyes never leaving the two of them.

Nick groaned, the sound lost in the thumping music. He might have come out here to help Micah tease his husband, but Ryan was going to be the death of him. In retaliation, Nick dragged the tip of his nose up Micah's throat, making him gasp and tip his head back. He slid his other hand down until he could get a grip on Micah's ass and really press them together, rocking to the beat of the song.

As soon as their hips came in contact, his rapidly thickening cock found an answering hardness in Micah's pants. Fuck. His eyes flicked down. He couldn't see Micah's face, but he felt it when Micah's fingers tightened on the back of his neck.

Unexpected erections happened from time to time, especially in a situation like this. But then Micah leaned in and nuzzled Nick's throat, lips just brushing his skin. Oh, hell. He shut his eyes and realized he'd been maneuvered into a trap a moment before Micah stretched up to speak in his ear again.

"Nick?" he asked, breathless and more than a little hesitant.

"Fuck, yes," Nick answered him, fingers threading through Micah's hair and tugging him back so he could see the agreement in Nick's eyes. Micah looked up at him, flushed and beautiful, his eyes dark and needy, his lips parted. It took everything Nick had not to kiss him. He ran his free hand down Micah's chest instead, finally getting to touch all that firm muscle as Micah's head fell back in acceptance and he clung to Nick's shoulders. He was perfect. Just short enough to fit in Nick's arms, but not so delicate that Nick felt like he had to be careful with him. He was all strength and grace in a compact package. Nick traced along the bottom of his ribcage and got a hitched breath and a shudder in response. "You're like a fucking fantasy come to life," he said, knowing Micah couldn't hear him over the music but not caring. It needed to be said.

Nick had just pulled Micah close again when the crowd shifted and Ryan stepped onto the dance floor. Ryan paused a short distance away, watching them move, his eyes taking in the way Micah clung to Nick, the way Nick had his knee pressed between Micah's thighs. Ryan's intense gaze made something in Nick's chest flare hot and bright, and in that moment he knew that whatever Ryan and Micah wanted—whatever they had planned—his answer was yes.

Ryan must have seen the desire in Nick's eyes, because he stepped up behind Micah and caught him by the hips, then leaned in and kissed his bare shoulder. Nick caught a glimpse of Ryan's tongue darting out to taste sweat-slick skin and groaned.

He would love to get his own taste, but for now, he was following their lead.

Micah gasped at the contact, then melted, letting his head fall against Ryan's shoulder with comfortable familiarity, eyes going half-lidded as his tongue slid over his lower lip.

Nick restrained himself from chasing after it. Barely.

The music changed to something slower and heavier. The kind of song that felt like vertical sex. The three of them fell into sync with the beat, hips rocking, hands drifting. At one point Micah slid his palms up Nick's back, under his shirt, and groaned, loud enough that Nick could feel it over the bass. He met Ryan's eyes over Micah's head and was startled by the want in them. He'd assumed this was for Micah's benefit, but unless he had completely lost his touch, Ryan was just as into it.

He raised an eyebrow in question and Ryan raised one in return, tilting his head toward the dimly lit hallway that led to the bathrooms.

Nick might be new in town, but he was more than familiar with what went on in this type of place. He nodded his interest—whatever they wanted to do, he was willing.

Ryan dipped down to speak in Micah's ear, and Nick watched Micah's lips part and his gorgeous skin darken in a blush that spilled halfway down his chest. His eyes opened and he looked up at Nick, desire warring with hesitance.

Nick lifted his hand and skimmed his thumb over Micah's plump lower lip. His breath caught in surprise when Micah opened his mouth and sucked it inside, tongue flicking over the tip before he released it again with a pop. Then he pressed forward so Nick could hear him. "You really want to?" he asked, breathless. Nick couldn't feel his heartbeat over the deep bass, but he guessed it was racing.

"Yeah," Nick said, giving him a playful leer. "I'm up for anything, sweetheart."

Micah snorted a laugh, then ducked his head and pressed closer, mumbling something into Nick's throat. Nick wasn't about to let him get away with that. Sliding his fingers into Micah's hair, he tugged until he could see his face. Nick swiped his thumb over one flushed cheek.

"Have you ever—um," Micah said, then paused, tongue darting out briefly as he gathered his confidence. "So— There's this glory hole..." He trailed off, and his teeth sank into his lower lip.

Nick grinned wickedly. "Fun."

Micah snickered, relaxing, his hands smoothing over Nick's shoulders. "I've never tried it," he admitted, then glanced back at Ryan, probably for support.

"Yeah?" Nick asked. "You wanna give or receive?"

"I want to be on my knees," Micah said, soft enough that Nick had to read his lips. He groaned at the thought of that gorgeous mouth wrapped around his cock. Yeah. He had absolutely no issue getting his cock sucked by this pretty boy.

Nick's eyes flicked to Ryan, not sure of the boundaries here. It didn't matter how much his body was thrumming with desire, how hard his cock was—he refused to overstep and mess this up.

The next thing he knew, Ryan's hand was cupping the back of his head and drawing him down so he could press his lips to Micah's throat. Nick groaned at the heavy, masculine scent of sweat and Micah's cologne. Before he could second-guess, he let his tongue dart out to taste. Micah shuddered and clutched at him, so he did it again, following it with a sucking kiss that made Micah's hips arch and grind against his. He glanced up to see Ryan watching them, approval and want in his expression. Then Ryan took Micah by the hand and tilted his head in the direction of the restrooms again.

The three of them made it down the hallway and into the bathroom, which was fortunately empty—not that that would have stopped Nick. He wasn't shy, and his dick was hard enough that any reservations he might have had were left on the dance floor.

Micah aimed for the last stall, presumably where the glory hole was located, his movements jittery with what Nick could only assume was nerves, despite Ryan's steadying hand at the small of his back.

Nick paused at the adjacent stall and called Micah's name. When he had his attention, Nick ran his thumb along the hard line of his cock through his pants, watching as Micah tracked the movement, his pupils blowing wide as his lips parted eagerly. "I've got a surprise I think you're gonna like," Nick said with a smirk.

Micah snorted, nerves momentarily forgotten, and stepped closer. "A surprise, huh?" he asked, his hand sliding down Nick's chest, fingers catching on his belt.

Nick snagged the wandering hand and lifted it, dropping a kiss on the back before he winked and ducked into the stall.

Micah gave a little "eep," then laughed. There were shuffling sounds and murmurs, then the other stall door closed and latched.

"You ready, baby?" came Ryan's deep voice from the other side of the heavy plastic.

Nick licked his lips, his eyes falling to the round opening cut in the wall and padded out with thick tape. He could see flashes of movement through it. Micah moaned, soft and breathless, and the slick sound of kissing reached Nick's ears. He palmed himself through his pants and shut his eyes, imagining the two of them wrapped around each other, tongues twining.

A gasp echoed through the empty space, followed by the sound of a zipper. "You want me to fuck you while you suck Nicky off?" Ryan asked, desire deepening his voice to a growl.

Micah whimpered. "Oh god." Long fingers curved through the glory hole, clutching at the opening.

Nick decided to ease him into it, stepping forward to brush his clothed erection against the back of Micah's hand. There was a startled sound before the fingers moved, tracing the shape of him through his pants.

The opening wasn't large enough for Micah to do much more than that, but when his plush mouth appeared next to his fingers and his tongue pressed to Nick's zipper, Nick groaned and fumbled to get his fly open.

He gripped the base to steady himself, then directed his hard cock back to the opening, his other hand braced on the wall. As soon as his flushed cockhead with its Prince Albert piercing came into view, Micah made a choked sound that ended on a groan. "Holy fuck," he managed.

Nick chuckled. The appreciation the piercing got from lovers was almost as satisfying as the jewelry itself.

Hot, shaky breath feathered over the sensitive skin as Micah hesitated. Nick held still, prepared to back off if Micah changed his mind, even though he was aching with arousal. Thankfully, Micah was all in. His tongue flicked out to taste the piercing, and they both groaned. The shock of pleasure settled low in Nick's belly, and he eased forward as Micah gave his cock tentative licks that quickly became more eager. When Micah finally took the head in his hot, wet mouth, Nick hissed, his eyes falling shut, his other hand leaving his cock to grip the top of the wall.

Damn, that was good. Tight suction and an eager tongue. With his eyes closed, he became more aware of noises from the next stall. The slap of skin on skin, Micah's pleased grunts, and the deep rumble of Ryan's voice.

"Look at you, baby. That's so fucking good. How far can you take him?" Ryan growled. A moment later, Nick's breath hitched as fingers pressed to Micah's cheek, rubbing his cock through the thin skin. He took the hint and eased forward until his hips were flush with the wall, his cock bumping the back of Micah's throat.

Micah's breath hitched around a moan, and he jolted, sucking hard. Nick registered a slick, rhythmic sound and cursed as he realized what was happening on the other side of the thin barrier. He heard Ryan murmur encouragement and, after seeing them the night before, could easily picture him stroking Micah's smooth, flawless skin as he fucked into his husband. It made Nick's cock throb and his balls draw up tight, his orgasm approaching quickly as Micah sucked him with perfect pressure. He couldn't help wishing he could twist his hands in Micah's hair and watch as Ryan pushed him to the edge.

He managed to bite out a warning, which Micah ignored. Nick's orgasm rushed up and over him, each pull on his cock making him jolt, a long, low groan escaping through his clenched teeth. He spilled down Micah's throat in long pulses and eventually had to ease back when he got too sensitive.

He leaned against the wall, chest heaving. He hadn't expected that to be so intense. Hadn't expected the raw need that had overwhelmed him right at the end.

Micah's gradually increasing gasps and Ryan's harsh breathing told him the other two men were getting closer to their own release. They were both the kind of stunning that people paid money to watch. He leaned his forehead against the partition and let the mental images wash over him.

Micah's fingers were wrapped over the edge of the glory hole again, and Nick stroked them before he could think better of it.

He'd blame his cum-drunk brain for that later. In the moment, he soaked in the small contact as Micah twisted their fingers together and clung.

Micah's breathless cry when he came made Nick's spent cock twitch, and he scrubbed his free hand over his face in an attempt to pull himself back together. Reluctantly, he stepped away from Micah and slumped against the far wall of the stall. Time to get back to reality. He fixed his pants without bothering to open his eyes. The wall was his friend, given how shaky his legs were at the moment.

He could hear Ryan murmuring to Micah and knew he needed to move. Clean up and get back to their table. He wanted another drink or five.

Before he could convince himself, the stall door swung open. Nick blinked his eyes in time to see Micah poke his head in, cheeks flushed and looking thoroughly fucked. "Hey," Micah said, eyes darting up, then away.

"Hey."

Micah gathered his confidence and straightened. "You good?"

Nick chuckled. He was better than good. "You let me know if there's anything else on your bucket list you need help checking off. I'll make myself available."

Micah grinned, a laugh bubbling in his throat. His ass was sore, his limbs loose and tingly. His jaw ached, and he could still taste Nick on his tongue. Holy shit. That had been the hottest thing ever. Porn was *not* lying to him. "You'll be my first call," he told Nick.

He glanced back at his husband, who was radiating smug satisfaction. As he should be. He and Nick had totally blown Micah's mind. Ryan rolled his eyes at their banter.

Nick stepped out of the stall, his pants already put to rights. When Micah had jimmied the door, Nick had still been recovering, his breathing heavy and his skin flushed. Now he looked perfectly composed again.

It made Micah want to muss him up.

As always, Ryan saved him from himself, wrapping one arm around Micah from behind and reaching out with the other to snag the front of Nick's shirt and haul him closer, similar to how they'd stood while dancing. "Ready to get out of here?" Ryan asked, the question directed to both of them.

Micah nodded, fidgeting in an effort to keep his hands to himself. He really, really wanted to touch Nick. Maybe suck him off again somewhere where he had access to more skin. Because the glory hole, while fun, had limited things. What would it be like to get down on his knees for the two of them? He had a sudden, vivid mental image of having a thick cock in each hand as he took turns with them. He shivered and sank his teeth into his lower lip so he wouldn't beg for that right then.

"What do you say, Nicky?" Ryan murmured, stroking his hand up and down Micah's arm.

Nick startled, his eyes lifting from where he'd been staring at Micah's mouth. Micah's cheeks heated, and he couldn't contain a pleased smile.

The corner of Nick's mouth curled up. "Yeah. I think I'm done dancing for tonight."

Ryan huffed a laugh and shook his head, then led them toward the door. Micah reached out, and Ryan laced their fingers together, tugging him along. He was still dozy from coming so hard and perfectly content to let Ryan tow him.

After a brief stop at their table to retrieve Micah's discarded shirt, they made it back to the truck, and Micah crawled into the middle of the front bench seat. With Nick next to the door, Micah slumped sideways against him. Nick didn't hesitate to wrap an arm around him to help keep him in place. Micah looked to the left and met Ryan's calm eyes.

"You good, baby?" Ryan asked.

"Yeah," Micah answered with a grin, hugging Nick's arms around him and resting his head on a strong shoulder. "He's not a bad pillow. A little hard, maybe."

Ryan laughed. "Not surprised. He's all muscle."

"He can hear you," Nick muttered, his head back against the seat, eyes closed.

Ryan put the truck in gear and pulled carefully out of the parking lot. Micah appreciated how responsible his husband always was when they needed to drive home. He hadn't been counting, but he knew Ryan kept his drinks to a minimum when they were out.

Micah dozed against Nick for the twenty minutes or so it took them to get back to the ranch. Nick smelled good. Fresh and woodsy with a hint of leather.

Back at the house, he dragged himself from the truck and zombie-walked upstairs to face-plant on the bed. He wasn't used to nights out anymore. The drawback of being married to someone who claimed his clubbing days were ten years behind him. He tried to kick his shoes off without lifting his head and hummed happily when his leg was caught in strong hands and he felt the laces being loosened. Yes. This was the best part of having a husband.

Someone chuckled. Oh. He must have said that out loud.

"You think that's funny?" Ryan asked.

Micah nodded into the pillow, but Nick was the one who answered. "I think you need to up your game if this is his favorite part," he teased.

Micah giggled as one of his shoes was tugged off and dropped to the floor with a thump. He tried to lift his other leg to help, but it was snagged out of the air.

Ryan huffed. "You making suggestions?"

"Nope," Nick chirped back. "I've had enough of married life. I'm just here to steal your bathroom."

The door of said bathroom clicked shut at the same time that Micah's other shoe fell to the floor, and hands reached under his hips, unbuttoning his pants and dragging them down. He lifted up helpfully and got a teasing smack on the ass in reward.

Micah hummed and squirmed but only got an additional pat before Ryan dragged the blankets out from under him.

A few minutes later, Nick was across the hall and Ryan was crawling into bed and gathering Micah into his arms. Micah snuggled in and slung one leg over both of Ryan's, pillowing his head on Ryan's bare chest. Ryan's hand fell to his back and rubbed in slow, soothing circles until Micah was a happy puddle.

"You feeling good, baby?" Ryan murmured into his hair, his tone soothing, like he wasn't sure if Micah was still awake or not.

Micah understood what Ryan was asking. They'd never done anything like that before. Still, as soon as Micah realized Nick was interested, there'd been no going back. He might have chickened out by asking that they play with the glory hole, but that was only because he'd needed to maintain that bit of distance, just in case they had it wrong and this ended badly. In the end, he kind of regretted not following his gut and inviting Nick to their bed. He felt like he might have cheated them out of something really spectacular. All of which he explained to Ryan.

"It's okay to take this slow," Ryan said when Micah finished his sleepy, rambling word vomit. "And I don't think it needs to be a one-time thing if you don't want it to be. I just want to be sure you enjoyed yourself and you aren't regretting anything."

Micah chewed on his lip. He got what Ryan was asking, checking in after something so new and intense. But as he examined his emotions, he only felt good.

He'd worried there might be some jealousy. Maybe some weird reaction like he'd somehow betrayed Ryan, but there was none of that. Just a relaxed hum in his brain and the knowledge that he'd definitely be down for doing it again.

"I'm great," he answered finally and felt a tension he hadn't noticed leave Ryan. "How about you?" he asked. There was a chance they weren't on the same page here, but he knew Ryan wouldn't hesitate to tell him if that was true. It was part of why they worked so well together. They trusted each other with everything.

Ryan huffed softly, his chest rising and falling under Micah's cheek. "I wish I had it on video. You were so fucking gorgeous. And the look in his eyes when he came out of that stall? You rocked his world, baby. It was stunning."

Micah's face went warm, and he turned to hide it in Ryan's throat. "Yeah?" he asked, feeling shy.

Ryan gave a pleased growl in reply and dragged Micah closer until he was draped across Ryan's body, his legs falling open over Ryan's thighs. A broad hand skimmed down his back, and fingers dipped possessively between his cheeks.

Micah spread his legs helpfully, but Ryan didn't go further, just touched him, hand cupping his ass.

"I wish I could have seen his face. Seen how good you were making him feel while you swallowed his cock," Ryan said, his voice a warm rumble under Micah's ear, his words making Micah's dick twitch. Micah had thought nearly the same thing. He swallowed.

"Do you think..." He hesitated, his heart suddenly beating a little too hard.

"I think," Ryan said, his finger pressing in where Micah was still wet and slippery. "Nicky would definitely be down for more."

Micah moaned, goose bumps breaking out across his skin as he rocked down into Ryan's touch.

More was an exciting thought.

Sadie was the first horse to notice Micah entering the barn. Her eager whicker set off all the others. There was nothing cuter than a barn full of thousand-pound animals calling for their breakfast.

It was still dark out, the sky only showing hints of pink behind the mountains. Micah was a little early, but he was awake, so he figured he'd get a head start on the day. It was going to be a busy one, with back-to-back trail rides.

The sounds of hungry animals died down as Micah filled their buckets. When he was done, he topped off the cats' food bowls while Pumpkin and Peppermint wove between his legs. The bowls went on top of a cabinet so the dogs—who had eaten up at the house—couldn't get into the kibble, and the cats hopped nimbly up to enjoy their breakfast.

Micah loved mornings in the barn just as much as he loved lazy ones in bed. He leaned over the door of Lex's stall, stroking the paint gelding's neck as he chowed down on his grain. Back when Micah was still in high school, Lex was the first horse he'd trained himself. He'd started out as a standoffish bastard, always biting or lashing out at the people and horses who walked by his stall. But once Micah had formed a bond with him, he learned that it was all just a front. A reaction to conceal how on edge he was after years of living in bad conditions. It had taken time, but Lex became one of their most reliable trail-ride leaders. And now he was actually Micah's, a present for his recent birthday. Maggie had joked that Micah trained Lex so well, it had taken Ryan that long to afford him. Though everyone in attendance knew Maggie probably would have given the horse to Micah if he had just asked.

He was so glad Maggie had gotten through the surgery and was going to be okay. It had been too many years since she'd been able to move comfortably, and Micah knew she'd love to get back on a horse at some point. A big impetus for the surgery had been an article Micah found talking about athletes returning to their sport after a joint replacement. The person with the bad hip they interviewed had been an Olympic show jumper. Once Maggie read the piece and Ryan showed her some research on recovery rates, she'd finally decided to go for it. Really, things had been bad enough that Micah didn't think she had anything to lose, but it wasn't his body, so he couldn't judge.

Still, it was going to be incredible if he could ride the trails with her again. He missed it desperately. He bet Nick did too. Maggie had told him stories about her nephew, and she made it sound like he was born to be on a horse.

Micah's brain caught on the idea of Nick riding a horse in jeans, chaps, and nothing else, and his traitorous cock took interest. Because of course it did. He sighed and let himself picture just how good Nick's bulge would look, framed by leather straps. His skin went uncomfortably warm at the direction his mind kept dragging him—which was right into the gutter. He hated how easily he was blushing these days. He'd thought he'd outgrown it, but apparently there were still things that could embarrass him.

"Man," Izzy said from behind Micah, making him jump—which made Lex snort and toss his head before going back to eating. Izzy was standing at the bottom of the stairs to the hayloft apartment where he lived, looking like he hadn't spent half the night dancing and accepting free drinks from his adoring fans. "How early were you up?" he asked as he strolled over, travel coffee mug in hand. This close, Micah could see that his eyes were a bit red-rimmed after all and felt better about the mild headache he'd woken up with.

Micah shrugged. "Early enough to do your job for you." He gave Lex a final pat and headed for a stack of hay bales along one wall. He pulled one down and cut through the twine, then started tossing flakes into the horse's stalls. Hopefully, Izzy would do whatever he was up so early to do and leave Micah to his thoughts.

Izzy snorted. "You know I'm never first shift on Sunday. You should be shocked I slept here at all."

Micah couldn't argue with that. Izzy was a self-described "ethical slut"—he'd happily fuck anyone with a dick and some interest—who found a new bed to spend the night in every weekend. "Why *are* you here, anyway?" he asked. It wasn't like Izzy to be both home and awake on his morning off.

Izzy shrugged. "Alice asked me to pick her up later, and my hookup lived in the wrong direction, so I did him in the back seat of his Tesla, then made fun of Elon Musk. He was more than ready to drop me off."

Micah shook his head. Only Izzy could get away with something like that. Micah would never dream of it. Even back when he was hooking up with randoms in clubs.

"Now," Izzy said, "tell me about last night. Don't think I didn't see what the three of you were up to out on the dance floor. Are you and Ryan starting something with Maggie's nephew?"

Micah groaned, his face burning. Again. Fuck, he'd thought Izzy was distracted by the Tesla guy. How the hell was he supposed to explain this? It wasn't like they'd talked about anyone finding out.

Izzy took in his face and laughed. "Man, it must have been hot as hell."

Micah shoved him away, though he couldn't contain his grin. "Shut up."

"No way," Izzy pressed. "Baby had a threesome. I want all the spicy details."

"Ugh. You're the worst. I'm not giving you details."

"I guess I'll just have to let my imagination fill in the gaps," Izzy said with a leer in his voice.

Micah groaned. "You suck. I'm going to pick up breakfast in town, and I'm not getting you anything."

Izzy laughed as Micah headed toward his truck, leaving his annoying friend behind. Man, Izzy was lucky Micah loved him.

An hour later, it was fully light, and Micah pulled back up to the house, a large bakery bag on the seat next to him. The bakery had only been open a few months, but it had quickly become one of his and Ryan's favorite spots for breakfast. When one of them got up extra early, they usually ended up making a pastry run.

When he walked into the kitchen, Ryan was leaning against the counter while coffee brewed. Micah dropped the bag off on the table and went over for a good-morning kiss, smiling into it when Ryan hummed and pulled him closer.

"Morning, baby," Ryan said when they broke apart, concern clear in his voice. "You were gone early."

Micah shrugged and went to grab plates. "I woke up early, so I figured I'd get the day started."

The brewing coffee sputtered to a stop, and Ryan filled their mugs, leaving an empty one on the counter next to the pot. He dropped a kiss on Micah's temple as he handed over his perfectly doctored coffee. "Nicky should be down in a minute. He was getting dressed."

Micah bit the inside of his cheek to hide a smile. He liked the way Ryan called Nick "Nicky." It was cute. He grabbed another plate from the cabinet and set three spots at the table.

Ryan didn't say anything, but Micah could tell he was amused. Micah had gone a little overboard at the bakery, and despite what he'd told Izzy, there was more than enough for him and Alice too. He'd take some down later.

He was just sitting down to eat when he heard Nick's footsteps on the stairs. He jumped back up and went to pour him a coffee.

"Morning," Nick drawled as he wandered into the kitchen. He looked half-asleep, shirtless and in sweatpants, his hair tousled. Micah wanted to squish his cheeks, but that would probably be weird, so he settled for returning the greeting and asking how he took his coffee.

"Strong," Nick said as he came to a stop next to Micah and stared at the coffee pot.

"Not a morning person?" Micah couldn't keep the grin out of his voice.

"This isn't morning," Nick grumbled. "It's the middle of the fucking night."

Ryan chuckled, leaning back in his chair. "Micah's been up at least two hours."

Nick gave him an incredulous look. "What the fuck is wrong with you?"

Micah laughed and handed him his coffee, black. Tired Nick was hilarious. "You get used to it."

Nick shook his head and headed for the table. "I think the country air has rotted your brain. There's nothing normal about this time of day." He dropped into a chair and lifted the mug to his lips, groaning as he took his first sip. The sound took Micah right back to the bathroom stall, and he shifted uncomfortably, his eyes going to Ryan's.

Ryan gave him a wink that made Micah's cheeks heat. Dirty bastard knew exactly where Micah's brain had gone just then. He huffed and sat back down, grabbing his favorite bear claw from the bag and passing the rest to Nick. Ryan already had a plain croissant, because he was a boring-breakfast person. Who didn't want sugar in the morning? Micah's husband, that was who.

Nick peeked into the bag, and his eyes widened. He pulled out a cinnamon roll. "These look amazing."

"They're the best," Micah agreed, his mouth full of sugary goodness.

Nick took a bite, and his eyes closed in pleasure. Micah felt a rush of warmth at the obvious enjoyment on his face. Nothing made Micah happier than taking care of the people who were important to him. And Nick was easily taking a place as one of those people.

It was probably too soon, but Micah was starting to wonder what it might take to keep Nick around.

# TEN

RYAN

RYAN STUCK THE SHOVEL back in the wheelbarrow and paused to wipe the sweat from his brow. It was a pleasantly cool day, but nothing got your blood pumping like hauling gravel down a quarter mile of driveway. It was the second time he'd had to do it this year, and he was fed up. If the town didn't come out and repave the spot, he was going to march down to city hall with one of Nicky's ruined tires and dump it on the town manager's shiny mahogany desk.

Ryan wasn't a fan of the new guy they'd hired. He seemed to think that only things within the city limits should be a priority—which was just untrue. Ryan missed the previous manager, who had retired after doing the job longer than Ryan had been alive. Mr. Jones would have had this mess fixed the day after it happened.

Ryan dumped the rest of the gravel into the pothole and smoothed it out as best he could. It would suffice for now, at least. They'd been lucky that it was Nicky whose car had been damaged, rather than a client who might blow up their online reviews. That shit was impossible to manage. Ryan didn't want to be the guy who left a nasty response to a complaint about something that was completely out of their control—the number of bugs on the trail, to name one recent example—but he also didn't feel right ignoring reviews. Which was why Archer took care of that part of the business. Archer had a way of pointing out how absurd someone was being while still sounding like he was apologizing for the inconvenience.

Ryan smirked as he imagined the review Nicky might leave them. Hopefully the night before had made the flat tires worth it. Arousal simmered in his gut as his thoughts drifted to the handsome man who'd strolled into their lives. He and Micah had made a stunning picture out on that dance floor, limbs entwined, hips pressed together.

That wasn't the first time Micah had enticed Ryan from his seat by getting close to another dancer. It was a game that always ended in a good time for the two of them, either once they got home or, if they were feeling adventurous, in a private corner of the club. But it had never been like it was with Nicky. Micah had never truly been interested in the person he was dancing with, and neither had Ryan.

Apparently, that made all the difference, because Ryan hadn't felt a hint of jealousy when he saw Nicky's hands on his husband's skin. He'd only wanted to get closer, to find out how their new friend would react if Ryan did the same to him. It wasn't as much of a surprise as he would have expected, and, paradoxically, that was probably the thing that surprised him the most.

Ryan was familiar with how things like this could work. He'd had his fair share of threesomes, including a long-term relationship with a couple in college. But Micah was less experienced. They'd had extremely pleasurable adventures with toys and new and exciting locations, but adding a third to an encounter was something they hadn't considered... until now. Ryan had known it was going to be good—he always got off on Micah's pleasure—but he hadn't expected his own reaction.

He wanted more, and he wanted it with Nicky. Micah had been gorgeous and needy, sucking Nicky like he couldn't get enough, his skin flushed with pleasure, his fingers bleached white where they were pressed to the wall keeping them apart. His husband loved blow jobs, both giving and receiving, and he was a talented provider. His hot little mouth was heaven on earth, and Ryan had wanted to know what Nicky looked like on the receiving end of all that focus.

Nicky was hot as sin, entertaining as hell, and—it seemed—just as interested in them as they were in him. Most importantly, Nicky felt like someone safe. They might not know him well, but Ryan could tell he had no desire to hurt them. The way he'd watched Ryan undress Micah for bed put any final concerns about that to rest. The softness of his gaze and the gentle curve of his smile as he'd joked about Ryan needing to up his game said everything Ryan needed to know. Nicky cared. And in Ryan's experience, that was the most important thing.

That didn't mean Ryan was going to push for more, and he would watch that Micah didn't either. If anything else happened, it would be because all three of them wanted it.

A sedan coming up the road interrupted his thoughts. The pothole was still on the dangerous side, and he gestured for the driver to go around. Instead, the car came to a stop, and the driver rolled down the window.

Ryan stuck the shovel in the mound of gravel and stepped up to the car. "Can I help you?" he asked. Maybe it was a potential guest stopping by to check the ranch out. It happened from time to time.

The driver was a heavyset, middle-aged man with graying hair and a thick mustache. Ryan nearly did a double take at the suit and tie, which were out of place in these parts. Even the people who worked at city hall were more likely to sport polos and khakis.

"Is the driveway accessible? I have an appointment with the owner."

Ryan frowned. "There must be a mistake. She's not in right now."

The man's eyebrow hooked up. "This is the Lauder property, isn't it?"

Ryan gave a nod. "Yes. But—"

The man didn't let him finish. "Well, I have an appointment with *Mr.* Lauder to discuss the sale of the property."

Everything in Ryan froze, but he still managed to say. "There must be a mistake, Mr...."

"Russell Miller. I'm here on behalf of Calvin Developers."

Ryan's mind raced. What the hell was going on? Was this Nicky's doing? And did Maggie know? No. There was no way. He squared his shoulders. "My apologies, Mr. Miller, but there's been a miscommunication. Mr. Lauder isn't available to meet."

Miller's eyes narrowed, and he frowned. "And who are you?"

"Ryan Avery. I'm the ranch manager." Ryan held out a gloved hand and kept his face carefully neutral as Miller eyed it, nostrils flaring in dismay, before shaking it.

"Do you know when Mr. Lauder will be available? I can't wait long."

"I'm not sure. Not for several hours at least."

Miller huffed and pulled out his wallet, handing Ryan a business card. "Please have him contact me as soon as possible."

Ryan glanced at the card. *Russell Miller, Real Estate Developer.* He kept his face impassive as he nodded and tucked it into his pocket. "Will do, Mr. Miller."

Miller looked skeptical but gave Ryan a nod, rolled up his window, and drove off.

Ryan quickly spread the rest of the gravel and stalked back up the driveway, trying not to let his assumptions get out of control. It was possible Nicky didn't know anything about this. It could be some kind of miscommunication.

He left the wheelbarrow in the yard and barreled through the screen door. It smacked shut behind him with enough force that Nicky, sitting on the couch with a book, looked up, startled. His teasing look quickly morphed into confusion as Ryan stared him down. Ryan took a few deep, steadying breaths. He didn't have much of a temper, but this combination of anger and confusion was pushing his restraint.

"Care to tell me why I just turned away a real estate developer who claimed he had a meeting with you about selling the ranch?"

The color drained from Nicky's face, and if he hadn't been sitting already, Ryan would have forced him into a chair. "I'm not sure—"

"Don't bullshit me, Nicky," Ryan growled, his mood darkening further as he saw Nicky's shoulders tense. "What the hell is going on?"

Nicky's book fell from his hand as he reached up to scrub a hand over his face. "Goddammit." He shoved himself to his feet and grabbed his cell off the end table. "I need to make a phone call."

Ryan stopped him with a hand on his shoulder, then pulled it back when Nicky turned to face him. He read the turmoil in Nicky's green eyes and gave in. "All right. But then I'm gonna need you to explain."

Nicky looked away but gave a sharp nod before striding out onto the deck, the phone already pressed to his ear.

As the back door was closing behind him, the front one swung open and Micah walked in, his forehead creased with concern. "You okay? I saw the wheelbarrow in the yard."

Ryan tried to hide his grimace. The last thing he wanted was to upset Micah before he had any answers. Hell, he wasn't even sure what the questions were at this point. Did Maggie know this was going on? He couldn't imagine she did. The ranch was her whole life. She would never sell it, and she definitely wouldn't allow it to be sold when she wasn't even there.

Micah crossed the room while Ryan was trying to come up with an answer that wouldn't set off alarm bells. He reached out, palm cupping the back of Ryan's neck. "Ry? What is it?"

Ryan wrapped an arm around Micah's waist and dragged him closer, taking comfort in his solid warmth. Things were so different than they had been back when they first met. They might joke about the age difference between them, but in reality, Micah was his equal in everything. His partner. And he couldn't ask for anyone better. He dropped a kiss on Micah's temple, breathing in the soothing scent of Micah mixed with hay and horses.

"I'm not sure," he said finally. "But Nicky has some explaining to do."

Micah looked even more concerned at that half answer. "Is he okay? Are *you* okay?"

Nicky strode back inside, his expression mutinous, but slowed to a halt when he saw Ryan and Micah watching him. "Fuck," he growled. For a minute, it looked like he was going to chuck his phone across the room. Instead, he shoved it into his pocket and dug both hands into his hair with a growl. "My fucking father," he bit out through clenched teeth.

Micah stepped toward him, hand outstretched to offer comfort. Ryan halted him with a touch on his arm, then felt a flash of guilt when Nicky noticed the gesture and winced. Ryan didn't apologize, though. He didn't think Nicky would lash out at either of them, but he didn't really know the man, did he?

Nicky turned away from them and walked to the sink to splash water on his face, then braced his palms on the edge of the counter and hung his head. "I thought I'd have more time."

Micah pulled away from Ryan and went to Nicky, laying a hand on his shoulder. Ryan couldn't help the rush of warmth he felt in that moment. Micah couldn't stand to see anyone he cared about hurting. He was a much better person than Ryan, who wanted the facts before he made a decision. "Hey," Micah said, his palm against Nicky's back. "Let's go sit. I'm sure we can figure things out." He rubbed soothingly, the way he'd treat an anxious horse, until Nicky nodded and stepped away from the sink, his face flushed and damp. Micah handed him a towel with an uncertain smile. Nicky huffed but took it and dried his face, then followed the two of them to the living room.

When Micah and Ryan were seated on the couch with Nicky in an adjacent armchair, Nicky finally started to explain.

"My father is in the process of divorcing his third wife," he said, his hands clenched so tightly together that his fingertips were white. "They have a prenup, but all of the assets acquired during their marriage need to be split fifty-fifty."

Ryan frowned, not sure what that had to do with anything, but let Nicky continue.

Nicky dragged a hand over his face, exhaustion in his eyes. "Are the two of you aware that Phillip owns the ranch?"

"What?" Micah shook his head. "No. That's not— The ranch belongs to Maggie. Her father left it to her." He looked to Ryan for help, but he was equally bewildered.

"Micah's right. Maggie's owned the ranch for close to thirty years."

Nicky's shoulders sagged. "She did until about five years ago. I don't know all the details, but she was having financial problems and transferred ownership to my father."

"Who told you this?"

Nick sighed. "I understand it's hard to believe. I didn't until my father showed me the paperwork. The ranch is legally his, and he's been supporting it financially since the transfer."

"And now he needs the equity to pay off his ex-wife," Ryan said, putting the pieces together.

Micah's fingers bit into the muscle of Ryan's thigh. "What does that mean?"

"It means Phillip is planning to sell Split Rock out from under Maggie while she's away having surgery."

Nicky grimaced but didn't correct him.

"No," Micah choked out, his voice wet. "No, he can't do that."

Ryan wrapped an arm around him and folded him against his side. "We aren't going to let him." He turned back to Nicky. "Explain what you mean by supporting the ranch. The business is profitable."

Nicky shook his head, some of the emotion leaving his expression as he started talking business. "I've been over the accounts in detail. It's been in the red for at least eight years. Most months it's only operating because my father is making up the difference."

Micah was already shaking his head. "That's not true. Last year was our best ever. The business is growing like gangbusters. We've even been talking about hiring more help."

"I'm sorry, Micah," Nicky said, and he sounded like he meant it.

Micah's hands balled into fists, and he opened his mouth to argue. Ryan squeezed him to make him wait. "You said there are records of this?"

Nicky pressed his palms to his thighs as he heaved a sigh. "I have a copy of the paperwork upstairs."

"And it shows that Phillip is the owner?" Ryan asked rhetorically, getting a nod from Nicky.

"Well, fuck that." Micah's voice shook with emotion. "It has to be fake. Maggie wouldn't have given the ranch away without telling us."

She wouldn't. And didn't, Ryan knew. Micah wasn't aware, but Ryan had helped Maggie update her will just last month. She was leaving the ranch to Micah, something she wouldn't do if she didn't believe she owned it. Ryan rubbed Micah's arm, hoping to steady him. It didn't matter that Maggie wasn't actually related to them, or that they were her employees. She was family, and Split Rock Ranch was home—and they wouldn't hesitate to defend it.

"You said you thought you had more time," Micah said. "What did you mean?"

Nicky sighed and dragged a hand through his hair, dislodging the curls and making it stand on end. "It wasn't supposed to happen this way. When I left New York, my plan was to talk to Maggie and explain things. Then meet with the real estate developer sometime next week. I never wanted to blindside anyone." He shook his head sharply, his jaw clenched. "I didn't know about the surgery, but I'm sure Phillip did. Maybe he thought it would be easier this way." Nicky didn't look like he believed that.

Micah didn't either. "That's bullshit."

Ryan had to agree. "I'd like to see this paperwork," he told Nicky, who agreed and went to retrieve it.

As soon as he was gone, Micah shot to his feet and started pacing. "We need to call Maggie and tell her. She can... She can... I don't know. She can tell us this is all a mistake." He started patting his pockets for his phone. His hands were shaking, and Ryan grabbed them in his own.

"Take a breath, baby."

Micah tried to pull away. "No, Ry, we need to *do something*." His voice cracked, and his lower lip wobbled. Ryan's heart hurt. He hadn't seen Micah this upset since one of the horses got injured and things were touch-and-go for a while. Even then, he'd managed to hold it together.

Ryan stood and took Micah in his arms, squeezing him until he buried his face against Ryan's chest. "We'll figure it out. I promise."

Micah let out a shuddering breath and nodded.

Nicky returned moments later with several folders of paperwork.

Ryan grabbed his spare glasses from the end table and flipped through, but it was exactly as Nicky had said. The deed was in Phillip Lauder's name. That made things complicated. "Okay. Nicky, I can see how this all looks straightforward from your side of things. I have to tell you, though, as the manager here, there's no reason that the ranch shouldn't be in the black. I see what goes in and out every day, and I can guarantee we've been profitable for years." He held up the deed with Phillip Lauder's name clearly visible. "And as far as this goes, Maggie would never have knowingly transferred ownership. So we've got two stories that don't match up. I don't want to jump to conclusions, but the only explanation that makes sense to me is that this deed is a forgery." He paused, but Nicky didn't protest—which made Ryan wonder just what was going through his head.

"If your father forged the transfer paperwork, it's going to be extremely difficult to prove. As Maggie's financial manager, he's had access to her accounts for years and could easily have taken the opportunity to falsify her signature." He went back to the deed of title, examining it more closely. "But, unless we can find proof, it will come down to whether a judge believes him or Maggie."

Nick's voice held a little bit of hope, despite Ryan basically accusing his father of fraud. "You sound like you have experience with this kind of thing."

Ryan tipped his head in agreement. "Before I came to Split Rock, I was a lawyer. My license is inactive now, but I practiced in Florida. There's a lot of real estate litigation work down there."

Nicky's eyebrows shot up. "You left law to manage a horse ranch?"

Ryan shrugged, thumb tracing circles on the back of Micah's hand. He wasn't fond of talking about his life back then, but in this case his background could be useful.

"I left law because I hated it. It was my father's dream, not mine. When I realized I was never going to be happy doing it, I left. I was lucky to land here thanks to a good friend. It turned out to be the best thing that ever happened to me." He lifted Micah's hand to kiss the back of it and got a wobbly grin in return.

"Damn right." Micah turned his hand to lace their fingers together, then looked back to Nicky.

"If you're right, and my father forged these documents," Nicky started, his expression troubled, "there has to be a reason for it. It makes no sense that he would take the ranch from Maggie after all this time." He lifted a hand and pressed his thumb and forefinger to the corners of his eyes.

Ryan was intimately familiar with the emotions flitting across Nicky's face. The mixture of duty and frustration that came from having a parent you were loyal to but didn't approve of. He'd felt it many times when dealing with his own estranged father.

"Do you think you can get Phillip to back off for a few days?" he asked. "At least until Maggie and I have a chance to go over things and get a practicing lawyer involved?"

Nicky winced. "I'll see what I can do. I can try to get in touch with the developer and tell him we need a few more days to get things in order."

Ryan handed over the man's card. "That's his number—though I guess you probably have it already. It sounded like he wasn't staying in town, so that might help." He gave Micah's hand a final squeeze. "I'm going to give Archer a call. He'll need a heads-up."

"I'll get started on lunch," Micah said, straightening reluctantly. He headed into the kitchen, avoiding Nicky's eyes.

Nicky's lips pressed together in a frown as they watched Micah go. "Think he'll ever forgive me?"

Ryan took in the lines of exhaustion around his eyes and the defeated slump of his shoulders. "For what?"

Nicky scowled, like he thought Ryan was mocking him.

"No, really," Ryan said. "'Cause from where I'm standing, you're just the messenger. Last I heard, we're not supposed to shoot those."

Nicky snorted at Ryan's weak attempt at a joke. "I appreciate that. But I meant for not saying something sooner. Pretty sure what happened last night never would have if you'd known why I was here."

Ryan shrugged. "I don't think one thing had anything to do with the other, but if you're worried, ask him." He patted his pocket to make sure he had his phone, then headed for his home office.

"Ryan," Nicky called after him.

Ryan glanced back.

"Thanks. For being understanding. Not everyone would be, in your shoes."

"Trust me, Nicky. If I know anything, it's that we aren't responsible for the decisions our fathers make."

Half an hour later, after a conversation with Archer that involved some very creative swearing, Ryan exited the office. He could smell chocolate baking, which meant Micah had whipped up some of his famous brownies. They were one of his comfort foods, and Ryan felt a pang that he wouldn't be able to tell Micah he'd fixed this whole mess.

When he stepped into the kitchen, two sets of worried eyes met his. He walked over to his regular seat at the head of the table, Micah on his left and Nicky across from him. Bowls of soup and grilled cheese sandwiches sat in front of them. More comfort food, but it looked practically untouched.

"Well?" Micah asked. "What did she say? Did she know? What are we gonna do?"

Nicky kept his mouth shut but watched Ryan with just as many questions in his eyes. He was twisting his water glass in his hands, the only real sign of his anxiety.

Ryan sighed. "She was resting. The surgery took a lot out of her." At Micah's quick inhale he added, "She's doing well, just exhausted. I spoke to Archer, and he'll fill her in when he sees her tonight."

Micah took a deep breath and let it out shakily. "But everything went okay with the surgery?"

Ryan nodded and reached out to squeeze Micah's hand. "It went extremely well, according to the surgeon. She's already walking with assistance and should improve even more over the next few days."

Micah gave a relieved smile. The surgeon had been hopeful about doing a total hip replacement, saying Maggie was strong and it would be a straightforward recovery, but they'd still worried. Micah had wanted to take her to the hospital himself, but Maggie insisted she wanted him at the ranch, where he could be useful. She knew his husband well. Micah would have been a wreck in the hospital waiting room. Archer was much more able to maintain the levelheaded calm one wanted during that kind of thing.

Besides, Maggie wouldn't have stood for Micah's hovering. She was a strong woman and fiercely independent. She was used to bearing her problems on her own. It had taken a lot of convincing just to get her to let them help with transportation to and from her appointments around town and in the city when her hip made driving too difficult. And that didn't begin to cover the arguments they'd had when she decided she wanted Ryan and Micah to live in the house while she took over the one-level cottage directly behind it.

"So now we have to wait," Micah said, picking up his sandwich to take a bite when Ryan nudged him.

"I'm sure we'll hear from her first thing in the morning with directions on what we can do. Archer's going to have a hard time keeping her down there for the follow-up appointment," Ryan said as he retrieved his own sandwich from the oven. He wasn't someone who lost his appetite under pressure. He wouldn't have made it through law school if that had been the case.

Apparently the same wasn't true for Nicky, who was pressing his fingers to the corners of his eyes like he had a headache starting. "I should try my father again. I want to see what he has to say about the developer being here so early." He grimaced and pushed back from the table.

"You should eat first," Ryan said, trying to keep it a suggestion and not an order, but either way, Nicky shook his head.

"Save it for me, okay?"

"Okay," Micah replied to Nicky's back as he left the room. Micah bit his lip and watched him go, then turned to Ryan, a worried crease marring his forehead.

Ryan reached over and squeezed his hand, his heart warming when Micah flipped his palm up and laced their fingers together. No matter what happened with the ranch, Maggie, and Nicky, he and Micah would be okay.

NICK ROOTED THROUGH HIS bag for his migraine meds and swallowed them dry. The tension behind his eyes was building and flaring down his neck and shoulders. Fucking migraines were the bane of his existence. The doctor said they were caused by stress—which he thought was fucking obvious—and that Nick should try meditation. Like he had time for that. He sat on the edge of the bed and rested his elbows on his knees, rubbing slow circles against his temples in an effort to relieve the throbbing.

Closing his eyes, he sucked in a deep breath, his lungs filling with the familiar scent of the farmhouse. Even with the new residents, it still smelled like wood, old books, and a hint of leather. This had been his favorite place when he was a child, the one place there was no pressure to be who his father wanted him to be.

It was Nick's fault that that had ended when his mom died. He was the one who chose to stay away, to spend summers clinging to his only remaining parent. At thirteen, he'd been old enough for his dad to put him to work in his office. So fresh mountain air, sunshine, and horses became cool office AC, tinted windows, and the heavy perfume favored by his dad's executive assistant.

For a long time he tried to tell himself that's what he wanted out of life: to be powerful and respected, just like his dad. That lasted until freshman year of college, when he met Xavier.

Xavier had turned Nick's whole world on its head, not just because he was Nick's first openly gay friend, but because he introduced Nick to a world Nick hadn't known existed. A world that was loud, fun, and exhilarating. A world that didn't revolve around Nick's father. There was a reason that—despite their divorce—Xavier was still his best friend.

Nick should probably call him. He knew Xavier would offer his help... which was why Nick didn't want to get him involved. He refused to take advantage of Xavi's unfortunate sense of obligation. Not this time. Nick would find a way to fix this without Xavier's help.

Anger rolled in his gut when he thought about the events of the day. After listening to Ryan's assessment of the situation, Nick was questioning everything. What if Ryan was right, and Maggie had never needed Phillip's help to save her home or agreed to him taking ownership of the ranch? Nick knew his father wasn't perfect, but would he really go so far as to steal from his own family? And for what purpose? The divorce explained why he was selling the ranch now, but that didn't explain why he'd wanted it in the first place.

Nick didn't know what to think.

He stared at the floor, his spinning thoughts competing with his throbbing brain and reaching only one conclusion: he believed Ryan and Micah. The ranch wasn't, and had never been, failing. Hearing that it was doing well, plus seeing it with his own eyes, left little room for doubt. His father had lied. And if his reasons for taking over the ranch were fabricated, the rest of his explanations fell apart rapidly.

The question was, how was Nick going to fix this?

One step at a time. He called Russell Miller and left a message with the man's secretary, explaining that there had been a mix-up and he wouldn't be available to meet for a few more days.

Then he tapped the contact for his father and listened to it ring through to voicemail. He gritted his teeth. Phillip always had his phone on, so if he wasn't answering, it was by choice. That meant he had sent the real estate developer early on purpose and was now avoiding Nick's calls to prevent Nick from questioning him on it. Xavier would point out how passive-aggressive that was.

Nick waited through the voice message that made his dad sound like a politician on the campaign trail. "Hi, Dad. We need to talk." He paused, debating whether he should say more, but decided not to. That would only give Phillip more time to come up with excuses. "Please give me a call back when you get this," he said and hung up the phone, letting it fall to the bed next to him.

The worst thing was, after dealing with his father for all these years, Nick wasn't even surprised.

He *was* shocked, though, by Ryan and Micah's reactions to the situation. Micah had been devastated, of course, and Ryan had turned cool and analytical in a way Nick hadn't been expecting. But none of their anger had been directed at Nick. Despite the things he hadn't told them, the chaos his visit had caused, neither of them seemed to think he deserved any blame for it. Nick didn't particularly agree with that, but he wasn't foolish enough to argue the point.

He didn't know yet how Maggie would react, but he hoped she would give him the chance to apologize and help make things right. Because he wasn't going to let his father get away with this.

Even if he still wasn't sure how he was going to stop it.

The tension in his head was getting stronger, and he really needed to lie down, but he didn't want to be stuck in the dark with his swirling thoughts. He reached up to dig into the muscles at the back of his neck, hoping to relax them some, then rolled his head from side to side and consciously loosened his shoulders.

"You okay?" Micah asked from the bedroom doorway.

Nick looked up, annoyed that he'd forgotten to close the door. "Yeah," he replied. "Just a headache. I get them all the time."

Micah pushed the door the rest of the way open and crossed the room. He paused in front of Nick with his hand out, like he'd just remembered he should ask before touching him. "Can I, um." He gave a lopsided grin. "I'm pretty good with my hands. Ryan says it helps." His cheeks were pink, and Nick had to smile.

"I bet he likes your hands."

Micah's blush darkened, and he gave Nick's shoulder a light shove. "Asshole. Just turn around."

Nick shifted so Micah could kneel on the mattress next to him. He couldn't hold back his groan when Micah's hands went right to the tight, aching muscle between his shoulder and neck and dug in with firm pressure. Pleasure-pain radiated up his neck, and he shivered.

"Damn," Micah said. "You're like a rock." He nudged Nick toward the middle of the bed. "Take off your shirt and lie down."

"Usually that's my line," Nick teased but did as he was told. When he turned to look, Micah's gaze was sliding down, taking in the muscles he'd earned through lots of hard work in the gym.

"Oh, um," Micah stammered, then gulped. "Right." He kicked off his shoes and crawled up the bed, straddling Nick's hips, his hands on Nick's shoulders. "This okay?"

"Mm-hmm." It was fine. They'd been a hell of a lot more intimate at the club. Besides, the tension in Nick's temples was threatening to spiral. Micah could do anything he wanted if he thought it would help.

Micah's fingers dug back into Nick's muscles, drawing out another groan. Damn, he'd forgotten how strong Micah was.

Micah inched his way down, coaxing stubborn knots into loosening, occasionally shooting spikes of pain up through Nick's neck when he hit a particularly tight spot. Nick melted into the mattress. He couldn't remember the last time someone had given him a massage for free.

Micah worked at a knot below Nick's shoulder blade until the muscle gave up and released. That felt amazing. Nick was suddenly aware of his cock taking interest in the proceedings.

The heels of Micah's hands pressed into the muscles along Nick's spine and slid up to the base of his neck in a glide that turned Nick into a puddle.

"I think I'm jealous."

*Oh, shit.* Nick flinched at Ryan's voice and tried to lift his head. Before he could get far, fingers slid into his hair and pressed his head back to the pillow. Micah hadn't paused his massage, so the hand had to be Ryan's.

"Stay," Ryan said, amusement coloring his voice. Then his fingers slid to rub the back of Ryan's neck, making goose bumps spill across his skin.

"He's got a migraine," Micah murmured, working his way across Nick's shoulders.

"I'll be fine," Nick muttered into the pillow, his body heavy, his thoughts soft as the medicine combined with Micah's expert touch started to do its job.

"Lucky for you, we have some experience with headaches around here." The deep rumble of Ryan's voice was so soothing Nick wanted to roll around in it.

He hummed. He wanted to ask, but words felt like too much effort at the moment. He let himself drift until Micah slowed to a stop and eventually pulled back. Nick's last thought was that he needed to thank him, and he wondered if Micah would accept a blow job as a token of his gratitude.

Nick made his way down the stairs a few hours later feeling worlds better. His headache was nearly gone, and he wasn't nearly as fuzzy as he usually was post-migraine. There was no one in the living room, but he saw movement on the front porch.

Rain was coming down in quiet sheets, creating a cocoon that blocked out everything much past the edges of the roof. Ryan was sitting on one of the wicker couches with his bare feet up on the coffee table. Micah was sprawled out next to him, head on the armrest, feet on Ryan's thighs and a blanket over his legs. Ryan was reading, wearing a pair of dark-rimmed glasses, while Micah was doing something on a tablet.

Ryan looked up with a smile when Nick walked out. "Hey, how are you feeling?"

"Like Micah's got magic hands," Nick admitted.

Micah grinned at him. "Told you."

"No work this afternoon?" Nick asked.

Ryan tipped his head toward the rain. "We canceled the last trail ride. Tourists aren't going out in this weather, and the horses are in for the night. We also decided to put off family dinner until Maggie's home and all of this is settled."

Nick was relieved to hear it. He really wasn't up for socializing, and it was clear Ryan and Micah weren't either. "Mind if I join you?" Ryan gave him a "Go ahead" wave, and Nick took the seat. "Speaking of Maggie, have you heard from her yet?" he asked, dreading the answer.

"She and Archer are spending two more nights in the city for her to recover before they drive back, doctor's orders. In the meantime, she's going to work on finding a lawyer who's willing to help her fight this."

Nick held back a sigh. That was good. But it didn't sound like it would be fast, or easy. And what happened if Phillip tried to go through with the sale in the meantime? Could they stop him without any proof? All questions with no good answers.

"Let's play a game," Micah suggested suddenly, sitting up and gathering the blanket in his lap, his bare toes peeking out from below it.

Nick raised an eyebrow at him.

"We have cards."

"I'm decent at poker," Nick offered. He was more than decent, but keeping that to himself was half the game.

"Okay." Micah bounced to his feet, then turned to give Ryan a pleading look.

Ryan chuckled and stood. "No need to bring out the puppy eyes. I'll play."

Micah cheered and fist-pumped, then trotted inside.

With a shake of his head, Ryan met Nick's eyes, his own shining with humor. "This should be fun. Micah's got no poker face."

Nick snorted. "Are you allowed to tell me that? Isn't it against your marriage vows or something?"

"Nah. I promised to love him forever, not help him win at cards."

Nick followed Ryan into the house, where Micah had gathered two decks of cards and a box of poker chips. Micah flopped down at one end of the couch, Ryan took the other, and Nick claimed his favorite chair. Micah started to shuffle. "What are we betting?"

Nick glanced at Ryan and felt heat stir in his belly at the intense look he got in return. He sucked in a breath, trying not to look too eager—and failing. "I'm up for anything."

Micah went still and glanced up at them, lips parted. "Oh. Um." His eyes slid to his husband even as his cheeks went pink, and his tongue darted out to wet his lips.

"Your call, baby," Ryan murmured, his gaze softening when he met Micah's eyes. It made Nick feel better about going there. The last thing he wanted was anyone being pressured into something they didn't really want. But fuck if he was going to let an opportunity to get his hands or his mouth on one of them, or both of them for that matter, slip past.

Micah ducked his head and started shuffling the cards again. "Winner's choice?" he offered, then missed and spilled the cards across the floor.

Ryan chuckled and reached down to help him gather them up. "Sounds good to me. Nicky?"

Nick was very careful not to let on exactly how good that sounded. "Sure. It's a deal." He pushed up from his chair. "How about I grab us some drinks?" He took their requests and ducked into the kitchen, giving them a minute to talk and himself a minute to get his racing heart under control. Was this really happening? If he won, what would he ask for? He had so many ideas, but it wasn't like they'd discussed boundaries in any real way.

He stood at the sink and chugged a glass of water, willing himself to calm down. He would let things play out, he decided. Micah had set the stakes, and Micah could decide the rules.

He grabbed a bag of chips and snagged them all beers. Just then, his phone buzzed with an incoming call from Xavier. He silenced it, promising himself he'd call back later.

In the living room, Micah was still on the couch, but Ryan had moved to the other armchair, across from the one Nick had claimed. He passed out the drinks and sat. "What's the game?"

"Let's keep it simple," Micah said, dealing the cards. "Texas Hold'em."

Nick took a swig of his beer. "All right, let's see what you've got, pretty boy."

He held back a grin when Micah's eyes flew to his, then narrowed. "Is that how it's gonna be?"

Nick winked. He peeked at his cards: a pair of jacks. This should be interesting.

An hour later, Micah was losing spectacularly, while Nick was down about half of his stack. Micah tossed his cards in the muck after a raise and flopped back with a dramatic sigh. "If I see seven-deuce one more time, I swear..."

Ryan chuckled and gathered the pile of chips in front of him. "That's okay, baby. I'm sure the next hand will be better."

Micah stuck out his tongue and crossed his arms over his chest in an exaggerated pout. He was too cute. Nick wanted to reach over and ruffle his hair, just to hear him squawk in protest. "No one told me I was betting against two card sharps."

The next hand wasn't any better, if Micah's face was anything to go by, but Nick's wasn't all that great either. He eyed his relatively small pile of chips compared to what Ryan had collected and tried not to shift in his seat. The innuendo had been flying hot and heavy, and Nick had a pretty good idea someone, *Ryan,* was getting his dick sucked at the end of this. His mouth watered in anticipation, his cock perking up as his imagination tried to help him out.

Would it be bad form to throw the game just to find out what Ryan had planned? Not that he would—Nick was way too competitive for that. But meeting Micah's hungry eyes across the table made the idea almost worth it.

He slid a few chips in front of his cards. "Raise."

"All in," Micah said. Ryan called. They saw a flop of king, queen, and nine, mixed suits. Seeming to discount Micah's chances, Ryan turned his attention completely on Nick. They both checked the deuce on the turn. One of the two remaining kings completed the board.

Nick's gut tightened at the fire in Ryan's usually calm blue eyes. Nick licked his lips, his body responding with anticipation that made his heart race. He had trips; he could probably win this time.

Ryan glanced at his cards, then his mouth tipped up in a wicked smirk. "Well, *pretty boy*," he teased with the same nickname Nick had thrown at Micah, "you gonna bet?" His expression said Nick would be a fool if he did, and Nick's competitiveness flared in response.

"All in," he said, tossing a chip in front of him to represent the commitment, his heart pounding in his chest.

Ryan's mouth broke into a grin. "Call." He laid down his hand: a straight.

Nick blinked at the cards. How the hell... He tossed his king on the table. "Damn it."

Micah broke down laughing. "Oh, man. Your face." He grinned at Nick, eyes dancing with excitement and lust.

Nick couldn't help but chuckle in reply. He glanced at Ryan, whose focus shifted from Micah to meet his eyes. Ryan's expression made Nick shiver, and his breath caught. There was something about Ryan that just drew Nick in and made him want. He'd never experienced anything like it before, this burning need to find out more about the man—and to let Ryan know him in return. It was a little unsettling, to be honest. He pushed the confusing realization aside and spread his arms. "Well, winner, what's your prize?"

"That's the question, isn't it?" Ryan held Nick's gaze. "I know we have a bet, but you can say no at any point. It's just a game."

Nick felt something loosen in his chest. He trusted Ryan not to take advantage, but at the same time, it was nice to be reminded he had a choice here. "Are you planning to have me scrubbing floors? Because I'll go ahead and veto that right now."

Ryan shook his head. "I was thinking about you on your knees, but in a very different context."

Micah shifted and Ryan reached out, drawing him around the table and into his lap. Once Micah was straddling his thighs, Ryan's hands settled on Micah's hips.

"What about me?" Micah asked. "I lost worse than Nick did."

Ryan leaned in to steal a kiss. "Don't sound so eager about that, baby."

Micah's grin was wicked. "But you know I love it when you get all bossy." He looked over his shoulder at Nick. "It's hot, right?"

Ryan stood and laid Micah across the low table in one swift motion, cards and chips scattering. Micah gasped as his shirt was dragged over his head before Ryan peeled his pants and underwear down and off in one swift move. Before Nick could fully process what was happening, Micah was naked, hard cock slapping against his belly. Nick got another glimpse of the tattoo curling over Micah's shoulder before his view was blocked by Ryan stepping between them. Nick looked up and met glittering blue eyes, the desire in them stealing his breath.

"What do you say, Nicky? Is Micah right?"

Nick's lips parted, and it took him a few seconds to remember the question. Was Ryan hot when he got bossy? "Hell yes."

"Oh, fuck," Micah groaned, his skin going tingly at the roughness in Nick's voice. The kinky stuff wasn't always a part of his and Ryan's sex life, but when they indulged, holy shit it was incredible. They'd tried everything from blindfolds to bondage to some very fun toys. Playful spanking was a favorite for both of them, as was Ryan taking control and blowing Micah's mind. It wasn't anything they kept up outside the bedroom, but they were both adventurous when it came to sex, and willing to give their fantasies a shot.

Micah shifted against the hard wood of the table and shivered at how exposed he was. Spread out and on display for not one but two incredibly sexy men. He sank his teeth into his lower lip. He wasn't body shy by any means, but it was different to be so exposed when they were still fully dressed.

Nick's eyes raked over him like he was a delicious offering, and Micah squirmed. God, he was so hard he was practically leaking, and no one had even touched him yet. How was this real life?

Ryan stepped to the side and jerked his chin at Nick. "Lose the shirt."

Nick didn't hesitate, just ripped his shirt over his head and tossed it aside. So many muscles. And those nipple piercings. Micah wanted to feel them under his tongue. He looked to Ryan hopefully and got a smile in return, as if his husband had read his mind.

Ryan stepped up behind Nick and rested his hands on denim-clad hips. Nick's eyes went half-lidded, and his head tipped back when Ryan's palm slid down over the clearly defined line of his erection and gave it a squeeze. "Fuck," Nick bit out. "Some warning would be good." Despite the protest, he rolled his hips into the touch, his lips parting on a sigh.

"Fair enough," Ryan said as he turned his head and flicked his tongue against Nick's earlobe. "I want to strip you naked and watch you suck off my husband. Then I'm going to jerk you off until you come all over him. Sound good?"

Micah's brain short-circuited as red-hot desire shot through him. He almost didn't hear Nick's groan of agreement, but he saw Nick's head jerk in a nod.

Ryan's hand slid up to tug at one of Nick's pierced nipples. Nick's back arched, and Micah slid his hand over his own chest, mirroring the action. That earned him an approving growl from Ryan.

Ryan's deft fingers went to Nick's buckle next, opening his pants and pushing them down until his thick cock sprang free, the piercing at the tip catching the light. Micah's mouth watered with the urge to get his mouth on it again, to really take his time exploring and learning what Nick liked.

Once Nick had kicked his pants off, Ryan urged him around to the end of the table. Micah took the opportunity to watch his ass flex as he moved. The guy was flawless, like a sculpture, and hard in all the right places. Micah wanted to lick every inch of him. His eyes flicked up to Ryan, and he grinned when he caught his husband staring as well. Oh yeah. They were definitely on the same page when it came to Nicky Lauder.

Despite watching him move, Micah still startled when Nick dropped to his knees and his hands landed on Micah's thighs. He looked up and found Nick watching him intently. He was waiting for permission, Micah realized. He pulled his heels up to the edge of the table and spread his knees helpfully. "Gonna show me what you've got?" he teased, ignoring the way his heart was pounding. Nick's eyes slid to his straining cock, which twitched eagerly under his gaze.

Nick's lips curled wickedly as his hands slid up Micah's thighs and pressed his legs open wider. "You might want to hold on to something." Then he ducked down and sucked Micah's cock into his hot, wet mouth.

Micah yelped and flailed to grip the sides of the table, shocked by the suddenness of the pleasure that roared through him. He was still trying to get himself under control when a second set of hands joined Nick's, trailing from his belly to pluck at his nipples before one wrapped around his throat in a loose hold that made his breath speed up.

He moaned and tilted his head back to give Ryan more room. In return he got a deep, hungry kiss that made his toes curl and his cock throb in Nick's mouth.

Nick moaned and sucked harder, tongue swiping at the slit in a way that said he was chasing the flavor of Micah's precum. God, that was amazing. Micah rocked into the sensation as his higher brain functions abandoned him. All he could focus on was the hot-wet-tight of Nick's mouth and the familiar, grounding hold of Ryan's hands. He cursed and writhed, overwhelmed, body overloaded as Nick reached up and started playing with his balls, knuckles pressed to the sensitive place just behind them. Micah whimpered into Ryan's kiss as everything pulled tighter, sparks racing under his skin. Nick doubled down, sucking harder, and Micah's whole world went white. He panted and shook through his orgasm, one hand buried in Nick's hair, the other clinging to Ryan's shoulder.

When he came back to himself, Ryan had his arm wrapped around Nick's waist and his fist was slicking over Nick's flushed cock. Nick's mouth, red and wet from sucking Micah off, was open, low groans of pleasure escaping every time Ryan twisted his wrist just right. It was one of the hottest things Micah had ever seen, and if he could have gotten hard again, he would have. As it was, he sat up, then climbed to his knees and started kissing and licking his way across Nick's chest, finally, *finally* getting his mouth on the barbells through Nick's nipples and tasting the warm metal.

Nick hissed, moaning something that sounded like Micah's name and burying his hands in Micah's hair.

Micah slid his fingers through the neatly trimmed hair on Nick's chest, enjoying its roughness under his fingers. He'd always loved a guy with chest hair, maybe because he didn't have much of his own, and he wanted to rub his face all over Nick's. So he did, making his way down until he could lick the defined lines of Nick's abs and lower to where Ryan's hand was working him over.

When he gave the ring through the head of Nick's cock a flick with his tongue, Nick cursed and shook. Micah did it again. And again and again, until Nick bit out a warning. Micah was about to ask Ryan where he wanted him, when Ryan's fingers twisted in his hair and held him still. At the first hot splash of cum against his lips, he opened his mouth and stuck out his tongue, catching as much of Nick's release as possible. Ryan hauled him up, Nick caught between them, and kissed him hungrily, tongue sliding over Micah's skin to search out the remaining flavor. Micah moaned, shivers running through him, mind fuzzy from endorphins.

"You two are a fuckin' wet dream come to life," Nick slurred next to Micah's ear, making him grin.

When Ryan was done, Micah moved back enough that he could see Nick, whose eyes were half-lidded and filled with pleasure.

"Missed a spot," Nick murmured. Then his tongue darted out and licked the corner of Micah's mouth.

Micah didn't think, just licked the same spot, chasing Nick's flavor and getting a close-up view of Nick's nostrils flaring. Their lips were inches apart, and Micah could feel the heat of Nick's breath ghosting across his face.

He really, really wanted to kiss Nick.

Nick swallowed, his eyes on Micah's mouth.

Micah licked his lips again, taking a deep breath to ask—

Then Nick was drawing back. "And what about you, Mr. Card Sharp?" he asked Ryan. "You're the only one who hasn't gotten off. Seems like a strange prize."

Ryan chuckled, but Micah could see the tension in his frame, the desire in his eyes. "After that show, it's not going to take much."

Nick put a hand on his chest to push him back a step, then another, until Ryan sat on the couch, his knees spread. Nick slid gracefully to his knees, his back muscles flexing as he reached up to free Ryan from his pants. He hummed in appreciation as he closed his hand around Ryan's thick, leaking cock before glancing over his shoulder at Micah. "Maybe your husband wants to show me what you like?" he asked with a wink.

Micah scrambled off the table, not nearly as gracefully, and dropped down next to him. "Oh, hell yes," he said, leaning in to kiss the sensitive hollow of Ryan's hip.

Ryan hissed and cupped the back of his head as Micah mouthed along his shaft until he could flick over the tip and give it a good suck. Opening his eyes, he met Nick's, which were warm with amusement.

"Eager little cocksucker, aren't you," Nick purred, approval obvious in his tone.

Micah let his lips pop free, then grinned. "You have no idea." He dove back in, taking advantage of his knowledge of all his husband's sweet spots, like just under the head and the spot along his happy trail that Micah could nuzzle when he took him deep. After a minute, he felt an unfamiliar touch as Nick stroked the back of his neck, then eased him into a faster rhythm. Micah groaned, loving the minor loss of control. It made his own cock twitch and try to go hard again. Sadly, he wasn't eighteen anymore, so he was going to need more than a minute to recover.

He worked Ryan over until he felt Ryan's thigh muscles start to tense with his impending orgasm, then pulled off with a wet slurp and turned to Nick. "Your turn."

Nick's eyes went dark, and he reached up to thumb Micah's spit-slick lower lip. "You're sexy as hell, you know that, sweetheart?" He pressed lightly with his thumb, and Micah closed his mouth around it, sucking. Nick left it in place as he turned and brushed his lips over Ryan's cock. As he mouthed the tip, Micah automatically flicked his tongue, then groaned when he saw Nick mirror the action. He really was letting Micah show him what Ryan liked.

Micah glanced up when Ryan's broad palm settled in his hair, the other falling to the back of Nick's head. He worked Nick's thumb faster, and Nick did the same to Ryan's cock.

Ryan growled out a curse, and his fingers tightened as he started to thrust into Nick's mouth. Micah hollowed his cheeks and let his teeth scrape skin ever so lightly and saw Nick do the same.

Ryan's hips stuttered and pressed deep as he came, Nick swallowing around him. Micah moaned at the sight of Nick's throat convulsing and gave his thumb another eager pull. This was definitely one of the hottest moments of his life, and they hadn't even fucked.

Things were surprisingly easy with Nick. Once they recovered, cleaned up, and found their clothes, they decided that pizza and another movie night sounded perfect. Micah ended up sprawled across the couch again, this time with his head in Ryan's lap and his feet in Nick's. He was pleasantly full from the carbs and sated from his orgasm. He'd probably have fallen asleep right there if the movie weren't so good.

"Tomorrow will be busy," Ryan murmured as the credits rolled, his fingers scratching over Micah's scalp. "Two of the groups that got canceled today rescheduled, and we won't have Archer back in time to take them out."

Micah hummed. It would be tight, but they'd dealt with worse. They still had Izzy and Alice. Neither of them led trail rides, but Izzy was great with the guests, and Alice could run the barn almost single-handed when they needed her to.

"I'm happy to help," Nick spoke up, his voice filled with tired contentment. "It's been about a dozen years since I was on a horse, but I'm not too bad at following directions."

Micah perked up at that. "I thought you only rode as a kid."

Nick gave Micah's ankle a squeeze. "There's enough social capital in the horse world that Phillip agreed to lessons up through college."

"You should come out with me tomorrow," Ryan said. "I could use another responsible adult for the long trail. It's a three-hour loop up to the high meadow and back, with a picnic lunch in the middle."

"That would be perfect," Micah said. That way he could handle the shorter group rides, and Alice and Izzy could keep things running smoothly in the barn.

Nick chuckled. "As long as you promise to take it easy on me. Like I said, it's been a while."

"I don't know, you seem like the type who likes to ride hard," Ryan teased.

Micah snorted at the terrible pun. "I'll ride you hard, Daddy," he snarked, wiggling his ass against the cushions.

Ryan reached down and dug his fingers into the sensitive spot on Micah's side, making him yelp and giggle. "Brat."

Micah noticed Nick watching them curiously and gave him a "What?" look.

"Just how kinky are you two? Should I prepare myself to find a St. Andrew's cross in the basement?"

That sent Micah into a fit of laughter, even as his cheeks heated. "Not *that* kinky," he gasped, a grin splitting his face.

Ryan was grinning as well. "We like a little spice, but only in the bedroom. Neither of us are into the lifestyle."

"I get it. My ex likes the more adventurous side of things. It's part of the reason we never would have worked out."

"How long were you together?" Micah asked. He'd been curious based on some of the comments Nick had made, but he didn't want to bring up bad memories.

"Xavier and I were really only ever friends," Nick said, making Micah's eyebrows go up. "His grandfather was a good man, but very old-fashioned. When he died, he stated in his will that Xavier could only inherit if he was married before he turned thirty. Lucky for us, gay marriage was legalized after he passed. I don't think he would have approved of us as a couple." Nick rolled his eyes. "We stayed married long enough for the lawyers to work things out—there were a few cousins that didn't approve of me being a man and tried to sue—and then we waited another year for the attention to die down." He laughed softly. "It isn't like Xavi's against marriage—the man's a damn romantic. But putting a deadline on finding love is bullshit. People should be allowed to make those decisions in their own time, not under threat of losing their home and inheritance." Nick shrugged, looking suddenly uncomfortable with his rant. "Anyway, it all worked out in the end."

Oh wow. That wasn't what Micah had expected at all. It gave him a whole new perspective on who Nick was. Nothing was more telling about a person than what they were willing to do for their friends.

"So that's why you were open," Ryan said, sounding intrigued.

Nick nodded, his hands folded across his stomach. "We weren't exactly compatible in bed. We tried it when we were younger, but our wants don't match up. We had a lot more fun with someone between us." He winked at Micah.

Micah could see how that was a good solution, though it just made him curious about what Xavier was into that Nick wasn't. "You should invite him down here. I want to meet him."

Nick chuckled. "Gonna replace me with my kinky ex?" he teased, nothing but warm humor in his voice.

"Hell no," Micah scoffed as he planted his feet more firmly in Nick's lap. "We picked you. No take-backsies."

That made Nick laugh. "No what now?"

Micah huffed. "You know what I mean." Nick was theirs. At least for the moment.

Their recently renovated en suite was Micah's dream bathroom. Back in the days when they shared the loft apartment over the barn, he never would have thought he'd want a fancy bathroom, much less have one. But part of their deal with Maggie when they moved into the house was that they were going to fix things up for her. The bathroom had been second on the list, after the kitchen. It was more than worth it, Micah now knew as he stood warm and sleepy under the hot spray.

The shower door slid open, and Ryan stepped in with a rush of cold air that made Micah shiver, but it was quickly replaced by the heat of Ryan's body against his back and muscular arms wrapping around him. Ryan stole the sudsy shower puff and dragged it across Micah's collarbones and down his chest. Micah moaned, letting his head rest on Ryan's shoulder. "That feels awesome," he murmured, pressing a wet kiss to Ryan's jaw in thanks.

Ryan hummed and continued to wash him, paying special attention to his cock and balls—not enough to get him hard, but enough to have him melting further. "Nicky wanted to kiss you earlier."

Micah's brain stuttered at that, but he was too relaxed to have much more of a reaction. "You think?"

"You wanted to kiss him too," Ryan added, no judgment or accusation in his voice.

Micah licked his lips and pressed back into Ryan's body. "Yeah," he admitted, not sure what to say but not trying to deny it.

"Why didn't you?"

That got Micah's attention. "I don't know. I guess... it felt like it might be too intimate?" He closed his teeth on his bottom lip, remembering the heat in Nick's eyes as he licked the corner of Micah's mouth. Too intimate and like it might be crossing a line that he couldn't come back from. "I don't want to screw this up," he admitted.

Ryan dropped a kiss on his shoulder, lingering for a moment with his lips against Micah's skin. "What if I told you I wanted to kiss him too?"

That made Micah's breath catch, and he turned in Ryan's hold so he could see his expression. "Do you really? You're not just going along with it?"

Ryan grinned at him and ducked his head for a wet kiss that threatened to derail the conversation. When they paused for breath, he said, "Baby, I already told you how stunning I think the two of you are together. And how much I like Nicky. I'm getting just as much out of this as you are."

"So kissing is on the table?"

Ryan gave his nose a playful nip. "Kissing is on the table as far as I'm concerned." He slid his soapy hand down Micah's back to brush over his hole. Micah gasped and arched his back, trying to get pressure where he wanted it.

The tip of Ryan's finger slipped in easily, with just enough friction to make Micah moan.

"What about this?" Ryan asked. "Do you want him to fuck you?" He rocked his finger back and forth gently as Micah's body flushed with heat.

He ducked his head, hiding his face in Ryan's neck as he thought about it. He definitely had some fantasies that involved more than one cock, but he didn't feel like that's what Ryan was asking. This felt bigger, more important. "I need to think about that," he decided, squirming at the loss when Ryan's fingers slid away.

"That's perfectly okay." Ryan reached up and eased Micah's head back until their eyes met. "Like I said, I'm with you, baby, one hundred percent. Whatever happens."

Micah smiled up at him. "I know. I love you."

"I love you too." Ryan stole another kiss. "Want to get out of here and let me show you how much?"

Micah absolutely did. The questions about Nick and exactly what his place in their lives might be could wait. There was no rush.

# THIRTEEN
NICK

THE SKY WAS BRIGHT blue and the sun perfectly warm the next morning as Nick watched Micah and Ryan get everything ready for the trail ride that was about to go out. The trail ride Nick was going on. He wanted to go, no question, but he was also more nervous than he'd anticipated. It had been more than a few years, and he didn't want to screw anything up and disappoint Micah and Ryan.

He took a deep breath and let it out slowly as he groomed the horse he'd been assigned. Micah had assured him that Honey was a total sweetheart and would take good care of him. Nick had a few carrot sticks in his pocket, just in case he needed a little extra bribery.

Honey, presumably named for her color, heaved a sigh and pulled another mouthful of hay from the holder in the corner of her stall. "I sure hope you go easy on me, girl," Nick said under his breath as he ran the brush along her flank. "I'd like to be able to walk under my own power when we get back."

A chuckle behind him made Nick twitch and turn around, only to be met by amused blue eyes under a halo of blond curls. Izzy was leaning against the stall door, watching him.

"Hate to break it to you, man, but it's a three-hour ride. If you haven't been on a horse in a while, your ass is gonna *hurt* by the time you're done." Izzy's eyes tracked down Nick's body appreciatively. "Though I'd be happy to help you out with that later."

Nick started to respond with a quip about his ass being taken but hesitated. The last thing he wanted to do was make things awkward, since he was pretty sure Izzy didn't know Nick had hooked up with his bosses.

Damn it. Now he'd let the silence hang too long.

Then Izzy gave a put-upon sigh. "Wow, you are not subtle at all," he said with a roll of his eyes. "Micah already told me about the club."

Nick choked. He'd assumed anything they did would be kept quiet for the sake of not ruffling any feathers. You never knew how people would react to the idea of three men hooking up, especially if two of them were married. Some people had very strong opinions about other people's lives, and they weren't afraid to share them. Nick and Xavier had lost a few friends during their marriage when said friends didn't understand how they could be open. Of course, their situation had been complicated by the fact that the two of them weren't actually together, but that was beside the point. People should be able to do what was right for them and their relationship, no outside opinions necessary.

That didn't seem to be a problem here. Izzy pushed off the stall door, shaking his head. "Kinky fuckers," he muttered. "I'd have loved to be a fly on the wall for that. Not that I have any desire to see Micah naked. Not my type." His gaze ran over Nick again. "Still, might be worth it." He gave a cheeky grin.

"Sadly, you'll never know." Nick swung the saddle onto Honey's back and did up the cinch.

Izzy chuckled, a practiced sound. "Don't worry about me, I'm perfectly capable of making my own fun."

Nick didn't doubt it. Izzy was a gorgeous man, well over six feet and built like a runway model. His cheekbones were sharp enough to cut a man, and his blond curls gave him an angelic look that Nick would bet good money was a facade. Despite his smiles and easygoing nature, there was something sharp about Izzy that told Nick to tread carefully. He'd met more than his fair share of that type living in New York and LA, and he knew to trust his instincts. Still, the man seemed like he was a good friend to Micah and Ryan, so Nick was happy to play along until Izzy proved otherwise.

"You should get out there. Micah's starting his spiel for the trail ride, and you don't want to miss it."

Nick thanked him and gathered up the reins, leading Honey out to where the rest of the group was milling. The horses were lined up along the fence, so he tied Honey on the end, then stepped closer so he could hear the instructions. Micah wasn't leading this ride, but Ryan said he was better at the customer service side of things, so he usually did this part.

As Nick walked up, Micah had the guests hanging on his every word.

"Now, this is the end that you want to pet." He smoothed his palm over a horse's nose. "And that is the end to avoid." He gestured to the horse's rear. "He may have a cute butt, but those legs pack a punch, so make sure you stay out of the way. Both from the ground and when you're out on the trail. No one enjoys a nose up their ass, least of all the horse in front of you." That sent the group giggling, and Nick couldn't help but laugh. He wondered how difficult it was for Micah to not turn that into a rimming joke.

The scuff of a boot was the only warning he got before a hand landed on his shoulder and gave a squeeze. He glanced over to see Ryan watching Micah with fond amusement in his eyes. "Just in case you're wondering, he has a whole speech filled with innuendo for when we do our Pride Week rides in June. I keep waiting for him to slip up with the wrong crowd, but he never does."

That made Nick grin. "I'm sure he's got tons of material. Just the amount of leather alone..." He let that trail off, getting a soft huff from Ryan.

"You're not wrong. He keeps suggesting a themed ride, but I told him pants are required under chaps."

That made Nick bark out a laugh, and Micah looked up, catching his eye and shooting him a bright smile. "You all are in luck for this ride," Micah said. "Not only do you get my smoking hot husband as your trail guide, but you also get Nick over there as additional eye candy. I'm honestly jealous. I'm gonna be stuck here with Milo and Rascal, and they're cute and all, but it's not the same."

That earned him another round of laughter as he wrapped things up. Then he and Ryan made the rounds, introducing riders to their horses and helping them mount.

Nick hopped into the saddle, surprising himself with how natural it still felt. Honey was experienced enough that she stood still while he got settled.

Micah stepped up next to him and made a show of checking the cinch and adjusting the stirrups. "I really am jealous. I wish I could go out with you two. Stupid responsibilities." He pouted at Nick, all big brown eyes and jutting lower lip.

They were angled away from the group enough that Nick took a risk and ducked down a little to brush his thumb over Micah's mouth. "How about we make it up to you when we get back?"

Micah's eyes went dark as his pupils dilated, and he made a teasing, teeth-snapping motion at Nick's thumb. "Gonna hold you to that," he said huskily, his tone making a ball of lust settle low in Nick's gut.

Nick sat back up, resisting the urge to duck lower and catch that sweet mouth in a kiss. That would be pushing things too far. Instead, he raised an eyebrow. "Not if I do first."

Micah's eyes ran over his face for a moment, and then he jolted. "Oh. Wait right here," he said, then jogged back into the barn.

Nick watched him go, bemused. Micah returned quickly, carrying a cowboy hat that he handed up to Nick.

"For the sun," he said with a grin.

Nick eyed it and shrugged. It wasn't his first time wearing one, and it would help. He put it on and looked over in time to see Ryan watching him intently. They were too far apart for Nick to read his expression, though.

Micah whistled quietly. "I like it. Totally ups the hotness factor." He nodded. "Now you just need some flannel and a few days' worth of stubble, and you'll fit right in."

Nick shook his head. If his ex-husband could see him now. At the same time, the picture Micah was painting sounded a lot more comfortable than it should. What would it be like to let go of the tailored clothes and two-hundred-dollar haircuts? To trade in his designer jeans for worn Wranglers?

He didn't hate the thought. Not at all.

Maggie's mountains were just as stunning as Nick remembered. As a kid he'd loved it here, but he hadn't really appreciated the beauty of the place. The trail was wide and well maintained as it snaked through the fields leading to the base of the mountain.

Once they reached the canopy of the forest, the trail became lined with thick strands of mountain laurel and huge oak trees that blocked out the sun and kept the riders cool. The sound of a hidden stream trickling through moss-covered rocks competed with the thud and clink of the horses' shod hooves against the occasional stone in the path.

Nick breathed in the crisp, clean mountain air—the scent of damp earth and growing things so different from the smog of LA or the exhaust and food trucks of New York. He swayed with Honey's gait as she picked her way nimbly along the trail, following the horse in front of her at a lazy pace. The combination of sounds, scents, and movement made something in his chest unknot—something that had been wrapped tight for longer than he could remember.

It felt a lot like coming home. Nick shut his eyes and concentrated on the sensation of peace. When he opened them again, they were approaching the first overlook, a break in the trees that gave the riders a panoramic view of the rolling blue mountains.

Ryan paused the ride to let people pull out their phones and snap pictures. As they waited, he circled back to Nick. "How does it feel?"

Nick looked out at the mountains and stroked his palm along Honey's neck. "Good," he admitted. "Makes me wish I hadn't stayed away so long." He looked down at his fingers as they slid through the thick strands of Honey's mane. It would be just his luck to finally make his way back here, only to lose it again. He clenched his jaw and took a steadying breath. Damn his father for putting them all in this position.

"Hey," Ryan said soothingly. "Don't think about that right now. That's not why I asked."

Nick nodded but didn't trust himself to respond right away.

"Just enjoy the day, Nicky."

Nick took another deep breath and let it out equally slowly. Ryan was right. There was nothing he could do about his dad while he was out on the ride, and he didn't want to ruin something so nice with dark thoughts about the future.

Ryan sidestepped his horse closer and reached out to squeeze Nick's knee. "You should ride up at the front with me so I can point out the best sights."

"You use that line often?"

Ryan laughed, low and warm. "First time." His gaze dipped to take Nick in from head to foot. "You look really fucking good on a horse, Nicky."

Nick felt his lips split in a grin. He could make a dirty joke, but he didn't feel the need. He let the warmth of the compliment settle as he followed Ryan up to the front of the group, then waited a little ways back while Ryan got everyone moving again.

A young woman, probably in her mid-twenties, rode up next to him and gave him a not-so-subtle once-over, then smiled flirtatiously when he glanced at her. "You seem to know what you're doing," she said, tilting her head to make her long hair spill over her shoulder. "Do you have any tips for a newbie?" Her full lips pulled into a pretty pout.

If Nick swung that way—and weren't already focused on Ryan and Micah—he'd probably take the bait. As it was, he smiled back politely. "Just relax and enjoy yourself. It's a beautiful trail."

She licked her lips and tried again, leaning on the saddle horn to show off the low vee of her top as she stroked her horse's neck. "You've been here before?"

"I grew up here," Nick admitted. "Haven't been back in a long time, though. My ex-husband isn't exactly the country type."

She blinked, and her mouth formed a little O before she straightened into a more natural posture. "Well, welcome back." Her smile this time was friendly instead of flirty. "I'm a summerbird. Like a snowbird in Florida, but reversed."

Nick smiled. He hated having to get rude before people got the picture that he wasn't interested. It was a relief when they caught on quickly.

He ended up chatting with the woman, whose name was Samantha, for a while, making her laugh with some of his stories.

When the trail widened, Ryan waved him forward. Nick jogged Honey up and fell into step next to him.

"You good?" Ryan asked, the corners of his mouth tight.

Nick tilted his head, trying to decide if that was annoyance in Ryan's expression. "Yep," he replied, nudging Honey close enough that their knees bumped lightly. "Just telling Samantha back there about the time I forced Xavier to go riding with me.

He complained about bruised sit bones for days." When that only got him a snort, he continued, "What I didn't tell her was that he claimed it was worse than the one time he let me top him."

Finally, Ryan cracked a grin. "A shame," he murmured, eyes on the path in front of them.

They continued on in peaceful companionship as the trail snaked up the side of the mountain. After an hour or so, they reached a break in the tree line that opened up to a large grassy area. The view was spectacular, nearly 180 degrees of unobstructed blue-green mountaintops vanishing into the distance. Off to one side, a stream cut through the clearing, crystalline water with large rocks along the bed. Ryan led them over to give their horses a drink, then dismounted.

"Welcome to the high meadow," he announced to the group. He directed them to tie their horses to the hitching post nearby and grab some lunch.

Nick followed Ryan to a large cooler sitting in the shade. He raised an eyebrow when Ryan opened it to reveal box lunches and bottled water.

"Izzy drove the food up this morning on the fire road," Ryan explained. "He'll come back for the trash later today. It's a lot easier than trying to pack it up and having something go wrong." He flashed Nick a wink. "Ask Micah about it sometime."

Nick huffed in amusement and chose a lunch, then found a quiet spot on a rock to take in the view while he ate. A few minutes later, Ryan settled next to him.

Wind blew through the clearing, tugging gently at their clothes and hair. It would be cold if not for the bright spring sun. "Aunt Maggie and my mom used to bring me up here for picnics," Nick said as he unwrapped his sandwich. "I'd forgotten this spot existed."

Ryan made a thoughtful sound. "Maggie's mentioned you spending summers here as a kid."

"Until I was thirteen. When I was little, my mom and I would come down for the summer to escape the heat at home. Dad was always too busy with work, so it was our time together. I loved the ranch and the horses and seeing Aunt Maggie. She was closer to my mom than she was to my dad, even though he's the one she's related to. When Mom died, I stopped coming." Nick took a bite of his sandwich to stem the flow of words. Ryan wasn't interested in listening to him whine about things that happened decades ago.

"I can understand you wanting space. Everyone reacts to grief differently."

Nick shook his head. "It wasn't that. Dad thought the ranch was a waste. Not profitable enough to sink effort into that would be better spent on other things. He had me start working in his office the next summer." Nick swallowed down the bitterness that memory brought up. He'd been so excited to spend time with his dad that he hadn't protested not going to the ranch. But it hadn't been what he expected. He'd spent months handing out mail and fetching things for Dad's secretary, hardly getting a glimpse of the man who was supposed to be raising him unless someone happened to open the door to his office when Nick was passing by. Some nights, his dad even sent him home with the driver so he could work late. Nick might as well not have been there at all. It had only gotten worse when his dad started dating, and suddenly there was a new woman to compete with for attention.

At the time, he'd been determined to work harder, getting better at the tasks he was given so his dad would notice and be proud of him.

He took off the hat Micah had given him and ran a hand through his damp hair. "It took until college to realize it wasn't what I wanted."

"You were trying to stay close to the parent you still had."

Nick gave a one-shouldered shrug. "I suppose. Not that it was effective. By the time I graduated college, my father was on wife number three, and I was more employee than son." He took a swig of his water, letting the icy liquid wash away the tightness in his throat.

Ryan's hand dropped to his knee and gave it a squeeze. "I imagine being here has brought it back up again."

Nick leaned into the touch. "More than I expected," he admitted, keeping his eyes on the horizon and pretending he didn't appreciate the support.

"My father decided I was going to be a lawyer practically before I was born." Ryan's tone was light, but Nick recognized the hurt behind it. "My mother went along with it, because that's what a good wife does. I went to the best schools. Private preschool and elementary. And then boarding school starting in seventh grade. I was the dutiful son, even when I started to want things I knew my father wouldn't approve of. First it was horses, which annoyed him but he accepted. Then I realized I was just as interested in the boys I was in school with as I was the girls who came for social activities. I kept that one to myself."

Nick could imagine that wouldn't have gone over well with the type of man Ryan was describing. His own father hadn't had a problem with his sexuality, probably because his mother knew long before Nick himself did, and she smoothed things over with Phillip.

"I made it all the way through law school and three years practicing before I burned out spectacularly. My dad wasn't interested when I told him I needed a break, so I left." Ryan finished his water in several long gulps. Nick was briefly distracted watching his throat move. "My buddy Keegan had just become a vet here in town, and he knew Maggie was hiring a ranch manager. He helped me get the job. It was meant to be just something temporary until I figured out what I wanted to do. I never looked back."

"I'm sure Micah had more than a little to do with that."

Ryan squeezed his knee, reminding Nick that his hand was still there. "Micah's known what he wanted since he could stand up and say 'horse.'" Ryan shook his head. "I think the only time he ever doubted himself was when he left for college. But that ended up working out. It gave me a chance to get my head out of my ass and notice what an amazing man he'd become."

"You two belong in a Hallmark movie."

Ryan raised an eyebrow. "Watch a lot of those, do you?"

"Not me. My ex. They're Xavi's guilty pleasure. You'll never believe me if you meet him, but he's a closet romantic."

"You should invite him up. I promise we won't put him on a horse."

Nick laughed. The idea was strangely appealing. He knew he needed to get back to Xavier, who'd been blowing up his phone ever since Nick left town with only a text asking Xavier to check his mail while he was gone.

He finished his sandwich and balled up the wrapper, then stood, taking Ryan's as well. "I'm not going to let Phillip get away with what he's doing. I need you and Micah to know that."

Ryan stretched his arms out on top of his bent knees, hands hanging loosely, his face in profile to the sun as he squinted up at Nick. "We know you won't, Nicky."

Nick hoped the bright sunlight was hiding the uncharacteristic heat in his cheeks.

# FOURTEEN
MICAH

Micah's brain was his worst enemy some days. Though he'd learned to manage his ADHD over the years, stress could still made things hard for him. His mind wanted to run off at full speed, and he couldn't predict if it would be toward or away from the problem. Sometimes he flailed around, unable to accomplish anything useful, and others he was so hyperfocused on a solution that he'd let the rest of the world burn if it meant he could finish the project.

Getting out on the trail usually helped, but today it only made him more scattered. His mind kept jumping from "What's going to happen to the horses if the ranch is gone?" to "What if this is the last time you ever see this view?" and "What if you have to move so far away you never see your friends again?"

He tried to keep up a good front, laughing and joking with the guests who were riding the short loop trail. He thought he did a pretty good job, but when the last of them were in their cars and driving away, he felt like a weight was crushing his chest. He ducked into Lex's stall to untack him and brush him down, letting the familiar shifting of the horse's weight and the sounds of the gelding munching on hay soothe him.

He needed to get it together. He knew Maggie wasn't going to give up their home without a fight. But he was really scared. This place, these people and animals were everything to him. He'd never dreamed that he could lose them.

He pressed his face into Lex's neck, hiding in the gelding's short hair. It wasn't fair that Maggie's brother could put them through this. That some asshole from the city, who hadn't set foot on the ranch in more than twenty years—if he ever had—could upend their lives like it was nothing. Micah didn't hate many people, but he *hated* Phillip Lauder.

"Micah?" Alice asked, her voice hesitant in a way she so rarely was.

Shit. The last thing he wanted was to explain this mess to Alice when he didn't have any answers. She didn't deserve the upheaval and was even less equipped to handle it than Micah was. Plus, her brother wasn't here to help her process. He subtly wiped his damp eyes and straightened, giving Lex a grateful pat.

"What's up, Allie?" he asked, forcing his voice to sound normal and not like he'd been seconds away from a breakdown. He glanced back to see her frowning at him from the stall door.

"Are you feeling sick?" she asked, almost hopefully. Micah huffed a laugh. He knew she didn't want him to be sick, but physical upset was much easier to fix than emotional.

"Just tired."

Alice made a sound like she didn't believe him. "You're not usually the tired one. That's Archer."

Micah cracked a smile. "That's 'cause Archer doesn't sleep enough when the art bug bites him on the ass."

"He's been working hard recently. He's got a space at the art show this summer, and he wants to get some visibility."

This was the first Micah had heard of that, which was honestly just like Archer. He might be Micah's best friend, but he kept some things, his art in particular, private. Micah didn't know why. Archer's paintings were amazing. He could easily make a living with them if he did more than a show here and there.

But Archer insisted that he was happy with the way things were, so Micah tried not to push too hard. Still, if he was going to have a space at the downtown art festival, Micah would promote the heck out of it. Archer's talent deserved some recognition. "Has he told anyone yet?"

"Just Maggie, since he needs that weekend off. It's a busy one here, too, and he didn't want to leave her understaffed."

Yeah, that could be a problem. There would be tons of tourists in town for the show. But they'd make it work.

If Split Rock Ranch still existed, that was. Crap. Now the rock was right back in Micah's gut. What would his friends do if the ranch got sold?

Izzy would land on his feet. He always did. Archer would too. He could get a job pretty much anywhere in town he wanted. Things would be trickier for Alice. She was great at her job, but she was pretty terrible at having a boss. She and Maggie had an understanding that worked perfectly for both of them, but someone else might not be as flexible.

And what about him and Ryan? Sure, they could find something else... but what if they couldn't find a place that would hire both of them? What if they had to move? Micah couldn't leave his dad, or Maggie. He'd never wanted to live anywhere but here. This was home. His spiraling thoughts pressed down on him, and try as he might, he couldn't shut them off.

"You're definitely not okay," Alice said, backing away. "I'm gonna call Izzy."

Micah let his back hit the wall and slid down to sit in a pile of loose hay. Lex shifted over after a minute and nudged him with his nose, breathing gentle puffs of air against his cheek. Maybe he could scrape together enough money to take Lex with them to wherever he and Ryan ended up. Boarding a horse somewhere you didn't work was expensive, but they could figure it out.

"Oh, good," he heard Alice say. "Can you please fix him?"

He cracked a smile that quickly crumpled. Then Ryan was sliding down to sit next to him. "What happened, baby?" Ryan asked, voice low and soothing.

Micah shook his head, then slumped over, resting against Ryan's shoulder and closing his eyes. "I'm scared," he admitted. "I'm so scared we're gonna lose everything."

Ryan wrapped an arm around him and hugged him close. "We'll figure it out." He sounded certain, but Micah couldn't see how.

"You know we can't afford to buy the ranch. We haven't even got a down payment. And all our savings is in the house renovations."

Ryan gestured, and then Nick was crouched down next to them, holding out a bottle of water. Micah didn't realize he'd started crying again until Nick's thumb brushed a tear off his cheek. How embarrassing. He ducked his head and tried to wipe his face on his shirt, then took a few grateful gulps of water.

"Sorry. I'm a mess. We don't even know what's gonna happen, and I'm already acting like it's over."

Ryan turned his head and dropped a lingering kiss on Micah's temple.

"It's not over," Nick said, voice rough. "I told Ryan I'm not going to let Phillip get away with this—and I won't, even if I have to sell everything I own and pay for it myself. I won't let you lose your home, Micah."

Ryan reached out and palmed the back of Nick's neck. "Let's wait to hear from Maggie before we make any drastic decisions."

Nick shut his eyes and nodded. He had dark shadows under his eyes, and his forehead was creased with tension. Micah felt a flare of sympathy. It couldn't be easy for Nick to admit that his closest family member was the bad guy here, to offer to go against him for people who were virtually strangers and an aunt he'd barely seen in the last twenty years.

Micah tangled his hand in Nick's shirt and tugged, leaning up at the same time to press his lips to Nick's startled mouth.

There was only a brief pause before Nick was kissing him back, his knees hitting the straw on either side of Micah's splayed legs as he cupped Micah's face with his palms.

Micah moaned when Nick's tongue slid across his lower lip, electric heat licking up his spine and making his skin tingle. He opened his mouth eagerly, letting Nick in as he was pressed back against the stall wall.

The kiss was firm but gentle, an exploration, their tongues gliding against each other, their mouths angling for more. When they parted, Micah was sure he was blushing scarlet, his lips wet and tingling from Nick's stubble. He was still trying to catch his breath when he opened his eyes and lost it again at the uncertainty on Nick's face.

He looked to the side and caught Ryan watching them with a smile. Micah returned a shy grin. "Um. So, that happened."

Ryan chuckled and leaned in to kiss Micah's forehead, then turned to Nick.

Nick met Ryan's eyes with a mixture of want and apprehension, his lips red from kissing Micah.

"Come here," Ryan said, then tugged Nick in with a hand on the back of his neck.

Micah's heart was slamming against the inside of his chest as their lips brushed, tentatively at first and then more firmly. He couldn't tell who deepened the kiss, but it went from testing to hungry in a matter of seconds. Their mouths opened at the same time, tongues sliding together with a slick sound. They were light and dark, Ryan's sun-bleached beard against Nick's dark stubble, Ryan's ruggedness against Nick's city-slick appeal. It was like watching live-action porn just inches from his face, and the sight made him squirm, cock thickening in his pants. He bit his lip against a desperate moan.

Ryan eased back, giving Nick a final kiss that left him panting and wild-eyed. They both looked at Micah, and he smiled in return. The expression felt shaky, a reflection of the butterflies swarming in his gut, but that was more excitement than anything else. Despite what they'd already done, this felt like a turning point. An understanding on all of their parts that something had shifted and this—they—were more than a fun hookup. At least, Micah hoped they were all on the same page about that.

"What—" Nick started, his voice wrecked. He cleared his throat and tried again. "I think I missed a meeting," he joked. "Want to fill me in?"

Micah snickered and ducked his head. Okay, maybe words were necessary. "I just really wanted to kiss you. And Ry said he did too." He peeked up at Nick, trying to gauge his reaction. "And we were wondering if you were interested in—well—more kissing. And maybe some cuddling? And just—more? 'Cause you're hot, and sexy, and we like you a lot and want to see what could happen if we let it?"

Nick and Ryan both looked amused when his ramble ended with a question. He gave them a winning smile and straightened up, wiping the last of the salty tear tracks from his face.

"Nothing needs to change if you aren't comfortable with it," Ryan, always the practical one, added.

Micah should have said that. He nodded instead. "Yeah. We don't want you to be uncomfortable."

Nick caught Micah by the hips, tugging him into his lap. Micah looped his arms around Nick's neck automatically, putting them nose to nose. "You're sweet. I'm interested. Definitely interested." Nick leaned in and nipped at Micah's lower lip again, making his breath catch. "But let's take it easy here. There's a lot up in the air, and I don't want whatever this is to get tangled up with the ranch and the crap my father is trying to pull."

Scratch that. Maybe Nick was the practical one. Micah pouted and glanced at Ryan. "But—" Ryan gave him a look that Micah recognized as a signal to be patient. He sighed. "Okay. But just so you know, kissing and fucking are definitely on the table."

"I thought we already had you on the table," Nick said.

That made Micah's cheeks burn, and he squirmed in Nick's lap, *accidentally* grinding their cocks together. Nick groaned, and his hand flew to Micah's ass to still his wiggling hips.

A moment later, familiar fingers twined in Micah's hair and tugged his head back. Ryan's lips pressed firmly to his. Then Ryan turned and did the same thing to Nick. "On that note," he said, satisfaction gleaming in his eyes. "We need to get back to work. There's another trail ride coming in in thirty minutes, and we have horses to tack up." He helped them both to their feet.

Micah's knees were wobbly, and he felt like he was on an emotional roller coaster, but Ryan pulled him into a tight hug that steadied him. He tucked his face into Ryan's neck and breathed him in for a moment, then straightened. "Okay. We've got this."

They were getting the horses put up for the night when Micah's phone started to play Pat Benatar's "Heartbreaker," the ringtone he'd set for Archer when he'd been on an oldies kick back in high school—and refused to change, because Archer had "Bad Boys" from that old Will Smith movie for him and this was payback. He tugged off his gloves and pulled the phone out of his pocket, his heart in his throat at the idea that there was news. It didn't occur to him that if there were, Maggie would be calling Ryan, until he'd already answered.

"I hope you're being careful, buddy," was the first thing Archer said. Micah went hot from his cheeks to the tips of his toes. How the hell did Archer know what Ryan, Nick, and he had been up to? Izzy was the only one who had a clue, and as far as he was concerned, they had just danced at the club.

"What?" he managed to croak out.

"With this guy, Dominic, staying with you. I don't trust him not to go behind your backs looking for other ways to screw over the ranch."

Wait. What? "What do you mean, you don't trust him? You don't even know him. And he goes by Nick. Not Dominic."

"I've heard plenty," Archer said, his voice tight. "I'd keep him at arm's length if I was you two. He's a slick sonuvabitch."

Micah gaped at the phone, wondering what planet Archer was living on. And where he was getting his information. "Nick is great. He's a mess over this whole thing and wants to help make it right."

"Are you sure about that? 'Cause from the conversation Maggie just had with her brother, it sounds like this whole thing was Nick's idea."

Micah went light-headed. He gripped the edge of the stall door. That wasn't right. Nick was helping them. He'd promised he wasn't going to let his father get away with this. "You're wrong," Micah managed. "Nick is on our side. He wants to stop the sale as much as the rest of us do."

"Does he?" Archer sounded skeptical. "What I heard is, he's there to meet a real estate developer and get the sale underway. He has all the paperwork."

Micah shook his head numbly, blinking spots from his vision. It took him a minute to realize he was holding his breath, and he let it out with a whoosh. "Phillip's forcing Nick into this."

"I don't know, JB," Archer said carefully, pulling out the old "jailbait" nickname. Micah swallowed at the hesitant tone. "You didn't hear this guy on the phone. Maggie had him on speaker so we could record the conversation for the lawyer. He's... I just don't think we can trust a word either of them say."

Micah straightened his shoulders. "I'm telling you, Arch. Nick's not like his father."

"I hope you're right, buddy," Archer finally allowed. "Because we don't have the best news."

Micah cringed, his nails digging into the wood. "The lawyer can't help?"

"Well, the guy we met with won't help," Archer said, sounding exhausted. "Maggie's chances of winning in court aren't good, and without that, it's hard to find someone interested in taking the case. Plus, with Phillip in control of her accounts, she can't afford to pay the fees up front."

Micah's heart sank. "What's she gonna do?"

"Right now, I'm not sure. She's going to have a glass of wine and make some more phone calls."

"Are you coming home soon?"

"Not yet. We have an appointment with another lawyer tomorrow. If it finishes early enough, I'll drive Maggie back after. If not, we might be here another night. She's also going to see if she can get a loan from the bank."

"That's not fair," Micah said before he could stop himself. "The ranch is hers. She shouldn't have to buy it back from someone who stole it."

Archer sighed. Micah could picture him sprawled out in a chair, one leg over the armrest as he ran a hand through his shaggy blond hair. Archer never could sit right in a chair. "I know, but we're exploring all the options. We're not going to let some crooked developer buy it and tear the place down to build vacation homes."

Micah had to take a steadying breath before he could answer. "Is that what their plan is?"

"We're not going to let them, Micah."

Micah nodded but couldn't seem to make himself speak. It was like his worst nightmares were coming to life. "I gotta go, Archer," he finally managed. "We're just wrapping up for the night."

"Yeah, I know it's about that time. Listen, don't say anything to Allie, okay? There's no reason for her to worry about this when we don't know what's going to happen yet."

"I know," Micah said. "I wasn't planning to."

"Thanks, buddy," Archer said. "I don't want her upset when I'm not there to help."

"Yeah. We got you."

Archer probed Micah a little bit more about the day, but Micah was distracted. Through the kitchen window, he could see Nick up at the house, moving around. Ryan was in the office, finishing up the day's paperwork. Suddenly all Micah wanted was to drag both his men to bed, pull the covers over their heads, and pretend the rest of the world didn't exist. Maybe things would be better in the morning.

# FIFTEEN

## NICK

THE CHICKEN WAS BROWNING in a pan on one burner, water boiling on another. The aroma of garlic sautéed in oil filled the air while Nick diced veggies for a simple stir-fry. He enjoyed cooking, but only for other people. If left to his own devices, he'd pull something from the freezer and reheat it. But when he could cook for friends, he tended to pull out all the stops. Stir-fry was disappointing, in a way. He'd like to impress Ryan and Micah with what he could do, but he hadn't had time when they got back from the trail ride. Maybe he could try cooking for them again tomorrow night.

That was, if Maggie wasn't back by then and Nick wasn't looking for a hotel to stay at. He still wasn't sure how his aunt would be feeling about him by the time she made it home.

Nick pushed that thought away and focused on the food. A few minutes later he heard the screen door open and then slap shut, followed by dog nails on hardwood. It made him smile, and he looked back to greet the two men who he was quickly becoming more attached to than he'd ever expected.

Micah gave him a wobbly smile, then said he was going to shower and thumped up the stairs.

Nick watched him go with a concerned frown. "Is he okay?" he asked Ryan.

Ryan stepped over to wash his hands at the sink, then leaned into Nick's space to steal a slice of pepper from the cutting board. Nick let him. There was plenty. "He says he is."

That was a non-answer if Nick ever heard one. "He's not, though, is he? How could he be?"

Ryan opened the fridge and pulled out two beers, offering one to Nick, who took it gratefully and twisted off the top. "I don't think any of us are going to be okay until this mess is settled." He leaned against the counter, watching Nick thoughtfully. "Will you help me distract him tonight? He's not gonna sleep otherwise."

"Of course," Nick agreed instantly. "What can I do?"

Ryan leaned in and kissed Nick's cheek. "Just be you. You're really fucking distracting, Nicky."

Nick turned his head to catch Ryan's lips as he pulled back. Ryan growled, and Nick found himself backed against the counter, his mouth claimed in a deep, hungry kiss that went on until his cock was hard and his knees weak. Then Ryan stepped back with a satisfied look.

"Just like that," he said as he turned to pull plates and silverware out of the cabinets.

Nick attempted to pull himself back together and look unruffled but knew he was failing spectacularly. He swallowed and turned back to the stove to dump the pasta into the boiling water and subtly adjust himself in his sweats. The chicken sizzled and popped in the pan, much like Nick's blood was doing in his veins. He'd figured things would be different after their conversation in the barn, but clearly he'd underestimated how different. Just as he got himself back under control, he heard Micah come down the stairs.

"It smells amazing in here. What are we having?" Hands landed on Nick's hips and a chin on his shoulder as Micah peered past him into the skillet. At least he sounded better. And he felt fantastic, molded to Nick's back like that. He had to be wearing sweats, because his soft cock was nestled right up against Nick's ass.

Giving up on any thoughts of subtlety, Nick reached back with one hand and wrapped his arm around Micah's waist, holding him in place. Micah hummed in his ear in response and hugged him around the middle.

One step at a time, Nick told himself. He'd meant it when he said he didn't want to get whatever this was with Micah and Ryan tangled up in the mess Phillip was causing. No relationship—no friendship, for that matter—could survive problems that combined family and money. Nick had seen more than a few fallings-out due to debts and changes in circumstance.

He was going to help stop his father, and then he could decide if he'd let feelings get involved. It was the right thing to do.

When the food was ready, Nick dished it up and they settled around the big wood table, chatting as they ate. They didn't have as many rides booked the next day, so Micah would be working with the horses he was training while Ryan took the two groups out. Ryan offered Nick a spot again, but Nick declined. He was currently sore in places he hadn't remembered could *be* sore. The idea of another few hours in the saddle made him cringe.

Micah laughed and offered to fill the bath in the en suite so he could soak.

"Or we could open up the hot tub," Ryan said as he gathered their plates and took them to the sink to wash.

Micah lit up at that. "Oh. Hell yeah." He turned to Nick with a breathtaking smile that Nick knew he would never be able to say no to. "It's a perfect night for it. Nice and cool, and all the stars will be out."

"I didn't bring a suit," Nick pointed out, though he was pretty sure that wouldn't be an issue.

Micah waved him off. "No one's around but us."

Nick raised an eyebrow at him. "Does that mean you're joining me in this naked hot tub adventure?"

Micah went pink to the tips of his ears. It was so cute that Nick had to reach out and stroke a thumb over his flushed cheek.

Ryan leaned over the table with a fresh beer for Nick, handing Micah what looked like a cider. "I'll get the towels and meet you out there."

Nick levered himself up with a groan. Sitting on the hard wooden kitchen chair had made him stiffen up, and not in the fun way.

He followed Micah out onto the dark deck. There was a light on down by the barn, and some spilling through the patio doors, but otherwise it was nearly pitch black, the moon only a sliver in the sky. Micah flipped the cover off the hot tub, and steam billowed up into the air.

Micah hit a button to turn on the jets and underwater lights, then kicked off his shoes and stripped out of his shirt and pants, which left him in nothing but loose boxers. Then he shoved those past his hips as well, giving Nick a glorious view of his perfectly firm ass as he bent to gather his clothes and drop them on a nearby chair.

Taking a steadying breath, Nick followed his lead, stripping down and putting his clothes aside. The air had a bite that made him shiver and hurry to follow Micah up and into the tub. He set his beer in a cup holder and sank back with a groan as the hot water closed around him. Holy shit, did that feel good. "Whoever's idea it was to install a hot tub is a genius." He ducked his head quickly, ran his fingers through his hair, then sat back and stretched his arms out along the edge of the tub. When he looked up again, Micah was watching him with parted lips.

"It was Ryan's idea," Micah said absently, his gaze tracing over Nick's chest and down to where the rest of him was hidden by the water.

"Well, your husband is a brilliant man. I hope you rewarded him appropriately."

Micah flashed a grin. "It was before we were together. But trust me, we've gotten good use of it since, and he's been rewarded more than once." He slid from his seat and toward Nick, the submerged lights reflecting off his wet skin and throwing the defined cut of his muscles into sharp relief.

Nick raised an eyebrow as he watched.

When their knees bumped, Micah climbed into Nick's lap, straddling his hips, and settled his bare ass on Nick's thighs, only inches away from his cock, which was rapidly getting on board. He reached out with one wet finger and slid it down the line between Nick's pecs. "The first thing I noticed about you was how perfect you looked—hair styled, leather jacket, designer sunglasses." His lips twitched up, devilish, his eyes glittering with wicked humor. "I like you better like this. Wet, naked, and messy." His hand dipped below the water, continuing to trace muscles he couldn't see. "You're not as slick as you want everyone to think, are you, Nicky?"

Nick blinked. That was the first time Micah had called him anything other than Nick. He liked it. He didn't move as Micah's fingers wandered closer to his rapidly hardening cock.

"Ryan saw it before I did, I think. You'd do anything for family, even when you know it's going to hurt. That's why you have a shell—to protect the soft parts."

Nick tried to focus past the arousal, not sure what Micah was getting at. "Doesn't everyone do their best to protect themselves? No one likes to be hurt."

"That's fair," Micah agreed. "But I think you keep the shell in place so no one will know if they leave a mark." Micah leaned in, ghosting his lips along Nick's cheek. "You have big heart that you're keeping hidden so you don't get hurt again," he said in Nick's ear. His tongue darted out to give the lobe a lick. "I hope you decide to let us in."

Then he sat back and looked over Nick's shoulder with a bright grin. "The water's perfect," he said as Ryan appeared.

Within seconds, Ryan was naked and climbing into the hot tub. His thick, soft cock caught Nick's eye as he stepped over the lip, and Nick swallowed as his mouth began to water. Ryan settled in the seat adjacent to them, and Nick dragged his gaze up to meet amused blue eyes.

"See something you're interested in?" Ryan asked.

Nick gave a nonchalant shrug. "I guess that depends."

"Ryan mostly likes to top," Micah offered helpfully. "I'm vers, but I usually prefer to bottom." He wiggled in Nick's lap to demonstrate.

Nick had to hold back a laugh at how not subtle Micah was when he wanted something. It was impressive how he could go from murmuring hard truths in Nick's ear, to big eyes and biting his lip like he was ready to beg to get fucked. "Well, isn't that lucky. I'm vers too, no preference. I like things that feel good, and sex feels good, no matter what position it happens to be from."

Micah grinned and leaned in until they were nose to nose. "So, does that mean you'd be up for Ryan fucking us both, here in the hot tub? 'Cause that is definitely on my bucket list."

Nick groaned at the mental image and lost the battle to keep his hands on the sides of the tub. He tangled one in Micah's wet hair and grabbed his ass with the other, hauling him into a hard, filthy kiss, all teeth and tongue.

Micah moaned and surrendered, melting against him and letting Nick direct his movements. He felt fantastic in Nick's arms, hard, wet, and slippery as Nick held him close.

He heard the water slosh as Ryan moved, sliding into the spot next to him. When he and Micah broke apart for air, Ryan was there, catching Nick's lips in a demanding kiss that took the last of the breath from his lungs. Nick groaned and wrapped an arm around Ryan's neck, keeping him close. At the same time, he felt Micah shift and close a hand around both their cocks, lining them up and using the slickness of the water to stroke them together.

Someone's hand brushed his thigh right before Micah jerked in his lap and groaned desperately, hips squirming. Nick slid his hand to Micah's ass and found Ryan's fingers playing with his hole. A ball of lust dropped into his belly, and he was suddenly desperate for more. He broke the kiss and pressed his forehead to Ryan's damp shoulder, rocking into Micah's grip around their cocks.

“Fuck,” he groaned, pressing Micah to him as sparks gathered in his groin.

His groan turned to a hiss when Micah was tugged away—and with him that delicious friction. Nick’s eyes opened to see Ryan gazing down at him.

“Up. Both of you.” Ryan gripped Micah by the hips and positioned him on his knees on the bench, his elbows planted on the edge of the tub, his ass in the air. Micah rested his cheek on his folded hands and gave Nick a grin that Nick had to kiss from his lips.

As they parted for breath, he heard a crack, and Micah gasped. Nick saw his pupils blow wide with pleasure and his back arch.

Ryan gave his ass another playful smack, loud against wet skin, and Micah moaned, hips writhing to chase the sensation. He got one more smack and an admonishment to be still, then Ryan shifted to tug Nick into position as well.

“You spank me, and I won’t be held responsible for my actions,” he told Ryan, trying to sound threatening.

“Noted,” Ryan said, voice low and rough with arousal. “More for Micah.”

Micah laughed and then gasped when he got several quick smacks in a row.

The contrast of the hot water and the cold air made Nick’s head spin and his thoughts go fuzzy. He braced his knees on the slick plastic of the bench and waited. As long as whatever Ryan had planned meant he eventually got fucked by that thick cock,

Nick was on board, threats about spanking or not. He couldn't remember the last time he was so freaking horny.

"Please, Ry," Micah begged, his back bowing in encouragement.

Nick turned his head and saw Micah's lips part on a shaky exhale. A quick glance showed him Ryan's long fingers disappearing between Micah's cheeks. The water wouldn't make very good lube, but it was evidently enough for now.

A moment later, Nick made a rough sound as those fingers slid along his crack and danced over his hole. His back dipped involuntarily, offering his ass up to be plundered. God, it had been so long since he'd let someone top him. He was practically drooling for it, and Ryan's hum of acknowledgment told him he'd been found out.

A wet finger circled his hole, teasing the muscle into relaxing. Nick tried to keep his breathing even, but it still stuttered when Ryan eased in, the water enough to smooth the way but not to prevent the burn of the slight stretch.

Micah made a wrecked sound, and Nick dragged his eyes open, wondering when he had closed them. Micah had lifted his head and was watching with wide eyes and parted lips as Ryan worked first one finger, then two, into Nick.

"Oh, fuck," Micah breathed. "This is way hotter than I expected."

Ryan laughed and pressed his fingers deep. Pleasure jolted through Nick as Ryan grazed his prostate. Micah moaned for probably the same reason.

Nick needed more, needed a connection to Micah. He sought out Micah's mouth for a sloppy kiss. Micah returned it eagerly, their tongues sliding together as they shivered and groaned under the assault of Ryan's talented fingers.

Micah was panting into his mouth, his fingers scrabbling to cling to Nick's wet shoulder. Nick shifted closer and got his arm braced against the side of the tub, giving Micah something to cling to—and to sink his teeth into, he realized as Micah sucked a biting bruise into his shoulder.

Ryan pulled away and reached over the side of the hot tub to where he'd left the towels. When he returned, he was quickly rolling a condom down his length and spreading lube over it. Then, with a hand on Micah's hip and another on his shoulder, he thrust home.

Micah's shout was equal parts shocked and euphoric. His eyes rolled back and his mouth dropped open as Ryan fucked him, dragging Micah's hips toward him as Micah braced himself against the bench. Micah transformed into a writhing, babbling mess as he begged for more, harder, "yes, Ryan, yes."

They were stunning together: Micah lost in pleasure, Ryan with fierce determination creasing his brow. Nick reached below the water to stroke himself, unable to hold off. But then his hand was pulled away.

"You save that for me," Ryan growled, his voice so deep with arousal that Nick shivered, feeling it in his chest. Like hell would he argue.

He reached for Micah instead, pushing him up until he was balanced on his knees and sitting on Ryan's cock. Then he slid between him and the wall, slouching until he could suck Micah's pretty cock into his mouth. He let Ryan control the rhythm, pulling Micah back and then pushing him forward. Micah dug his hands into Nick's wet hair with a sob of pleasure, trembling under the onslaught. When he started coming, Nick swallowed eagerly, loving the salty-bitter taste.

After a minute, Micah pushed Nick away with a murmur about being too sensitive. Nick let him go and slumped against the wall of the hot tub, his eyes falling shut. The jets were buffeting him just right, and he groaned, the rush of water against his hard, aching shaft sending flickers of pleasure through him that weren't nearly enough.

He contemplated taking care of things himself, but Ryan's words were still echoing in his mind. Then strong hands gripped his hips and pulled him from the seat. He groaned and grabbed the side of the tub as he was flipped and arranged on his knees again. There was something overwhelmingly arousing about a man who could move him where he wanted—though the water was obviously helping in this case. He rested his chin on his folded arms and tilted his hips up in invitation.

Someone moved behind him before hands gripped his ass cheeks and a slick tongue dragged over his hole. Nick jerked in surprise, then moaned and leaned closer when it happened again.

"That's it, baby. Press that tongue in there. Get him nice and soft for me." It was Micah's mouth on him. Nick groaned, arousal pulsing at the realization.

Micah's sound of agreement was muffled, and the vibrations sent a shiver through Nick. He was more than ready, but fuck if he was going to stop Micah. He rocked back instead, losing himself as the slick probing lit up his nerve endings. He turned his head enough to catch a glimpse of Ryan rolling a new condom down his flushed cock and adding more lube. Nick needed that beauty in his ass five minutes ago. It had been way too long.

Ryan caught him staring. "You ready?" he asked, giving himself a slow stroke.

"I was ready in that bathroom stall," Nick admitted.

Before he could worry that that was too honest, Ryan growled and dipped down to claim his lips in a fast, hard kiss. Then he stepped behind Nick and urged Micah away, and Nick felt the blunt pressure of Ryan's cock pressing against his entrance. He bore down to let him in, and Ryan drove home with one steady thrust that made all the breath leave Nick's lungs.

He lost track of things after that. The world dissolved into sensation, pleasure assaulting him from all sides. Ryan's cock pounding into him. The jets of the hot tub caressing his skin from every angle. Somehow Micah got between Nick and the wall, all wet skin and full lips. Ryan dove forward to kiss him, sandwiching Nick between them.

When Nick's body started to tighten, Ryan hauled him upright and Micah ducked down to suck his cock into tight heat, swallowing around him. Nick shook as his orgasm crashed over him in waves, his release spilling onto Micah's tongue in long, drawn-out pulses.

He was vaguely aware of Ryan chasing his own release, sending aftershocks through Nick's body until Ryan buried himself deep with a groan, hands gripping Nick hard as he filled the condom.

Micah slept like a rock and woke up plastered to Nick's back. After a few minutes of sleepy confusion at being trapped between two warm bodies, he remembered dragging Nick to bed with them on the premise that it was more convenient in case he needed the bathroom. Nick and Ryan had been amused by his logic and gone along with it. Micah had fleeting thoughts about waking one or the other of them up with a blow job that could maybe turn into another round of fun, but when he saw the clock, he had to let the idea go. It was too early. Still the middle of the night, as Nick would point out.

Micah managed to wiggle out from between them and grinned when Ryan grumbled in his sleep and dragged Nick into little-spoon position. They were so cute he had to stop and snap a picture with his phone, saving it as his wallpaper. That was the stuff fantasies were made of.

After a quick trip to the bathroom, he jogged down the stairs to let the dogs out and start the coffee. Milo gave him a baleful look from his bed before hopping up and heading for the door.

Micah promised to throw the ball for him later. Poor guy wasn't getting nearly enough attention this week.

His phone buzzed on the counter while the coffee was brewing. It was early enough that it could only be Izzy or Archer—Izzy still awake, or Archer up way too early, like Micah. He snagged it on his way to fill the dog bowls and thumbed it open.

It was Archer, checking to see how things were. Which probably meant he was up worrying about the fate of the ranch, just like Micah. Micah took a steadying breath as the rock of anxiety he'd been ignoring got bigger. He fired off a thumbs-up in response and shoved the phone back into his pocket. Thinking about the what-ifs was only going to send him into a tailspin. For now, he was going to focus on what he could do. In the office were a whole bunch of old files with bank statements and bills. Maybe he could find something that would help.

Having done their business, the dogs ate, then flopped back in their beds in protest of the early morning. Micah grabbed a mug of coffee and headed to the study that they mostly used for storage and work when the weather was too nasty to walk down to the barn. In the closet were a dozen or so file boxes filled with papers. Micah dragged the oldest-looking one out, settled on the floor, his coffee next to him, and opened the lid. He stared down at the disorganized mess of receipts and invoices with a sigh. This was going to take forever, but maybe there was something in here that would help them prove that Maggie owned the ranch and would never, ever give it up.

His eyes were starting to cross when he heard his name being called. He blinked up at the surprisingly bright room. He wasn't sure how long he'd been sitting there, but he was stiff and his coffee had gone cold.

Ryan was watching him from the office door, a bemused look on his face. "What are you doing, baby? How long have you been up?"

Micah shrugged and looked at the piles of paperwork surrounding him. "Dunno," he muttered, rubbing at his gritty eyes. "I remembered these files were in here, and I thought I'd see what I could find."

Ryan stepped carefully across the room and reached down to haul him to his feet.

Micah only discovered that his legs were asleep when he staggered and Ryan had to catch him so he didn't land on the floor again. "Crap," he groaned as pins and needles attacked his limbs. "Ow, ow, ow."

Ryan kept him upright with an arm around his waist until the feeling wore off. "Find anything interesting?"

Micah rolled his aching shoulders. "A lot of old bank statements and bills, invoices, and canceled checks. A waste of time, I guess." He slumped, suddenly exhausted again.

Ryan rubbed his back soothingly. "You never know what could come in handy if we have to go to court." He pressed a kiss to Micah's temple. "I'll help you look through the rest of the boxes later. Right now, you need breakfast. Nicky's cooking."

Micah breathed in and noticed the scent of bacon and what might have been pancakes. His stomach grumbled loudly, and Ryan arched an eyebrow at him. Micah gave a sheepish grin in return.

He followed Ryan into the kitchen. Nick was at the stove in just a pair of low-slung gray sweats, his toned back on display. Micah had no choice but to walk over and plaster himself to all those muscles, leaning up on his toes to nuzzle the back of Nick's neck. He was regretting getting out of bed before anyone else woke up.

Nick laughed and reached back to squeeze Micah's hip. "Morning, sweetheart," he said, voice still rough from sleep.

Micah hid his smile and didn't comment on the pet name. "Morning."

Nick gave his hip a smack. "Get yourself some more coffee while I finish here." He had several burners going: thick slices of French toast frying in one pan, bacon in another, and eggs in a third. Micah's stomach let its approval be known.

He did as he was told, then settled next to Ryan at the table and leaned over to give him a good-morning kiss as well. "You missed some fantastic hand jobs this morning," Ryan said. "Turns out Nicky and I are both fans of morning sex."

Micah gaped at him, heat flooding his body at the mental image. Definitely not fair. "I love morning sex," he said petulantly.

Nick set a plate piled with food in front of him. "Anytime, sweetheart." He gave Ryan a plate as well, then went back for his own.

As they ate, Micah and Ryan discussed their plans for the day. There was plenty of work to do on the ranch, particularly after a busy weekend. The horses needed to be taken care of, the farrier was due to come by, and there was a list of repairs that needed to happen.

"This is why we've had only one bathroom for six months," Micah reminded Ryan. "There's always more projects than there are hours in the day."

"I'm happy to help," Nick offered. "I probably wouldn't be any use with the bathroom, but put me to work. I'll chip in where I can."

Micah and Ryan were happy to accept that offer. With Archer still out of town, they could use an extra set of hands. It warmed Micah's heart that Nick wanted to help. When Nick had arrived at the ranch, in his designer clothes, Micah never could have imagined it, but now that they were getting to know him better it was obvious that Nick wasn't who he first appeared to be.

They decided that Nick would help with the horses while Ryan did repairs and Micah did his training work. Izzy would handle the stalls, and Alice had her own set of tasks to accomplish. There weren't any trail rides scheduled, so that made things easier.

It was later than usual when they made it down to the barn, Nick in Archer's old boots and clothes borrowed from Ryan. Izzy was finishing up feeding when they arrived. He gave Nick a lingering once-over that ended when Micah shoved his shoulder.

"Don't be an asshole," he muttered in Izzy's ear. "He's helping."

"Oh, I appreciate the help," Izzy replied, luckily keeping his voice down. "I also appreciate the view."

Micah scowled, annoyance flooding him. "Keep your appreciation to yourself, buddy."

That made Izzy throw back his head and laugh. Micah scowled harder. "Oh, man. I can't fucking wait until Archer gets home. This is going to be epic."

Micah folded his arms over his chest, but Ryan interrupted before he could say anything.

"I'll get Nicky started, and then I'm going to be in the shed, changing the oil in the farm vehicles. Call me if you need me?"

Micah leaned in for a kiss. "You got it." He shot Nick a grin, too shy to kiss him in front of Izzy, and got a wink in return. Then he headed out to get his first horse of the day ready to go.

It ended up being the perfect morning. Each time Micah went into the barn and saw Nick at work the warm feeling in his chest grew. Having Nick here felt right. Natural. Like this could be real life: him and Ryan including Nick in their work, their lives, and their bed. The idea made him ache with want. But Nick had been there less than a week, and they had no clue what the future was going to hold. For all Micah knew, once the ranch was safe, Nick would go back to New York, and they'd never see him again.

That was a sobering idea, and Micah refused to entertain it. Nick fit too well with them to leave and not come back. Micah and Ryan would just have to tie him to the bed and convince him to stay. The thought made him grin and blush at the same time.

"What's that look for?" Micah's head jerked up. Archer was leaning in the stall door, his muscular arms folded across his chest, one dark blond eyebrow raised in question.

"What look?" Micah asked, trying to wipe any of his tells off his face. Unfortunately, Archer had known him way too long. "The look that says you're having dirty thoughts and you don't want anyone to notice."

Micah's cheeks burned, and he wished he had something to throw at Archer, but his hands were empty. "Asshole," he grumbled but stepped over to give Archer a hug. "How did it go?" he asked as Archer squeezed him equally tight in return.

"It was rough. The surgery went great, but the rest..." Micah's heart sank. "We don't have any news yet," Archer finally said. He sounded exhausted, and when he stepped back, Micah could see the deep shadows under his eyes.

A rock of guilt settled in Micah's stomach. It was an asshole move that he'd let himself be distracted by Nick and Ryan while Archer and Maggie were losing sleep trying to find a way to save the ranch. "How's Maggie?" he asked, looking toward the house in hopes that he might see her out on the deck.

"Pissed." Archer chuckled darkly. "Her brother is a fucking piece of work. You should have heard the bullshit that came out of his mouth when she finally got him on the phone." Archer bared his teeth in a sharp grin. "The guy better not show his face around here is all I'm saying."

"What did my *wonderful* father have to say?" Nick asked, making "wonderful" sound like a curse as he stepped into sight outside the stall.

Archer's expression went dark, and he glanced back, then turned away from Nick dismissively. "Anyway," he continued, ignoring the question, "I'm just here to take Allie home. I need to sleep for a week, and I don't want to come get her later."

"We can give her a ride," Micah offered, but Archer waved him off.

"It's fine. Maggie wants to talk to all of you, and I need to fill Allie in on what's happening." Archer shut his eyes for a moment, visibly gathering himself. Micah winced. That conversation was going to be hard for both of them. It wasn't fair to keep Alice in the dark, but at the same time, the idea of losing the ranch was going to be a huge trigger for her.

"Let us know if you need anything," Micah said, pulling Archer into another hug. "We rescheduled family dinner for Thursday night."

Archer nodded and clasped Micah's shoulder. "Thanks, JB. I'll let you know if we're up for it." He turned away, leveling a long look at Nick, who was watching them quietly. "I hope you're as good a man as my friend here thinks," he finally said before turning and stalking away.

Micah winced, then met Nick's gaze. "So, that was my best friend, Archer."

Nick stepped into the stall, pulling the door partially shut behind him. Micah licked his lips as he took in Nick's messy hair, dirt-streaked forearms, work gloves, and old jeans. He shifted closer. Damn. Scruffy Nick made Micah want to climb him like a tree.

Nick smirked, obviously reading Micah's expression. He stepped closer, backing Micah against the wall and caging him in. Micah's heart raced, and his cock twitched against his zipper. He tilted his chin up at the same time that Nick dipped down and brushed their mouths together in a chaste kiss. "The things I want to do to you later," Nick murmured.

"Hey, JB, we're leav— What the fuck?" Archer's furious voice made Micah flinch and Nick jerk back. Oh, crap. Micah met Nick's startled eyes a moment before Archer's hand closed over Nick's shoulder and ripped him away. "Get your hands off him!"

"Archer, don't—" Micah began, but his words were drowned out by a feminine scream. He dove for the two men even as Archer slammed Nick into the wood planks of the stall, making the whole thing rattle and dust rain down on them.

Nick groaned, looking dazed, one hand gripping the fist Archer had balled up in the front of his shirt, the other raised to protect his face.

"No!" Micah shouted, jumping on Archer's back like a spider monkey and grabbing his arm. "Stop. Stop!"

"Stop!" Alice shrieked as she shoved into the stall and got between Nick and Archer.

"Allie, move," Archer growled even as he lost his balance and was forced to take a step back.

Nick, being a smart man, slid farther behind Alice's petite frame, effectively making further attack impossible.

Footsteps pounded down the aisle, and Ryan and Izzy appeared in the doorway. "What the hell is going on here?" Ryan growled in the deep, take-charge voice that made Micah's tension leave him in a whoosh. His feet hit the straw, but he didn't let go of his death grip on Archer's arm, not sure whether Archer would keep trying to throw punches and not wanting to let him do anything he would regret later.

Archer was shaking in his hold. His fists were still clenched as he looked between Alice and Micah in confused betrayal. "Ask your husband," he told Ryan, jerking his hand out of Micah's grip and backing away.

"He saw Nick kiss me," Micah said. "It was mutual, and Ryan's part of it too," he added to Archer's profile, just in case that hadn't been clear.

Archer shook his head and gave Micah a bewildered look.

Ryan grimaced and scrubbed a hand over his face, then met Nick's wary eyes. "You okay, Nicky?"

Archer twitched, either at the nickname or at the sentiment.

Ryan took a step forward, then hesitated. Alice was still between Nick and her twin, white-faced and wide-eyed. "Alice," Ryan asked, "can I check on him?"

She gave a sharp nod but didn't move.

Ryan went around her and laid a careful hand on Nick's shoulder. Which was when Micah noticed Nick was gripping it with his other hand. "Can you move it?" Ryan asked.

Nick rolled it carefully, then did the same with his neck. "Just a bruise, I think. I didn't have time to brace myself."

Ryan's hand slid to the back of Nick's neck and rested there.

Micah heard another whispered "What the fuck" from Archer and turned to gauge his expression. Archer's brow was furrowed with confusion and exhaustion, and he shook his head. "Okay," he said, voice taut with disbelief. "Obviously I got whatever the hell this is really wrong. But I haven't slept in two days, and I'm too fucking tired to deal with it right now." He held out his hand to his sister. "Allie?"

Alice moved to his side and gripped his arm tight enough to make Archer wince, then hid her face in his shoulder.

Archer pressed his lips to the top of her head, still eyeing the rest of them mistrustfully. "I'm sorry," he murmured to Alice, free hand stroking her back.

"This is my safe place." Her words were muffled by Archer's shirt, but clear enough. "It's safe here."

Micah wrapped his arms around himself and gripped his elbows, feeling sick to his stomach. Out of the corner of his eye, he saw Ryan murmur something to Nick and lead him out. That would help. Alice hated an audience when she was struggling with her emotions. He kept his distance from the twins, not wanting to make things worse. Still, he couldn't leave without saying anything. "I'm sorry. I should have told you about Nick."

Archer shook his head, a muscle jumping in his jaw. "Yeah, you fucking should have." He shook his head. "You actually trust the guy?" he asked. "Not with"—he waved a hand toward the spot Nick had been standing—"whatever that is. You trust that he's not helping his father."

"I really do, Arch. So does Ryan."

Archer gave a sharp nod. "All right." He dragged a tired hand through his hair and glanced away. "I'll back off, then. I shouldn't have jumped to conclusions."

Micah bit his lower lip as Archer murmured something to Alice and got a quick nod in return.

"Can you apologize to him for me?" Archer asked. "We need to get home and relax."

Micah nodded. "Of course. You need sleep. Do you think you'll make it to family dinner?" If Alice ended up having a meltdown, neither of them would be up for socializing for at least a couple of days. And Archer hadn't even told her about the sale yet. It was going to be a rough night in the Beckett household.

"We'll try," Archer said, and Micah knew that was really all he could offer at the moment. Archer gave Micah a tired smile as he led his sister out. "Don't think you're off the hook, JB. I'm gonna need details."

Micah returned a weak grin and rubbed the back of his neck sheepishly. "Yeah. I promise."

The barn was deserted, so as soon as Archer and Alice pulled away, Micah made his way up to the house. He followed the low voices into the kitchen and found Nick at the table with an ice pack on his shoulder and Ryan starting coffee.

He beelined to Nick's side, concern pushing aside everything else. "I thought it was just a bruise." He placed a gentle hand on the wrist holding the ice in place, anxiously meeting Nick's eyes.

"It's hardly anything," Nick said. "Your husband just likes fussing."

Micah dragged a chair over so he could sit with his knees against Nick's thigh. "He doesn't usually fuss for no reason." He gripped Nick's thigh, needing to hang on to him in some way.

"I promise it's nothing," Nick repeated, turning to kiss Micah's forehead.

"He's still going to keep ice on it, though, to keep the swelling down," Ryan ordered as he came back with four cups of coffee, two in each hand. Micah eyed the fourth one until Ryan added, “Maggie’s on her way over. She was just settling in next door.”

That made Nick blanch. He sucked in a deep breath and straightened in his chair. Micah could see the conflict on his face. Poor guy. “She’ll understand,” he tried, running his hand back and forth over Nick’s thigh soothingly.

Nick gave him an unconvincing nod and dropped the ice pack on the table so he had a hand free for his coffee.

The screen door creaked open and then slapped shut again, followed by paws scrabbling on the hardwood. Rascal came around the corner and headed for the food bowl to search for anything Milo might have missed earlier. She was going to be out of luck.

Micah shifted away from Nick as Maggie followed the dog in, leaning more heavily on her cane than usual. Though she was hiding it well, Micah could see the exhaustion in her frame. He hopped up to offer her his chair.

Nick stood at the same time, and he and his aunt met in the middle of the kitchen. Maggie eyed Nick up and down.

“Aunt Maggie,” Nick said, his voice thick. “I’m so sorry.”

Maggie scoffed, wrapping her arms around him in a tight hug.

Nick froze, then hesitantly hugged her back, his expression a mix of confusion and relief.

“Don’t you dare apologize to me, Nicky Lauder,” Maggie scolded. “My brother’s sins are his own. I refuse to let you take the burden for something that isn’t your fault.”

Nick deflated, his arms tightening around her as he pressed his cheek to the top of her head. "I feel responsible. I should have questioned him more."

Maggie huffed out a sound that Micah knew from experience was a combination of frustration and amusement. "Did he give you any hint what he was up to? Tell you that he'd faked the deed?"

"No, but—"

Maggie pushed him back to arm's length, gripping his shoulders firmly. "Then what on earth makes you think you could have stopped him? He's the one who decided his greed was more important than family, not you, Nicky."

Nick straightened in her hold. "Even so, I'm going to find a way to stop him."

Maggie reached up and patted his cheek. "You've always been kind, to your own detriment. Do you remember the time you insisted on helping the feral kittens in the barn?"

Micah grinned. He'd heard this story. It was one of Maggie's cautionary tales. "Didn't they scratch the hell out of you, and you had to go to the doctor for stitches?"

Nick rolled his eyes but held out his hand so that Micah could see the faint white marks on the back of his forearm. "Little assholes. They were pointier than I expected."

Micah laughed and glanced at Ryan, who was shaking his head in amusement.

"And you still caught them and found them all homes in the end. Despite being bandaged from your elbows to your wrists."

Maggie gave his arm a squeeze. "Let's not have a repeat of that, okay?"

He frowned. "I'm not letting him cheat you out of your home." He turned his head to include Micah and Ryan in the statement. "Any of you."

"None of us are planning to lay down so he can run us over." Maggie gave his arm a motherly pat. "Now, bring me the paperwork, so I can see what my jackass brother thinks he's going to get away with."

# SEVENTEEN

RYAN

NICKY AND MAGGIE HAD been locked in the study for several hours. The dogs, who refused to leave Maggie's side after her time away, were with them. Ryan refused to admit he was a bit anxious. Not for the reason Nicky had been—he knew Maggie wouldn't be upset with her nephew—but he didn't like not knowing what was going on behind the closed door. He was staying busy, but he couldn't help glancing in that direction from time to time. After all, he was Maggie's... Well, he wasn't her lawyer, because he didn't have an active license, but he could help with unofficial legal advice. He should really be in there. And it had nothing to do with checking on Nicky.

"Ryan, please stop. You're making it worse."

He paused in the middle of the living room and looked over at Micah, who was on the couch with his laptop. "Stop what?"

"You're pacing."

"I'm not—"

"You've been to the kitchen six times in the last fifteen minutes. I promise, there's nothing new in the fridge since the last five times you looked."

Ryan sighed and dragged a hand through his hair. "Sorry. I just need to be doing something."

Micah held out his hand, and Ryan took it, sitting on the sofa next to him. Micah wiggled close and curled up under Ryan's arm until he had no choice but to hug him. "It's gonna be okay," Micah said. "She's not gonna let him blame himself."

"I know she won't. But he's been damn stubborn about believing he's responsible. I don't like it."

Micah grinned and kissed his cheek. "My protective man."

"You're not any better," Ryan murmured, nuzzling his temple.

"Nope," Micah said, turning the laptop so Ryan could see the slew of windows he had pulled up, all with searches like "what to do if someone claims your property" and "proving ownership of property."

Ryan huffed a laugh and squeezed Micah tighter. "Love you, baby."

"I love you back," Micah replied. "Now, help me understand how a writ of sequestration works. I saw it on one of these sites, but the legal babble is making my eyes bleed."

When the door to the study opened and the first thing Ryan heard was Maggie's laughter, relief washed through him. He straightened where he was sitting on the sofa. Micah sat up at the same time.

Maggie stepped out first, leaning on her cane. Ryan made a note to ask how much walking she was actually supposed to be doing three days after surgery. Even though she was the toughest person Ryan knew, it was hard to see her in pain.

The hip replacement had been long overdue. She'd put it off for years, thinking the surgery would stop her from ever riding again. Micah had finally convinced her to talk to the doctor by pointing out that she wasn't able to ride *now*. And it turned out that, as long as the surgery went well, she had every chance of being able to get back on a horse again.

Nicky was right behind her. Both of their eyes were a little red, but otherwise, they seemed as relaxed as they could be.

"Promise me that that's a last resort," Maggie was saying as they entered the living room.

"As long as you agree that it's an option."

Maggie sighed. "All right, kiddo. If it comes to that, I won't argue."

Nicky ducked down and kissed her cheek. "Thank you."

"What's a last resort?" Micah asked, looking between the two of them.

Maggie raised an eyebrow at Nicky, but Nicky shook his head. "I'm going to start dinner," she announced, aiming for the kitchen. "You three decide what it is you want to tell me."

Ryan blinked and glanced back at Nicky, who was wide-eyed and very pink. "I don't even want to know how she guessed."

Micah gave them both a sheepish grin. "How does Maggie know anything?" he asked. "I'm pretty sure she knew about me and Ryan before our first kiss."

"Oh, she definitely did," Ryan answered. "She's one of the most perceptive people I know."

"Well, I'll leave the decision up to you two," Nicky said, resting his unbruised shoulder against the doorframe.

Ryan blew out a breath. "Considering everyone else who works here already knows something's going on, it seems silly to keep it a secret from Maggie. Even if we tried, she'd find out by the end of the day." He ruffled Micah's hair. "I'm surprised Keegan and your dad aren't already knocking on the front door to give us the third degree."

Micah laughed and batted his hand away. "It probably helps that family dinner got postponed. We all know I'm no good at secrets."

Nicky was watching them from the doorway, a soft smile on his face. "So... what are we telling her, exactly?"

Micah shrugged. "I think we can tell her we like you, and we're enjoying your company. There's too much going on to make any decisions past that."

Ryan watched Nicky's reaction to his own words being repeated back to him. He saw the agreement and the understanding, along with a flicker of disappointment. He nodded, though. "Probably best to leave out the details of where and when."

Micah made a face and chucked a throw pillow at him. Nicky caught it easily. "Yes. Please don't tell my surrogate mom anything about my kinky sex life, thank you very much."

"Oh, sweetheart," Nicky teased. "You are far from kinky."

Micah's eyes narrowed, and his lower lip jutted out. "Am not."

Nicky laughed as he turned toward the kitchen. "Ask your husband to tell you about the time Xavier and I went to a puppy-play party," he said just before he disappeared around the corner.

Micah's jaw dropped, and he turned to Ryan with big eyes. "They went where?"

Ryan shook his head, mentally thanking Nicky for leaving him with that one. "He's teasing, baby. You're just the right amount of kinky." He leaned over and gave Micah a soothing kiss. "You know I love everything we get up to."

Micah pouted against his mouth. "I totally have some kinks. Sexy ones."

Ryan tried desperately to hide his grin. "I happen to be a fan."

Micah was still annoyed. "I'll show him," he muttered. "Just wait."

Like hell was Ryan going to dissuade him. Micah's imagination was a beautiful thing.

They eventually followed Maggie and Nicky into the kitchen, where Maggie was throwing dinner together and Nicky was grabbing things for her so she didn't have to move too much.

Seated around the table, they went over the last few days, how Maggie's surgery had gone, and what the rest of the week was looking like. It was comfortable and familiar, and Ryan loved how easily Nicky slotted into their lives.

Ryan had never felt like anything was missing in his marriage. He and Micah fit—they had since almost day one. Even back when Micah was just a kid who worked on the ranch, Ryan had felt the way their lives lined up. How Micah's wants meshed with Ryan's needs and vice versa.

No one had been surprised when they finally started dating or when they announced they were engaged. Most of the reactions had been "It's about damn time," which embarrassed Ryan a bit. He didn't expect the guy who owned the general store to have a better understanding of Ryan's love life than he himself did. But Mac had just nodded in recognition and proceeded to call him Mr. Avery from then on.

Wanting more with Nicky wasn't the sort of thing he'd expected. Because there had never been anything missing, and he'd always assumed that people added others to their relationships to fulfill needs that weren't getting satisfied by their partner. Maybe other people did. But this didn't feel like that to Ryan. Nicky felt like... *more*. Like he added to what Ryan and Micah already had in a way that Ryan hadn't known was possible.

Micah and Nicky were right. It was definitely too soon to be thinking these thoughts. But there was no point in ignoring them either. Whatever happened would happen. Ryan didn't need to bury his head in the sand in the meantime.

He felt a knee bump his under the table, and when he looked up, Micah gave him a wink. A second later, a foot brushed his calf. Nicky didn't pause in slicing his chicken, but Ryan could see the curl at the corner of his mouth.

Ryan was careful not to react. If he did, he'd give away how much he wanted to abandon dinner and drag the two men teasing him up to bed. He took a bite of baked potato and kept his amusement to himself. Bed was the one place he hadn't had them yet.

Oh, they had shared the bed the night before, but none of their escapades had actually taken place on a mattress. That was something he should rectify as soon as possible. And maybe, if they were all in the mood, they could pull out some of those kinky things that Micah was so insistent on Nicky knowing about. They had a pair of padded handcuffs that would look fantastic around Nicky's wrists.

The three of them didn't make it to the bed that night. Ryan and Micah had an early start the next morning, and Nicky stayed up talking with his aunt. Micah offered to keep a spot warm for him, but Nicky slept in his own room. Ryan reminded himself that that was normal and he had no reason to be disappointed. Micah wasn't as good at hiding his feelings and needed some TLC when they first woke up. It was kind of a head trip to be reassuring his husband that the man they were sleeping with was still interested, but Ryan was happy to do it.

Nicky didn't come down for breakfast. Maggie, who had never needed as much sleep as a normal person, said they had been up past midnight catching up on each other's lives and Nicky had joked about sleeping until noon.

Ryan figured if Nicky still wasn't awake by lunchtime, he'd send Micah in to deliver a wake-up call. That idea made him smile. Who knew he'd be so into his husband being intimate with another man? Then again, Ryan had never understood his friends who were jealously possessive of their partners. To him, if a relationship had a rock-solid foundation—like his and Micah's—then there was no reason to put limits on it other than what felt appropriate for them. So far, everything about Nicky felt right.

And that wasn't even counting how gorgeous the other man was, or how much Ryan wanted Nicky under him again as soon as possible. Because that mouth, *damn.*

It was Wednesday, so he had a list of appointments to get through. Keegan was coming out to see the newest foal, born a few weeks ago, and it was getting toward the end of the month, so there was paperwork to prepare. They would also have to figure out who'd be handling their financials, since it obviously wasn't going to be Phillip anymore. Ryan was already responsible for paying their vendors—that wasn't a problem—but Phillip had handled things like the property taxes and the more complex accounting. Just thinking about straightening that mess out made his head hurt, and he had a flare of sympathy for Nicky and his father-induced migraines.

Around ten, he resurfaced from the paperwork when his cell rang. Keegan's name flashed across it, so Ryan answered with an absent, "Hey, buddy."

"I need you down at the front entrance," Keegan said without waiting for Ryan to finish.

The tone in Keegan's voice had Ryan on his feet and headed for his truck, the phone pressed to his ear.

"Stop right there, Corey," he heard Keegan say, the sound muffled, the phone probably held away from his mouth. He'd have to correct Keegan later about Finn's name.

Milo bounded after him, hopping up into the cab when Ryan opened the door. Ryan pushed him to the passenger seat, not wanting to take the time to get him back out and put him away.

He made it down the driveway in record time, his brow furrowing when the main road came into view and he saw several vehicles stopped there. He recognized Keegan's SUV and Archer's beat-up Jeep. He had no idea who the owners of the gold sedan or the town car behind it were. Keegan and Archer were parked in the driveway, while Finn's cargo van was just behind them, stopped perpendicular to the driveway and blocking access.

The real estate developer who had been trying to get to the ranch the other day, Miller, was standing next to the town car, while an older man sat in the driver's seat, a phone pressed to his ear as he talked into it emphatically.

Ryan shot his best friend a grateful look, then walked over to Archer and Finn. "What's going on here?"

Archer shrugged lazily. "Corey's truck is stuck in all this mud. We're waiting for a tow to pull him out. Unfortunately, it's gonna be a while, and our visitors there won't be able to access the ranch until we can get it moved."

Ryan blinked at the tires on the cargo van, which were, granted, a little ways onto the muddy grass—but nowhere near stuck. Then he looked at its driver, whose cheeks were flushed pink. "Finn," Ryan said with a nod of acknowledgment.

"Good morning, Mr. Avery."

Ryan flashed him a smile. "Micah told you to call me Ryan."

Finn's blush darkened. "Sorry, sir— I-I mean Ryan." He twisted his fingers together and cast an anxious look at the men by the sedan.

"Don't worry, kid. I'll get this taken care of." Ryan walked over to Miller. "Sorry about the trouble. Looks like you're going to need to come back another day."

The man gave the cargo van an exasperated look, then turned to Ryan. "How long do you think the tow truck will take?"

Ryan shrugged and shoved his hands into his pockets. "Hard to say. It could be hours. We're pretty laid-back around here, and Joey is the only driver in town. If he's busy, who knows."

Miller's lips pressed into a thin line. He clearly didn't believe Ryan, but there wasn't much he could do about it. Just then, the driver's door of the town car swung open and the silver-haired man climbed out. He was probably in his mid-sixties, tall, and relatively fit. He rounded the front of the car, and Ryan knew at a glance who he must be. Nicky had his father's eyes—though Phillip Lauder's lacked the stalwart sincerity that drew Ryan in.

"I hope you're here to get that van out of our way," Lauder said in a warm tone that immediately struck Ryan as false.

Ryan had to maintain his composure. If Lauder wanted to take that approach, Ryan would go along. "No can do," he drawled, playing up the regional accent that was common in these parts, even though Ryan wasn't from anywhere close. "Road'll have to stay closed until we can find someone with a truck big enough to handle that one."

Lauder twitched, his eyes narrowing and giving away his annoyance. "We're on a deadline."

"Sorry to hear that."

Lauder's nostrils flared. "This is absurd. We'll just walk up." He took a step, and his fancy shoe landed in the pothole, which had picked up some mud during the latest storm. He jerked back, his shoe pulling free with a loud squelch.

Ryan had to press his lips together to keep from laughing. "Rest of the road's not much better than this, and the grass is even worse. You might want to change into some boots," he offered helpfully.

"I haven't got boots," Lauder growled, shaking his foot to try to get the mud off. A clump of it came free and hit the hem of his suit pants. "Damn it all." Lauder spun back toward Ryan, seething. "I know when I'm being set up. You tell my sister we'll be back in the morning and she'd better allow us to tour the property. Otherwise I'll get the police involved, and she'll find herself evicted." He didn't wait for a response, just stomped to the town car and yanked open the door. "Russell, let's go."

The real estate developer gave Ryan a look that was tinged with amusement. "Have a good day," he said politely before heading back to his car. Lauder pulled out, tires spinning briefly on the gravel, and sped off. Russell followed at a more moderate pace.

Ryan turned back to Archer, Keegan, and Finn with a sigh. Archer was scowling after the departing cars. Keegan shot Ryan a look that said he'd better have an explanation, and fast. Finn looked like he might be on the verge of a panic attack. That was what Ryan needed to handle first.

"Finn, hey. Thanks for your help."

The young man swallowed and ducked his head, dark curls hiding his eyes. "You're welcome," he said softly, scratching at one thumbnail with the other. "Archer said you didn't want them on the property." He said it like a question, voice wavering.

"Archer was right. You really helped us out."

Finn gave a sigh of relief, his shoulders loosening. He peeked up at Ryan through the shield of his hair. "Should I leave the truck, in case they come back? You're my only delivery today."

Ryan glanced at Keegan, who shrugged. "I can get around it when I need to leave." He gestured to his work truck, which was more than capable of grinding through a muddy field in the middle of winter. The soggy grass edge of the driveway would be no issue.

Ryan made the executive decision to head to the house. At the very least, he needed to let Maggie and Nicky know what had happened so they could be ready when Lauder came back. He gave Finn a ride, offering him lunch at least for his trouble, and had to smile a little at the way the young man immediately wrapped his arms around Milo once they were in the truck. The dog was equally pleased to see him, riding nearly in Finn's lap as they bumped back up the driveway.

He parked in front of the house just as Maggie stepped onto the front porch, followed by Nicky. Ryan was relieved to see that Nicky looked more rested than he had the last few days.

Maggie's eyebrows went up when Finn jumped down from the truck and Keegan and Archer made an appearance as well. Archer ducked into the barn, probably to find Micah.

Ryan looked up and caught Nicky's eyes. "Phillip was here."

Nicky's expression tightened.

Ryan turned to Maggie. "He brought the real estate developer back. Finn here helped stall them by blocking the driveway with his truck, but Phillip said they'd be back tomorrow." Ryan paused, wondering whether he should tell them the rest.

"What else did he say?" Nicky asked, voice flat. "Because I know my father, and he wouldn't have left without making it clear he expects to get what he wants."

"He said he'd have us evicted if we didn't let them on the property."

Nicky blanched, and a muscle jumped in his jaw. "That sounds like him. Go straight for the nuclear option."

Just then, Micah jogged out of the barn, followed by Archer. "What is it? What happened?" he asked breathlessly. Ryan held out his arm, and Micah stepped to his side, tucking himself close.

"My father happened. Again," Nicky managed to get out. All the energy Ryan had noted before seemed to drain out of him.

Maggie gave his arm a firm squeeze and a little shake. "Don't give up now, kiddo. Because I'm not planning to."

Nicky managed a strained smile. "I'm not." He gave Maggie a brief side hug and made his way back inside.

When he opened the door, Rascal slipped out and trotted down the stairs, heading straight for Finn. Finn grinned and dropped to his knees to give the eager animal some love. Rascal climbed into his lap, licking his face and making Finn laugh.

That was a relief. The young man's anxiety had been palpable. Ryan turned to Maggie. "We're going to need a backup plan. Phillip isn't going to be put off for long, and as far as the law is concerned, the ranch belongs to him until we can find a way to prove otherwise."

"Um. I'm not sure, but I think... a landlord can't just evict you," Finn said from where Milo was now also flopped across his lap for belly rubs. "Even without a written lease, he has to give notice and serve you with papers."

Surprised, Ryan gave Finn a grateful nod and got pink cheeks and a ducked head in response.

Micah heaved out a shaky breath and hugged Ryan tighter. "So we have some time."

Ryan stroked his back. "We have time. And these things never go quickly. The courts are notoriously slow."

"I have an appointment at the bank," Maggie said. "They want to see proof of the ranch's real income—not the numbers Phillip fabricated for Nicky—before they make a decision on a loan."

"I can keep sorting through the paperwork in the study," Micah offered.

"That's good," Ryan told him. "We'll need that documentation for the bank and the lawyer. Anything we can show to prove Phillip's lies will be useful."

"I can help you," Finn said, then lowered his gaze back to Rascal. "I mean... if you want? I'm happy to." He dug his fingers into Rascal's fur and gave her a scratch that made her back leg thump enthusiastically. "As long as I'm not in the way."

"You're gonna regret that offer when you see how many boxes there are," Micah teased, getting a grin in return.

Keegan clapped Ryan on the shoulder. "I have a new foal to see to, but let me know if I can do anything."

"I'll help any way I can too," Archer offered. "I just can't stay too long. I need to get home to Alice."

Ryan's chest hurt. That meant she hadn't taken the news well. Not that he'd expected she would. "You should get going, then."

Archer was already shaking his head. "Nah. She wanted me out of the house. I'll head back with food in a while, but I'm trying to give her some space."

"I'll pack up some of that soup she likes," Maggie told him. "And you can take Rascal home for the night."

Archer flashed her a smile. "Thanks, Maggie, she'd love that."

They all split off at that point: Keegan to the barn, Maggie and Archer to the kitchen, Micah and Finn to the study, and Ryan to find Nicky and see if they could come up with something to get Phillip to back off until they could get the legal process started.

The ranch belonged to Maggie. They would prove it.

# EIGHTEEN
NICK

It was a good fucking thing his father hadn't made it onto the property, because if he had, Nick would probably be facing assault charges for punching the old bastard in the face.

By late that afternoon, he was still trying to reconcile what he'd previously thought he knew about the ranch—based on the records Phillip had shown him—with what Maggie had told him that morning.

Phillip had been deceiving them all for years.

Nick looked around at the worried faces of the people gathered in the living room of the farmhouse. Micah and Ryan were together at one end of the couch while Nick claimed the other. Izzy was in an armchair, and Maggie was across from him with her foot up on the ottoman. Ryan's friend Keegan was standing against the big stone fireplace, his hands in his pockets and a frown on his face. Finn, who had helped sort paperwork for hours, had returned home, saying that he needed to check on his grandfather but to let him know if they needed anything.

"First, I want to thank all of you for what you've been doing," Maggie said. "This situation would be much more difficult without you."

Micah reached out and gave her hand a squeeze before settling back again.

"Nicky and I have been going over the records I have here and comparing them to what he was shown by Phillip. The first thing I want you to know is that the ranch is most definitely profitable. It looks like, at the very least, my brother altered the figures to get Nicky to agree to participate in this mess."

What they didn't know was whether the falsified numbers had only been used to manipulate Nick, or if Phillip had been lying to the IRS as well. But that was something they could deal with down the road.

Micah looked furious, but Ryan kept him seated with a hand on his knee. Nick wished he could move closer and offer comfort as well. But that would raise questions that weren't currently a priority.

"That leaves the bigger issue of Phillip's claim that I gave him the property." Maggie sighed, looking tired and older than her years. The timing of this, with her recovering from major surgery, couldn't have been worse. Which Nick was sure had been Phillip's intention. "According to the state, Phillip owns the ranch."

The tension in the room skyrocketed at that. Micah looked stricken, Izzy was pale, and Keegan and Ryan were both tense with anger.

"Since he has a deed that lists him as the owner, it's up to Maggie to prove that he's lying and she never gave him the property," Nick supplied when it looked as if Maggie was struggling with her emotions.

"This is where I made a mistake," Maggie admitted. "Phillip was expanding his investment firm seven or eight years ago, and he convinced me to let him handle the ranch's finances—the taxes and whatnot, as opposed to the day-to-day operations Ryan takes care of. I thought we were helping each other out."

"You had no way of knowing that your brother would screw you over," Micah protested. "He's a crook. That's not your fault."

Maggie gave him a quick smile, her fondness for him clear. "Maybe not. But the results are the same. I believed that Phillip was taking care of things and didn't ask enough questions, and instead, he forged documents to claim I'd given him the ranch—and he's been siphoning money from my investment accounts to pay the bills on it, while doing who knows what with the actual income."

Nick had helped her uncover all this earlier by comparing the documentation he had with her own records, as well as financial statements he was able to access remotely, but he still felt sick to his stomach hearing her talk about it. The others in the room looked like they felt the same. Micah's face twisted like he was torn between raging and crying, while Ryan was stoic, but Nick could see the anger in his eyes. Nick didn't know Keegan or

Izzy well enough to judge their reactions, but they were clearly unhappy.

"We can take him to court, right?" Micah asked once the shock had settled some. "He won't get away with this, will he?" He clutched at Ryan's arm, white-knuckled. Ryan was probably going to have bruises later but didn't seem inclined to stop him.

"I need to find a lawyer who specializes in this kind of thing, and hope they're willing to help. Especially since I'm not sure where the money to pay them is going to come from."

With nothing left to share, they gradually went in their own directions.

Nick took the first opportunity to escape to his room. He had a phone call to make that was long overdue.

Nick had been too young to recognize it while his mom was alive, but Phillip only truly cared about two things: money and the prestige having it brought. There was never a time when he wasn't scheming to get more of one or the other. Looking back, it was why Nick and his mom spent their summers at the ranch while Phillip spent his at the office. Long hours working and entertaining clients were easier when he didn't have a wife and son waiting at home.

After Nick's mom died, it only got worse. Phillip became obsessed with the next winning investment, the next million-dollar payout. His second wife encouraged it. She was from a well-off family and was accustomed to a certain amount of glitz and glam. Nick still wasn't sure how she and his father got together to begin with, but their marriage ended up being as quick and reckless as their divorce was drawn-out and brutal.

By the time Phillip was dating Melissa—the woman he was divorcing now—Nick had been in college, working toward his own degree in finance. That was where he met Xavier.

Xavi came from old money, but he was one of the most down-to-earth people Nick had ever met. He'd grown up with the proverbial silver spoon but wasn't interested in taking the easy trust-fund route. He wanted a career, and he wanted to be good at it. He was also one of the smartest and most charismatic people Nick knew. They joked that he could convince a cat to like water if he just had five minutes and a good bottle of brandy.

Somehow, what started as mutual dislike of an eight a.m. class became a lifelong friendship. There was no one on earth that Nick cared about and trusted more.

The problem was that Xavier could be a bull in a china shop if he felt his loved ones needed him. Which was why Nick hadn't immediately asked him for help. The last thing he wanted was to take advantage of his best friend's generosity. Unfortunately, they were out of both time and options, and they needed the kind of help that Xavier was more than happy to provide.

Nick was just going to have to suck up his pride and ask for it.

Nick sighed and tapped the contact on his phone, listening to it ring.

And ring.

Seriously? After blowing up his phone for days, Xavier was choosing *now* to be busy? Nick let it go to voicemail and left a brief message asking Xavier to call him.

He knew Xavi would get back to him quickly. In the meantime, Nick would just have to prepare as much as he could on his own.

Nick was sitting on the back patio a few hours later when his aunt walked outside, leaning heavily on her cane, followed by Rascal. He started to get up to help her, but she waved him back down.

"I'm fine. The doctor says I need to walk on it and keep the strength up in the muscles." She lowered herself to the seat next to him with a sigh of relief. "I'm actually in less pain than I was, despite them cutting me open."

"It was that bad?"

"Yep," she said, giving the offending joint a pat. "I fell on the ice years ago, and it hasn't been the same since. You'd think it would have been a horse that did me in, but it was a trip to the grocery store." She rolled her eyes. "Ryan found me an excellent surgeon who specializes in joint replacement for former athletes, and the procedure went extremely well. He says there's a good chance I'll be able to ride again." She smiled at him. "Another reason to keep up with the rehab."

Nick found himself smiling back. What a relief that must be. He couldn't imagine Maggie not on a horse. It was her whole life. "That's great news."

"It is. I'm looking forward to being able to drive again too. I hate putting so much on the boys. They work hard enough without needing to take care of an old lady like me."

"They love you, though. Of course they want to help." Nick swallowed against the sour taste in his mouth. He should have been the one here helping Maggie, taking her to appointments. He was her family.

"Oh, don't look at me like that, Nicky," she scolded. "You have your own life. I would never have expected you to come all the way out here just because I need a little more help than I used to."

"Yet I came all the way out here because Dad told me to. Because he's too greedy for anyone's good and thinks he can get away with stealing from family." He dropped his elbows to his knees and let his head hang. God. What kind of person was he that he'd thought he could just get this over with and move on? That he'd agreed to do his father's bidding, even knowing what it would do to his aunt?

"Tell me something, Nicky," she asked. "When you came down here, did you expect me to roll over and let Phillip have his way?"

Nick scoffed at that. He couldn't imagine Maggie ever letting that happen.

"That's what I thought," she continued without waiting for an answer. "You were a good kid. A little rowdy, but kindhearted. Phillip may be my brother, but thank god you're more like your mom than you are him."

Nick smiled at that. That was a familiar message. His mom and Maggie had always joked that they wished they were siblings.

"I know this place is just as important to you as it was to her."

Nick huffed. "I didn't do a great job of showing it, staying gone for twenty years."

"You needed to stay close to your dad. I understood that, and your mom would have too."

Nick's eyes burned. He didn't want Maggie to excuse his behavior. He wasn't okay with what he had done, and it didn't feel right for her to give him a pass.

"Nicky," she said, her strong hand squeezing his shoulder. "You did what you needed to. I promise it's okay."

He gave a nod and dashed at his eyes before any tears could escape. "I'm not going to let him sell the ranch. I have savings, and I can get a loan. Maybe not for the whole amount, but it'll be a start."

"Oh, honey." Maggie sighed. "I appreciate it, but I'm not done fighting. Let's not give up quite yet."

Nick wasn't ready to stop fighting, either, but if he needed to drain every penny from his savings in order to save Maggie,

Ryan, and Micah's home, he would do that. He felt like his priorities were in the right place for the first time in years, and he wanted them to stay that way. "I'm waiting for Xavier to call me back. I'm sure he can help us find a lawyer who's willing to help."

She reached out and gave his knee a firm squeeze, her eyes warm and grateful. "Xavier's a good egg. I'm glad you stayed friends. You deserve to have people like that in your life."

Nick's cheeks went warm as his brain flashed to Ryan and Micah. They were the best kind of people. He wouldn't mind having more of them in his life once they dealt with Phillip and everything settled down.

"What's that face?" Maggie asked teasingly. "Do you have a new someone in your life you want to tell me about?"

Crap. He was probably blushing visibly. "Is now really the time?"

"It's the perfect time. I'm ready for some good news."

"It's more 'someones,'" he admitted, wishing he could melt through the floor. This was more uncomfortable than when he came out to his dad, who had only given him a strange look and said, "Don't let it interfere with your schoolwork." It had been the one time he'd been grateful his father wasn't overly invested in his life.

"Oh," Maggie said, warmth and a bit of humor in her tone. "Trying to decide between two men, or...?"

"Or." He nodded. "They're together."

She hummed but didn't sound disapproving. "You should talk to Ryan. He had a relationship like that once, I believe. I'm sure he could give you some pointers."

Nick's whole body burned. Sure, that's exactly what he'd do. Ask Ryan for tips about triad relationships when he and his husband were the other two-thirds.

Maggie chuckled at him. "I wasn't talking about sex, by the way. I'm sure you're more than capable of figuring *that* part out."

Nick laughed through his groan. "Thanks. I think," he managed.

Maggie clapped him on the shoulder and grabbed her cane to stand. Rascal hopped to her feet, watching hopefully. "I'll stop embarrassing you now. I have a few phone calls to make. Did the boys tell you about family dinner?"

Nick nodded. The regular Sunday evening meal had been rescheduled for the next night. He was actually looking forward to it. He just needed to make sure it wasn't the last dinner Maggie hosted as the owner of Split Rock Ranch.

It was late, so the knock on the screen door came as a surprise. Maggie had turned in early. Nick had taken Ryan and Micah up on their suggestion of beer and unwinding in front of the TV. It was quickly becoming a habit for them.

He was kicked back in a chair with his feet up on an ottoman. Ryan and Micah had taken over the sofa, and Izzy was curled up in the other chair under a blanket with Milo—who was really too big to be a lap dog—draped across him. Since Izzy lived on the ranch as well, he ate dinner at the house unless he had other plans. Micah had whispered in Nick's ear, "Plans means a Grindr notification," which made Nick smirk. He was more than familiar with that part of the single lifestyle. He didn't miss it.

That thought pulled him up short. Since when was he not single? He'd had a Grindr date not two weeks ago. He eyed Micah, relaxing with his head on Ryan's thigh and his feet tucked under a cushion. *No*, Nick reminded himself. He wasn't going to rush into anything.

Micah got up to answer the door, waving the rest of them to stay put. Izzy and Ryan exchanged frowns that made Nick tense. It was too late for unannounced visitors. He was about to go after Micah, worried that Phillip had decided to return ahead of schedule, when he heard a familiar voice followed by Micah's flustered "Come in."

Nick climbed to his feet as Micah and their guest entered the living room.

Dressed impeccably in a tailored, three-piece suit despite the late hour, all six foot five of Xavier looked out of place in Micah and Ryan's living room. Not that that would ever bother Xavier. He was as at home at the New York City Ballet as he was in a dive bar watching football and eating peanuts of questionable origin. It was one of the things that had drawn Nick to him: his ability to adapt and make everyone around him feel comfortable.

Showing up at the ranch, a place he'd never set foot before, without warning, was pushing things, though. Still, Nick crossed the room to greet him. "What the hell, Xavi? I called you nine hours ago."

"Oh?" Xavier drawled. "So you finally remembered phones work both ways?"

Nick rolled his eyes. "Shut it, asshole. I've been busy."

"Well, I had something to tell you that wasn't appropriate for a voicemail, so I borrowed a jet."

Micah's eyes bugged out at that. "You borrowed a whole jet?"

"That was totally unnecessary," Nick grumbled, annoyed that Xavier had gone to so much trouble.

Xavier flashed his perfect smile and eyed Micah in a way that made Nick a little uncomfortable. "I had a client coming out this direction already. We just took a slight detour."

"Still," Micah said, "private planes were involved. Who *are* you?"

Nick huffed in amusement at Micah's dramatics. "Xavier, this is Micah, Ryan, and Izzy." He gestured to them in turn. "Everyone, this is Xavier DeCain. My ex-husband."

Xavier had obviously introduced himself to Micah at the door, but Izzy's eyebrows went up. Ryan looked unsurprised, standing to offer Xavier his hand. "It's nice to meet you, Xavier. Nicky has told us good things."

"I would hope so. He married me once upon a time, after all."

"And divorced you," Nick shot back.

Micah laughed.

Xavier's wink to Micah made Nick's gut tighten with what he hated to acknowledge might be jealousy. If Micah thought Nick was smooth, he hadn't seen anything yet. Xavier made schmoozing into an art form. When he turned it on, he practically oozed charm—and not in a slimy way. He just *got* people. Understood what they wanted and gave it to them. It was a talent that awed Nick and one he didn't possess. He was capable of being charming, sure. But he didn't have the magic that Xavier did.

Micah went into host mode, heading off to the kitchen to get him something to drink. Izzy settled for a wave from where he was ensconced in the chair and half-buried under the dog.

Once Xavier was settled on one end of the sofa—Micah having dropped onto the floor near Nick's feet—Nick finally asked, "What are you doing here, Xavi? What's so important that it couldn't be a phone call or a voicemail?"

Xavier took a sip of his drink, his focus shifting from small talk with Micah about the drive from the airport. Nick mirrored him, fighting the urge to jump up and pace. "Well, things that you may not want a record of. To start..."

Nick refrained from rolling his eyes. It was too late in the day for a dramatic pause. "Can you just spit it out? I promise we're already on the edge of our seats."

"I wasn't sure if you wanted to speak in private?" Xavier didn't look at any of the others in the room—he was too polite for that—but his comment reminded Nick that Xavier hadn't been a part of anything that had happened in the last week. These were strangers to him, while to Nick, they were already more important than anyone he had waiting back home other than Xavier himself.

He couldn't think of a reason not to have them there. As soon as he'd seen the pity mixed with a touch of annoyance on Xavier's face, Nick had known why Xavier was there. It was an unfortunately familiar expression. "They already know about Phillip."

Xavier's shoulders lost some of their tension. "I wasn't sure how much you knew."

"We know he's trying to sell Maggie's ranch, which he doesn't fucking own," Micah said.

Nick shifted his knee until it brushed Micah's shoulder. Micah leaned closer in response, his arm pressing comfortingly against Nick's calf. Xavier noticed, of course, but he didn't say anything.

"It's more than that," Xavier said, crossing one ankle over the opposite thigh and settling back against the cushions. "Six days ago, I received a very interesting email. It was part of a chain between Phillip and a real estate developer by the name of Russell Miller."

When Xavier said the name Russell Miller, Micah straightened, gripping his drink tightly. How the hell had Xavier been included on communication between Nick's father and the developer trying to buy Maggie's ranch? Nick and Ryan exchanged a look, probably wondering the same thing.

"I'm glad the name is familiar," Xavier continued. "A month ago, Phillip reached out to inquire if I had any clients interested in purchasing a piece of property he had. He was ready to put it up for sale and wanted it done quickly."

Micah made a face at that. The lie made him want to rage. Fucking Phillip deserved to be in a cell.

"As it happened, I had been speaking with a real estate developer at an event the night before. I passed Phillip's information along to him and didn't think much more of it until I got the email I mentioned.

"I nearly deleted it, since it didn't seem to be meant for me, but then I saw Split Rock Ranch listed as the sale property. I remembered the name, of course. Nick had mentioned it more than once. And Nick had only just called, asking me to have one of my PAs pick up his mail because his father needed him to go to North Carolina."

"Why did he call you? Don't you live in LA?" Micah asked, confused. Then he was immediately embarrassed that he'd interrupted with something unimportant.

Xavier gave him a smile that made him feel uncomfortably warm. "Good attention to detail. I like you."

Micah tried to ignore the heat in his cheeks as Xavier continued.

"I have a place in New York as well, and we're in the same building. One of my PAs is there daily to water the plants and keep an eye on things." He moved smoothly on. "I ended up reading the email and saw several things that concerned me. Phillip—or maybe his secretary—had forwarded Russell paperwork that didn't match the value of the property they originally discussed. In fact, it severely undervalued it. When Russell asked Phillip about it, Phillip told him the second set of numbers was an error by an intern and to ignore it." Xavier looked around the room, taking in the dawning understanding on their faces.

"He accidentally sent Russell the fake numbers he used to get me down here. The ones that show the ranch failing," Nick said, leaning forward and gripping Micah's shoulder.

"He did," Xavier agreed. "And Russell isn't an idiot. He was concerned and sent them to me, asking if I was aware of it. I have to say, he was rather upset that Phillip might be attempting to defraud him or involve him in something shady, but I convinced him that since he was already in town, he should come out here anyway and tell Nick what he knew." He gave Nick a disgruntled look. "Of course, Nicolas here has been completely unreachable, and no one would let Russell meet with him."

Micah looked up at Nick, whose cheeks were going dark. "I thought your name was Dominic."

Nick made a face. "It is. He calls me Nicolas when he's annoyed with me, because he knows I hate it."

"Back to the subject," Ryan cut in. "That doesn't mean much. Lying to Nick about the value of the ranch isn't illegal."

Xavier nodded. "You're right, it's not, but lying to the government is."

Nick's eyebrows went up. "Oh, hell," he muttered. "My father is an idiot."

"An idiot under investigation by the FBI, unless I'm way off," Xavier said with a nod. "Two agents showed up at your apartment when my PA was there dropping off your mail. Spooked the hell out of him, by the way. They want to interview you. Unless you've taken up a side business breaking federal law, I think it's probably about your father."

Nick dragged a hand through his hair. "That's why you didn't want to leave a voicemail."

"A digital trail didn't seem like a good idea. Just in case I was wrong."

Wow. Micah glanced at Ryan, who gave him a subtle nod of agreement. Micah was definitely a fan of Xavier.

"I appreciate your discretion, Xavi. I promise I haven't broken any laws that I'm aware of."

"Except that one time in Vegas."

That made Nick chuckle, and his shoulders loosened a little. "Yeah. Except that one time in Vegas."

"I'm grateful that you came here to fill us in, Xavier," Ryan said, bringing them back on track yet again. "But do you have anything that we can use to stop Phillip from selling the ranch? Because so far, none of this will prove that he isn't the owner."

"I wasn't aware that he isn't the owner," Xavier replied. "So, no. I can't prove that." He looked at the group of them thoughtfully. "We're going to need to get creative."

For all Micah had wondered about Nick's ex-husband, nothing had prepared him for meeting Xavier DeCain. When he opened the front door, he'd had to look up, and up some more. Izzy was tall, but Xavier not only had a few inches on him, he was broader as well.

Despite the late hour, Xavier was dressed in a fancy suit. His dark brown hair—styled as if he'd just come from the barber—was a few shades darker than his penetrating eyes. If Micah was going to describe him, he would call him classically handsome. He somehow managed to pull off a neatly trimmed goatee, something Micah thought only mobsters were capable of. When he smiled and introduced himself, Micah could only think that there was no way his teeth were real. They were too straight and too white.

Micah had never been so torn. On the one hand, Xavier was kind of awesome. Micah couldn't imagine what it was like to have a bunch of celebrities in your contact list. While they'd been chatting, Xavier had gotten no less than three texts from "a client having a crisis." Xavier handled whatever it was without missing a beat in the conversation.

On the other hand, Xavier was a little *too* awesome. It made Micah want to climb into Nick's lap and stake his claim. The problem was that Micah didn't actually have any claim on Nick. More than ever, he was regretting their agreement to wait on making any decisions until the problem with Phillip was resolved. Now that Xavier was here, Micah was jealous of his easy banter with Nick. They knew each other so well, and Micah and Ryan barely knew Nick at all. Although they wanted to know him better. A lot better.

Micah settled for keeping his hand wrapped around Nick's ankle, letting the skin-to-skin contact settle his nerves. He relaxed a bit more when he felt Nick's fingers stroke the back of his neck. He flicked his gaze to Ryan, who gave him the hint of an encouraging smile. They weren't going to let Nick forget his promise now that his too-awesome ex was in town.

They spent some more time hashing out ideas for proving Maggie was the owner of the ranch, but they didn't come up with anything solid. Everything felt like "wait and see," and it had Micah on edge. He wanted this fixed. He wanted their home safe. And he wanted Nick to agree to be theirs.

Eventually, Izzy started nodding off and excused himself back to his apartment. They'd offered Xavier the second guest room, and, since it was nearly midnight, he'd gratefully accepted. Micah was fading as well, but with the bathroom situation, he had to wait until everyone else was ready.

He woke up with his head resting on Nick's thigh, his arms hugging Nick's leg, and gentle fingers carding through his hair. It felt so good that he kept his eyes closed and just drifted, listening to the conversation flowing around him.

"I have faith," Xavier said, voice smooth and confident. "You forget, I know your father as well as you do."

"I'm not doubting you, Xavi, but he's stubborn. What if it doesn't work?"

"There are still other options," Ryan interjected.

"Are they as good?" Xavier replied in a tone that said whatever they were discussing, he was the one who was right.

Nick made a frustrated sound, and Micah gave his leg a squeeze in support. "You awake, sweetheart?"

"Ahh. I wondered," Xavier said.

Nick's thigh tensed under Micah's cheek. "Whatever you're thinking, keep it to yourself," he grumbled.

"He's cute, that's all."

"They are," Ryan agreed.

Micah turned and hid his grin in Nick's leg, hugging him tighter.

"Oh," Xavier said, then chuckled. "I wasn't expecting that. Good for you, Nick."

"Fuck off," Nick grumbled, then tugged Micah up and into the chair next to him. Micah curled into his side and rested his head on Nick's shoulder, letting himself drowse again. There was a little more murmured conversation, and then it got quiet. He was breaths away from sleep when Nick brushed a kiss to his temple. "We can't sleep in the chair, Micah."

Micah grumbled and snuggled closer. He was comfortable, damn it.

Nick nuzzled him until he gave up and opened his eyes. Nick was looking down at him, his green eyes warm with amusement.

Micah smiled. "Hey," he said, then leaned up and stole a kiss.

"Hey, yourself," Nick replied. He nudged Micah until he reluctantly climbed to his feet, then took his hand and led him toward the stairs. "You can sleep soon," he promised. "Xavier's done in the bathroom by now."

Micah followed him, Nick's hand warm and comforting where it was wrapped around his. When they reached his and Ryan's bedroom door, Micah tightened his hold. "Stay?" he asked hopefully.

Nick looked past him into the bedroom, where Ryan was sitting up with his laptop, wearing his sexy reading glasses. Nick only hesitated a moment before he gave in. After they'd each taken a quick turn in the bathroom, Micah crawled into bed and gestured for Nick to lie next to him.

"Get the light, would you, Nicky?" Ryan asked as he set his laptop aside.

Nick did his bidding before crossing to Micah's side of the bed and sliding between the sheets.

Micah hummed happily and tugged Nick closer until he was pleasantly sandwiched between two hard, warm bodies. He leaned up to kiss his husband goodnight, then smiled when Ryan leaned across him to kiss a startled Nick as well. Micah wiggled around so he could get his own kiss, then shut his eyes and fell asleep to the sound of deep, even breathing.

They were all on edge the next day, waiting for Phillip to show up again. Maggie had been filled in on Xavier's news and expressed how pleased she was to see him again.

Micah tried not to dwell on how warmly she treated Xavier—or the fact that Nick had been gone when Micah woke up that morning. Micah had found him downstairs drinking coffee with Xavier and Maggie when he hauled himself out of bed later than he'd woken in years. They looked happy and comfortable, like family.

It threw his world off kilter a little bit. Micah wasn't used to being on the outside at the ranch, and he didn't like it. Still, he didn't begrudge them time together. He of all people knew how important family was. Whether they were related to you or not.

Waiting for the other shoe to drop was more nerve-racking than anything Micah could remember, including his wedding day.

Xavier and Nick were in the study, working their way through the paperwork Micah and Finn had sorted. Micah and the others still had jobs to do, with horses to take care of and several trail groups booked for the day. Alice, who was understandably upset, was staying home, so Micah needed to cover her chores as well.

He was alone in the barnyard when a line of cars came up the driveway. The first two he didn't recognize, but the third was a police cruiser. He left his rake leaning up against the side of the barn and headed to where the cars had stopped outside the farmhouse. An older, well-dressed man, who had to be Nick's father, stepped out of the first car. A heavier-set man climbed out of the second. The two of them met at the base of the stairs to the front porch, speaking in low voices. Micah reached the yard just as the front door opened and Maggie walked out, followed by Ryan.

Phillip's back straightened and his chin lifted when he saw her. She didn't have her cane, but Ryan had a hand under her elbow, not that she seemed to need it.

"Phillip," Maggie said, voice firm and cool as she stared him down. "I assume you're here to explain yourself."

Phillip sighed, long-suffering. "I know you're disappointed, but there's no need to cause a scene, Margo." He gave the real estate developer, Russell, a smile that said he was sorry for the inconvenience.

Maggie's eyes narrowed. "A scene?" she bit out. "You've on my property, claiming you own *my* ranch, and I'm the one causing a scene?" She gave a sharp laugh. "Go to hell, Phillip," she bit out. "I don't know where you got the idea that I would roll over and let you steal my home from me, but I *will* take you to court to prove you committed fraud if you force me to."

Phillip sighed, managing to sound totally condescending. "Don't be difficult, Maggie. The deed, the tax payments, and the insurance are in my name. That's all the courts need to establish who the real owner is." He gestured to the silent police cruiser behind him. "If you keep fighting this, I'll have no choice but to get the authorities involved and have you removed for trespassing." He actually sounded sad, like the whole situation was an unfortunate misunderstanding.

Micah knew his role today was to stay patient and let Maggie and Nick handle things, but something in him snapped, and he stormed forward. "That's complete bullshit," he snarled. "We all know you forged those documents. Probably not even very well. A good lawyer will tear you apart."

Phillip eyed Micah up and down, then gave a smirk that, though lacking all of Nick's warmth and humor, reminded him of Nick's just enough that he flinched. "They're welcome to try," he said before turning back to Maggie.

"We will," Micah spat.

The real estate developer caught Micah's eye over Phillip's shoulder and raised a questioning eyebrow. Micah clenched his jaw and gave a sharp shake of his head, hoping the man would let things play out.

The screen door creaked loudly, and Nick stepped onto the porch, followed closely by Milo.

"Dominic," Phillip said, disapproval thick in his voice. "You were supposed to have this taken care of before I arrived. What good was sending you down here if you couldn't do the most basic thing I asked?"

Nick's nostrils flared, but that was the only thing that gave away his agitation, as if his father saying things like that was normal. It made Micah's chest hurt, and he desperately wanted to go to him. "Hi, Dad."

Before Phillip could respond, Xavier walked through the still-open door, hands tucked into his pockets, his relaxed posture belying the tension of the situation. Phillip's eye twitched when he saw him.

"Phillip," Xavier said. "Lovely to see you again." It was impressive how Xavier made that statement sound like it meant entirely the opposite while keeping a pleasant expression on his face.

Phillip pursed his lips as he eyed Xavier. He obviously wanted to ask what he was doing there, but he turned back to Maggie and Nick instead. "I don't have time to go back and forth with you over this. The ranch is being sold, and that's final."

Micah felt like he was about to vibrate out of his skin just listening to this guy spout his bullshit. Sensing Micah's tenuous self-control, Ryan moved to Micah's side, laying a hand on his shoulder.

"Do you know what I find interesting?" Xavier said as he descended the stairs. "You're so eager to sell this property when, according to what I've seen, it's making a sizable profit each month. It would make more sense to buy out Narissa... sorry, *Melissa*, and keep a profitable business. It made me wonder if you need the cash for other reasons."

Phillip's face went red. "That's not any of your business. Why are you even here? This is a family matter."

"All right, Phillip," Maggie said. "Between family, did you honestly think I wouldn't talk to Nicky and realize the numbers you gave him were falsified?" She gave Phillip a disappointed look. "How much money would I find missing from the ranch's accounts if I compared the numbers he brought with him to the real ones?"

"I don't know what you think you're implying—"

"Enough," Nick cut in. Micah could see him trembling with anger, but his voice remained calm. "How long have you been stealing from Maggie?"

Phillip turned on Nick, his expression outraged enough that Micah flinched back into Ryan's chest and Ryan's hand tightened on his shoulder. "I can't believe you," Phillip spat. "You would take the side of someone you barely know over your own father? I'm disappointed, Dominic. I thought you were better than that."

# TWENTY

NICK

His father was so predictable. Nick deflated, then shook his head with a low, bitter laugh. Whenever Nick did something he didn't approve of, Phillip played the guilt card. Nick expected it at this point. And, honestly, he was tired. Tired of working to earn his father's approval, tired of making excuses for Phillip's behavior, tired of clinging to a relationship that had only ever been one-sided. "It's been a long time since I thought the same of you. I'm sad to say, I wasn't even that surprised when I found out you'd lied to me." He straightened his shoulders. "I'm done, Dad."

"You're making a poor choice, Dominic. You're going to wake up tomorrow and regret this," Phillip said, taking a menacing step forward and tapping a finger to Nick's chest.

Micah, standing with Ryan a few yards away, made a distraught sound, and next to Nick, Milo's hackles went up as he growled.

Nick reached down and grabbed Milo's collar to hold him back, just in case. Phillip was a large man, but he had never been a fighter. For all he could throw insults with the best of them, he was physically soft, and Nick didn't want the dog in trouble for protecting him. He threw Micah a reassuring glance, glad to see Ryan had ahold of him.

A car door slammed, and Nick looked past his father to see a man in a police uniform making his way across the yard. Nick tensed, not sure what Phillip had told the police to get them there.

"Hey there, Maggie," the officer called. He was trim and fit in his uniform, with neat, graying brown hair and eyes hidden behind mirrored sunglasses. He looked to be in his fifties and moved with the casual confidence of someone who was used to getting his way, no questions asked.

"Good afternoon, Sheriff," Maggie said with a tight smile.

The sheriff turned to Phillip, who was still standing aggressively close. "Mr. Lauder, why don't you take a step back." He rested his hands on his utility belt, a finger tapping against his badge.

Phillip huffed but did as he was told.

"Now," the sheriff continued, "can someone explain to me what's going on here?"

Phillip spoke before anyone else had a chance. "We're here to view my property, and my access is being blocked."

The sheriff raised a skeptical eyebrow and shot Maggie a glance. "Your property?"

"Yes," Phillip insisted. "I have a copy of the deed right here." He took a folded paper from his suit pocket and shoved it in the sheriff's direction.

The sheriff took it and gave it a cursory scan. "I see."

Nick tensed. "Sir, I don't think—"

The sheriff held up a hand, silencing him. "Now, what I find interesting is that I've known Maggie for thirty years, and I've never once heard mention of you owning the ranch, Mr. Lauder."

Phillip's lips pressed into a thin, angry line. "That doesn't negate a legal document."

"No, it wouldn't." The sheriff hummed as he looked over the paper again.

"Sheriff," Maggie asked, "do you happen to know, if I suspected my tax preparer of fraud, what I should do?"

"Well," the sheriff drawled, rocking back on his heels and looking over the tense group, "tax fraud, that's a federal crime. It's not something that would be handled at the local level. There's a form you would need to file to report what you suspect. Then I believe the IRS would open an investigation and, if appropriate, seek monetary penalties and possibly a prison sentence. Now, I'm not a lawyer, but I believe if the preparer's fraud has harmed you, you can also sue."

Phillip's face was turning an interesting shade of purple, and Nick wondered if his father was going to have a heart attack. He was less concerned about it than he would have expected.

"Is it hard to start that process?" Maggie asked innocently.

"Not at all," the sheriff replied. "I'd be happy to help if you needed it."

The grinding of Phillip's teeth was practically audible. Nick wasn't sure if he wanted to laugh or cuss him out for putting everyone through this.

Xavier reached into his jacket and removed a paper and a pen, holding them out to Phillip.

Phillip looked like he was going to be sick. "What's that?"

"It's a quit claim deed. It says you relinquish all claim to Split Rock Ranch and revert the ownership to Maggie."

"That's—" Phillip raised his chin. "A quit claim deed needs to be notarized to be valid. Even if I signed it, it would be worthless."

Xavier smiled. It wasn't a smile Nick would have wanted to be on the receiving end of. "I'm so glad to know you understand the laws pertaining to validity of signatures, Phillip," he said.

"No need to worry about that," Ryan cut in. "As it happens, given that this is such a small town, the sheriff here is a notary, so he can take care of the formalities."

Nick hadn't expected the sheriff to be a witness to, much less a participant in, their plan. He didn't look concerned at all, though, and he had mentioned that he'd known Maggie thirty years. Hopefully they wouldn't end up in more trouble than when they started.

Nick counted the seconds until, finally, Phillip snatched the pen from Xavier with a snarl and scrawled his name on the document. The sheriff stepped forward and waited expectantly until Phillip produced a driver's license for him to examine.

Micah let out a whoop that made Nick crack a smile, and his father shot Micah a nasty scowl.

"I think it's time for you to head out, Mr. Lauder," the sheriff said when he was done adding his seal to the deed. "And don't think for a second that I won't come down on you with all my authority if you continue to harass these people."

Phillip looked like he had something else to say, but Nick didn't let him. "Just go, Dad," he murmured.

With a final sneer, Phillip spun on his heel and stormed back to his car.

The real estate developer gave the group of them a bemused look, then turned to Maggie. "I don't suppose you'd be interested in talking about a sale price?" he asked with a wry smile.

"No, I'm not," Maggie said firmly. "Split Rock Ranch is not for sale."

He nodded. "Good to see you again, Mr. DeCain. Please reach out anytime."

Xavier smiled and shook his hand. "And you do the same, Russell. Thank you."

With a final glance up at the farmhouse, Russell headed back to his car. Once he was gone, the sheriff turned back to the group. "Everyone okay?"

"Yeah," Micah said. "Thanks, Dad."

Nick's head jerked around from where he had been watching Phillip drive away. Micah gave him a grin and then walked over to give his father a hug. When they stood next to each other, the family resemblance was obvious. Micah had his dad's build, broad shoulders, and sharp jawline.

When Micah stepped back, Ryan took his place with a strong handshake and clasped shoulder. "Good to see you, sir," he said warmly.

"You, too, son." Then he turned to Nick and Xavier. "Sorry for the subterfuge. I'm Paul Avery, Micah's dad. Thanks for your help here. Ryan filled me in on what's been going on."

Nick flicked a glance to Ryan, who winked, leaving Nick uncertain just how much Mr. Avery knew about what had happened in the last week. He decided to go with the easier assumption. "I apologize for letting it get this far," Nick started, but Paul waved him off.

"Don't apologize for things that aren't your fault," he said easily. "Now, tell me." He turned to Maggie. "Are we still on for family dinner tonight? I'm dying for some of your brisket."

Nick liked the sheriff a lot. It turned out that Ryan had given the sheriff the heads-up about Phillip's scheme and asked his father-in-law for help. Having him there to witness Phillip's signature on the deed had tied things up even more neatly than they'd hoped when they came up with the plan.

Paul was warm and funny, and it was easy to see Micah in him. It was also hilarious to see Micah groan and complain when Paul pulled out the dad jokes. Dinner was a small gathering. They'd determined they would put off the full family dinner until Alice was feeling up to attending, though she had been called and filled in on the resolution to the situation.

"Did Micah tell you I met his mom at the station?" Paul said to Nick as they relaxed around the firepit after the meal. "Her father was the sheriff before I was, and he was good friends with your grandfather."

Nick gave a little laugh. Small towns were something else. He wondered if it was something he could get used to. He looked at Micah on the other side of him, sitting between Ryan's legs in the big Adirondack chair, leaning back against his husband's chest. He flashed Nick a grin and a wink in return. Yeah, he probably could.

"His mom was a firecracker. And whip-smart, just like her son. He definitely gets at least fifty percent of it from her." Paul and Micah exchanged a warm look.

"Seventy-thirty," Micah quipped as Ryan chuckled.

"Maybe," the sheriff said. "Just remember, I'm the trained investigator." He glanced down to where the pinky of Micah's dangling hand was occasionally brushing Nick's in the shadows.

Micah blushed but didn't pull his hand away, so Nick didn't, either, though it was a struggle to continue looking nonchalant when his heart was suddenly racing.

Xavier spoke up from Nick's other side, thankfully drawing the sheriff's attention.

Then Ryan shifted over to murmur in Nick's ear. "Stay with us tonight."

Nick shivered and nodded, then took a healthy swig of his beer. It had never occurred to him to do anything else.

Xavier left the next morning, wanting to get back to work. Nick, though... it didn't take much effort from Micah, Ryan, and Maggie to convince him to stay longer. After that, it was easy to fall into a routine with Ryan and Micah.

He was quickly becoming used to waking up tangled in too many limbs, touches that quickly turned to wandering hands and extremely enjoyable morning sex, and the easy banter they traded as they shared the one bathroom before gathering in the kitchen for breakfast. It was a heady combination—and dangerous, because he knew it couldn't last. Soon he would have to start dealing with his real life in New York.

He'd been in contact with Xavier's lawyer, who had assured him that the FBI was only interested in interviewing him for the case they were building against his father. Apparently, Phillip's greed extended beyond what he had done to Maggie and included bank fraud as well as tax evasion.

It turned out that Phillip had been inflating his net worth for years in order to take out loans, and defrauding banks was a federal crime. His sudden desire to sell the ranch hadn't been because of his pending divorce, but because he needed the profit from the sale to pay off some of his debts.

Nick heard from frantic coworkers that, before Phillip even made it back to the city, the FBI had raided his office and taken his computer and copies of all their servers. It looked like, if the FBI had their way, his father was going to spend the next ten to fifteen years in federal prison.

It was surreal when he got a call from the mechanic a few days later. His car was ready to be picked up. Nick stared at the phone. The accident at the bottom of the driveway felt like it had happened months ago. He'd been so wrapped up in life at the ranch, spending time with Ryan and Micah and getting to know Maggie again, that he'd nearly forgotten why he'd stayed with them in the first place.

Izzy made a strange face when Nick asked for a ride to the body shop but agreed easily enough. It felt fantastic to be behind the wheel of his own car again after nearly two weeks, and he made the drive home faster than was strictly legal, just to enjoy it.

The road had been repaired a few days after Ryan went into town and had words with the guy in charge. Nick grinned as he drove over the newly smooth patch and turned up the driveway to the ranch.

There weren't any trail rides, since it was a Wednesday, so the horses were out in the fields. He spotted Honey, his favorite little mare, and Lex, Micah's gelding. As Nick pulled up in front of the house, Micah walked out onto the porch. Nick grinned and stepped out of the car as Micah closed the distance between them.

"Nice ride," he said, eye-fucking the Audi as Nick preened.

"Any time you want to test-drive it, you let me know," Nick replied, putting just enough innuendo into his tone that Micah laughed and his cheeks pinked.

Nick crowded him against the side of the car and dove in for a toe-curling kiss. Micah tasted like coffee and sex. "Just what were you up to while I was in town? And did you save any for me?"

Micah wrapped his arms around Nick's neck and leaned in for another kiss. "Absolutely," he murmured.

"Hey. Get a room, you two," Archer called from the barn.

Micah lifted a hand to flip Archer off, even as he took a step back from Nick. "I forgot to tell you. Now that everyone's home, Ry and I have the next two days off. We're going to head up the mountain to Keegan's cabin. Think I can talk you into coming with us?"

Nick winced. He'd been hoping to delay this conversation. "Now that I have my car, I actually need to head back to New York tomorrow."

Micah's face fell. He looked away abruptly, but not before Nick saw his eyes glisten. "Oh. Right. Of course. I shouldn't have assumed."

Nick felt like a complete asshole. He shouldn't have said it that way. "Sweetheart—"

Micah flinched. "No. No, I get it. You have a life to get back to. This was fun, but—"

"Hey." Nick grabbed Micah's arms as he tried to turn away. "Don't do that." He waited for Micah to meet his eyes, but he wouldn't. With a frustrated growl, he turned toward the house, pulling Micah with him. "Where's your husband?" His voice was too sharp, he knew, but he couldn't help himself. He was only having this conversation once.

"He was finishing the lunch dishes, but—"

Nick yanked open the screen door and ushered Micah inside instead of letting him finish. "Ryan?" he called.

"Kitchen," Ryan called back.

Micah squawked as Nick pulled him in that direction, coming to stop in front of Ryan and pushing a squirming Micah, who was grumbling about being manhandled in the not-fun way, into his arms.

Nick took a breath and tried to calm his pounding heart as he looked at the two men who'd come to mean so much to him in such a short time.

He didn't know what to say.

"Nicky?" Ryan prompted. Which was when Nick realized he was just staring at them silently.

He tried to sort through what he wanted to say and, in the end, ended up blurting it out. “I have to go.”

Micah looked at the ground, his fingers tightening on Ryan’s arm, but Ryan didn’t seem surprised. “Figured that was coming soon,” he said carefully.

Nick’s chest hurt, but he fought for composure. “Phillip was arrested this morning. The arraignment is Friday.”

“And you need to be there.”

Nick nodded, feeling like he was making the biggest mistake of his life.

“When do you need to leave?”

As soon as possible, was the honest answer. It was a ten-hour drive—without traffic. But instead, he said, “In the morning.”

Micah was looking at him like Nick had broken his heart, and Nick couldn’t help but feel he’d done the same to himself. “I want,” he started, then stopped to swallow his emotions and steady his voice, pasting a smile on his face that Ryan and Micah could probably see straight through. “We should keep in touch—”

“Cut the bullshit, Nicky,” Ryan said, half-frustrated, half-amused. He stepped forward and slid a hand to the back of Nick’s neck, drawing him in until their foreheads were pressed together. Nick let out a shaky sigh as Micah gripped his hand, twining their fingers together. “You’re gonna call us when you get home, and we’re gonna pick a weekend to come up and visit.”

Nick shut his eyes, embarrassed to find tears blurring his vision.

"Yeah," Micah chimed in. "You're a fool if you think we're gonna let you go that easily."

Nick huffed a laugh and shifted to pull Micah more firmly against his side. There was no way it was going to work long term, but fuck if he didn't want to try.

Alice, Archer, and Izzy joined them at the house that night. Maggie pulled out all the stops for his goodbye dinner, including several nice bottles of wine. He was pleasantly buzzed when Alice dropped down next to him on the sofa.

"You're coming back, right?" she asked, sounding sure of his answer. "'Cause it would be a huge mistake not to. We all like you, and we want you here."

Nick rolled his eyes and took another sip of his wine. "That's the second time I've been called a fool today."

Alice scoffed and shoved his arm. "Prove us wrong, then." She grinned, and Nick found himself smiling back.

"We'll see."

It was still dark out when Nick woke. He lifted a hand to rub the sleep from his eyes, wondering what was going on. His alarm hadn't gone off yet. Then he felt the hand stroking over his abs. They'd gone to bed naked, after several rounds of what Nick could only call lovemaking. It had been heavy and intense, tinged with a bit of desperation. It was also some of the best sex Nick had ever had, and after both of his partners taking him multiple times, he knew he'd be feeling it the whole drive home and then some.

Worth it.

He caught Ryan's hand and lifted it to his lips. "I know I didn't hear my alarm," he whispered as he brushed his lips against Ryan's palm.

Ryan's fingers curled around his jaw and tugged him into a long, deep kiss that left Nick breathless. Nick only broke it when he tried to press closer and Micah gave a sleepy grumble from where he was wrapped around Nick's back.

Nick had ended up in the middle after they wore themselves out and then cleaned up in the shower. Micah had insisted on being the big spoon, and Nick could see no reason to argue. Ryan had pressed against him on his other side, wrapping solid, muscular arms around him. Nick had fallen asleep quickly and slept hard.

"You've got about ten minutes," Ryan murmured, answering his unasked question. "Sorry. I couldn't help myself." He slid his hand to the back of Nick's neck and gave a squeeze. "Micah's not gonna say anything, because he's afraid of jinxing it, but I need you to know how special you are. This would never have happened if it wasn't you who turned up on our doorstep."

Heat swept through Nick, and he had to stop himself from saying too much by kissing Ryan, hard and fast. "You too," he whispered into Ryan's mouth. "This is all your fucking fault."

Ryan huffed a laugh and kissed him harder. "Come back to us soon, Nicky."

# TWENTY-ONE

MICAH

"How was court?" Micah asked, balancing his laptop on his knees as he reached for his water. It was hot today, which was unusual but not unheard of up in the mountains. Unfortunately, the farmhouse had never had central air. They had a split unit up in the bedroom, but the downstairs was roasting.

"Boring." Nick sighed. "We're in the evidence phase, so it's hours of forensic accounting babble interspersed with the lawyers asking for clarification." He leaned back in the seat at his kitchen counter, a take-out box from his favorite Thai place in front of him. Micah worried about his diet, but he tried to keep his mouth shut. Nick was under a lot of stress lately, and if getting takeout helped, Micah wasn't going to argue with him. Besides, that place was delicious. Nick had taken them when they visited.

That had been a fantastic four days. They'd gone in the middle of the week, right before the trial began. Maggie's summer help had started, two kids who were home from college, but things hadn't quite picked up yet, so he and Ryan snuck away.

New York City had been amazing. Micah had been there a few times—he'd been close enough, going to college in Boston—but it was different seeing it with someone who lived there. Nick took them to all his favorite spots, and Micah had fallen for him just a little more. It had been painful to leave at the end of the week, but Nick had promised he'd come back to the ranch as soon as he could.

Then the trial started. And kept going. Nick attended every day, listening to all the accusations against his father. Micah worried that he still felt responsible, but Nick promised him that wasn't it. He just felt an obligation, as his son, to be there, even if Nick fully believed Phillip belonged in jail.

Nick had cooperated fully with the FBI and turned over every bit of evidence he could find to help convict his father for not only bank fraud, but also fraudulent accounting on behalf of his clients. Phillip's company, Lauder Financial Management, would go down with him. The trial was national news, so there was no way anyone would invest with them again. It meant Nick was currently unemployed, but that wasn't exactly his priority at the moment.

"How many more days do you think it'll be?" Micah asked hopefully. Earlier in the month, the lawyers had been projecting a five-week trial. They were on week four.

"I wish I knew." Nick rubbed a hand over his face, shaking his head, and Micah felt a pang. He wanted so badly to hug Nick. He settled for distracting him, telling him about an "I want to speak to your manager" type his dad had encountered at the gas station. The story had Nick laughing, and that's how Ryan found them when he came in from closing the barn for the night.

Micah saw Nick's focus shift first, then heard the dogs and felt an arm drape over his shoulders and a kiss drop on his temple.

"Hey, you two," Ryan said, his voice warm with affection.

Micah watched Nick try to hide his emotions, but after months of video calls, Micah had gotten good at reading him.

"Ryan," Nick responded.

Micah turned his head to glimpse his husband in nothing but low-slung jeans, his tanned chest bare and smudged with dirt. He'd probably already dropped his sweat-soaked shirt in the laundry. Micah inhaled the scent of sweat, dirt, and horses, and it made his mouth water.

He looked back at Nick and caught him wetting his lips, his eyes locked on Ryan. Micah grinned. "Something I can do for you, Nicky?"

Nick groaned and reached below the line of the counter, probably adjusting himself. "I need to finish eating right now, but later? Hell yes."

Micah wiggled eagerly in his seat. He liked video sex with Nick—not as much as real sex with Nick, but it was a close second. Nick had a creative mind, and he was great at giving Micah directions. They'd spent some very satisfying nights with Nick telling Micah exactly what he wanted him to do to Ryan.

It wasn't as good as being in the same room, but it was still fun and sexy.

They eventually had to let Nick go so they could get to their own dinner with Maggie and Izzy. Sometimes Nick would join them, but he said he wanted to get cleaned up and told Micah to call him back when they were upstairs for the night.

Micah shut his eyes and sighed when the screen went black, needing a minute to push down the feeling of loss that got stronger every time Nick ended their calls.

"I miss him, too," Ryan said, hugging him from behind.

Micah clutched one of Ryan's arms and took a steadying breath. "It sucks," he managed to say without sounding too watery. "I never expected this to happen."

Ryan urged him up and around the couch so he could hug him for real. "Tell me."

Micah let his head drop to Ryan's shoulder. "It makes me feel like I did when I left you to go to college," he whispered, guilt pressing on his throat.

Ryan tucked his fingers under Micah's chin and tipped his head up. "Before he left, I told him he was something special." He kissed Micah's forehead. "He's got us both twisted up in knots, baby. And I'm not inclined to try to get loose."

Micah's eyes burned as relief swept through him, washing away the lingering guilt. "I think I might have some pretty strong feelings for him."

Ryan squeezed him. "I think I have those same feelings. Now the question is, what are we gonna do about it?"

# TWENTY-TWO

NICK

Nick sat on the hard wooden bench in the courthouse hallway and stared at his hands. He hated how familiar the sounds and sights of the trial recess had become. The buzz of voices, the clerks hurrying back and forth, and the witnesses and spectators from the gallery milling about as they waited for the bailiff to call them back in. He hadn't thought they would still be here after six weeks, but the trial had been dragged out by his father's lawyers' constant objections and filing of motions.

Nick was tired, and he wanted to go home.

The problem was, he didn't want to go home to his apartment near Columbus Circle. No, he wanted to go home to Split Rock Ranch. To Ryan and Micah. To Aunt Maggie and the people he was already thinking of as family.

It had been a long four months since he left to handle his father's mess. There was only so much he could do, but he'd been working to help Phillip's former employees find new jobs and to recommend new investment firms to the clients that somehow still trusted him.

The only bright spot had been the short four days Micah and Ryan had spent with him. They'd split their time between Nick's favorite spots in the city and Nick's favorite spots in his bedroom. As much as he wanted to pretend it had all been about pent-up lust, he knew it was more than that. Missing them felt like a fist wrapped around his heart. Some days it squeezed tighter than others.

There was a holiday weekend coming up, and Nick was hoping he could get out of town for part of it.

It wasn't that he didn't talk to them on a regular basis. They had video calls at least twice a week, and Micah was a texting fiend. Nick now had pictures in his photo gallery of everything from awkward foals to Micah with his gorgeous lips wrapped around Ryan's dick. Ryan had been the photographer for that one.

It wasn't enough.

He was pulling out his phone, intending to start it up and send Micah a "Happy Friday" text, when a pair of glossy leather shoes stepped into his field of vision.

"Hello, son," Phillip said. His voice was filled with false confidence but also rougher than the last time Nick had heard it. Phillip hadn't testified on his own behalf, so he hadn't spoken in court since the not-guilty plea.

Nick slid the phone back into his pocket. Then he climbed to his feet and folded his arms across his chest, looking down at his father. It was strange: after everything that had happened, he only felt blank, with a hint of annoyance. "Phillip," he said and watched his father's expression flicker.

Phillip cleared his throat and drew back his shoulders. Nick glanced around and saw the lawyers standing nearby, but they weren't paying attention to the conversation. "How are you holding up?" Phillip asked.

Nick would have laughed if the question were honest. Instead, he asked, "What do you want?"

Phillip huffed and shifted his weight. He looked older than he had the last time Nick had been this close to him. His skin was gray, and Nick could tell he was wearing concealer to cover the dark circles under his eyes. "Why do you go right to the assumption that I want something?"

Nick stared him down and didn't respond.

Phillip shifted again, then smoothed down the sleeve of his suit jacket. "My lawyers asked me to speak with you."

That put Nick's hackles up. "Did they?"

"They think it would help humanize me to the jury if you explained how we lost your mother and how I fought to give you a good upbringing. It could help them understand that this was a mistake that got out of hand."

Nick nearly laughed in his face. No. Just no. He was done. He turned on his heel and walked away.

"Dominic!" Phillip called after him, voice sharp with reproach.

Nick didn't stop. There was no reason to. Not when all he'd ever be to his father was a convenient tool, and there were people waiting for him who valued him as so much more. He went straight out the front doors and down the courthouse steps, ignoring the gaggle of reporters who began shouting questions as soon as they recognized him, the cameras flashing in his face.

"No comment," he said as he strode down the street, leaving his father for the last time.

Nick stepped down from his new Land Rover and shouldered his duffel bag, shutting the door and hitting the button to lock it. The SUV chirped twice as the locks engaged. He knew he didn't really need to lock it, but it was going to take some time for his brain to adjust to the country.

He took a deep breath, letting the clean mountain air fill his lungs. As he let it out, he felt like he also released years' worth of tension. It was finally over. Or maybe he should say, it was finally beginning.

"Nick!"

The familiar shout made him grin. He turned and dropped his bag to catch Micah as he flung himself into Nick's arms.

"Nick, Nick," Micah repeated in between breathless kisses, his hands cupping Nick's face, his knees gripping Nick's hips. "You're here. You're actually here," he mumbled into Nick's mouth.

Nick laughed and splayed his hands beneath Micah's ass to hold him in place as he kissed him back. "I'm here," he agreed, soaking in the warm, solid feel of Micah's body.

A few minutes later a throat cleared nearby, and Micah pulled back to look over his shoulder at his husband. "Nick's here," Micah said helpfully.

Ryan shook his head. A fond smile curled the corners of his mouth and made Nick's stomach swoop. "I can see that, baby." He pulled off his hat as he stepped forward and wrapped his hand behind Nick's neck in a familiar hold. Then he tugged him into his own kiss.

Nick groaned as Ryan took control of his mouth. He had to release Micah with one hand and grab Ryan's arm for support when his knees went weak. That gave Micah a chance to wriggle to the ground. Nick groped for him but missed, and then Ryan was pressing him against the side of the SUV, his hard body firm against Nick's. Nick wanted the moment to go on forever.

Then Micah made an impatient sound, and they finally broke apart. Nick glanced over to see Micah holding his duffel bag.

"Is this all you brought?" Micah asked. It was only a weekend bag, so Nick understood Micah's uncertainty. He'd brought more the first time, when he only planned to stay a few days.

He stepped out from between Ryan and the SUV, circling around to the trunk, which he opened to reveal it was filled to the ceiling. "I had to trade in the Audi, because it wouldn't all fit," he explained. "And Xavi is in New York at the moment, so he's bringing the rest when he comes to visit in a few weeks."

Xavier had insisted on helping with the ranch's running costs until Maggie's finances had been sorted out from Phillip's. They'd discovered that Phillip hadn't been paying the ranch's bills the last eighteen months, despite Maggie sending the money, so there had been property taxes due, as well as late fees, and unpaid insurance premiums. They'd been scrambling to deal with those bills until Xavier stepped in. And after hearing that it would hardly make a dent in Xavier's bank account—and insisting on paying him interest—Maggie had agreed to let him help. Neither Nick nor Xavier was going to tell her just how low her interest rate was if she didn't ask.

Xavier had declared he was going to be in town on a regular basis, which Nick was happy about. Xavi claimed he was "checking on his investment," but Nick knew it was more than that. He wasn't going to complain. He'd missed his friend, with Xavi living in LA while Nick was in New York.

Micah was staring at him with wide eyes, and Ryan looked torn between wary and happy.

"What?" Nick asked innocently.

"You're—" Micah's voice broke, and he tried again. "You're staying?"

"Well," Nick hedged, "Maggie doesn't have a guest room in the cottage, so I'll need to find a place. Know of anywhere with a comfortable bed and a working bathro—"

Before he could finish, Micah was in his arms again, peppering his face with kisses. "I love you. I love you. I love you," he gasped as he clung to Nick, tears streaking down his face.

Nick's heart did something ridiculous, and his eyes burned, but he smiled. "I love you too." He kissed Micah back, long and hard, before turning to Ryan, who was looking rather smug. "Don't give me that look," Nick complained as he pulled Ryan closer.

"What look?" Ryan asked, wrapping one arm around Nick's shoulders and the other around Micah's waist.

"The look that says you knew all along."

Ryan flashed a smile. "I guessed." He leaned in and pressed a sweet kiss to Nick's lips. "I knew, if we were patient, you'd figure it out too."

Nick *humph*ed. "Just for that, I'm not saying it back," he teased.

Ryan grinned. Nick felt the movement of his mouth. "Even if I say"—he shifted to whisper in Nick's ear—"I love you so goddamn much, and I'm so fucking glad you're here, Nicky."

Nick trembled and closed his eyes, enjoying their arms around him as their words sank into his skin. He'd never thought this could be possible, hadn't even let himself dream of it. "Asshole," he finally muttered, his voice wet. "I love you too."

A moment later he heard his name called again, and he broke away from his two... partners? Lovers? Boyfriends? They would work on it... and turned to greet Maggie, who was walking briskly across the front lawn to him, no sign of her cane or a limp in her step.

"Nicky," she said with a laugh. "I'm so glad you made it." She nudged Micah and Ryan away and wrapped him in a hug. He shut his eyes and hugged her back, loving her familiar strength.

"Thanks, Aunt Maggie. It's really good to be home."

# EPILOGUE
NICK

"WE SHOULD PROBABLY GET out there," Nick suggested, not all that convincingly, as Micah pushed him into the newly finished hall bathroom and shut the door behind them.

"We will," Micah agreed with a glint in his eyes. "Soon." He slid to his knees, nimble fingers already unfastening Nick's pants and pulling out his rapidly hardening cock.

Nick groaned as Micah sucked him down, not bothering to muffle himself. Everyone else was out on the back deck sitting down to family dinner. There was no one to hear his curse as Micah's tongue flicked over his Prince Albert piercing.

Micah hummed happily. "I love this," he said before sinking down and swallowing around the head, sending sparks of pleasure racing up Nick's spine. Nick sank his hands into Micah's hair and gave up any attempt at protest. Micah's mouth was heaven, and Nick was all for using the hell out of it. When Micah reached up to play with his balls, he let his head fall back against the door with a thump. Fuck, that was good. It hadn't taken Micah long to learn all his sensitive spots. He nearly choked on his spit, though, when Micah's fingers continued back and brushed the place where he was still wet and open from Ryan bending him over the end of the bed and fucking him raw not an hour before. He groaned when Micah pressed in gently, searching for his prostate. Sneaky little brat. He knew perfectly well that Nick was going to be oversensitive.

It didn't take much to push him over the edge, just a few careful strokes, the tight squeeze of Micah's throat, and the realization that Micah was jerking himself off while he blew Nick's mind.

Nick came with a shout that wasn't muffled at all, then waited, panting, with his back braced against the door, while Micah cleaned them both up.

"You want to tell me what that was all about, sweetheart?" Nick finally asked when his brain felt semi-functional again.

Micah shrugged. "Ryan said you were nervous about the full family dinner. I don't know why. You know everyone already."

Nick shook his head. It was hard to explain. And if having a touch of anxiety about finding his place with this group of people meant he got fucked six ways from Sunday, followed almost immediately by a surprise blow job, he wasn't going to argue. He gave Micah a kiss instead. "I'm feeling better already. Feel free to help me relax any time." He smirked at Micah's eye roll, then took his offered hand and let himself be led out to the packed deck.

All the usual suspects were there, plus a few extras. Archer and Alice were already seated at the table with their food, safely out of the chaos. Izzy was still in the process of filling his plate.

Keegan ushered Maggie away from the grill and to a chair because they all knew if they didn't stop her, she'd cook through the whole meal. That left Micah's dad tending the grill and chatting with Xavier, who was in town for the weekend.

Off to the side, Finn was looking unsure and holding tightly to a glass of something colorful. Nick had a feeling the drink was Izzy's handiwork and would go a long way toward helping the guy relax. Micah had invited Finn as a thank-you for his help back when Phillip had been up to his tricks, and also to hopefully get him to loosen up and feel more a part of the group. As Micah put it, the queer townies needed to stick together—although this place was about as queer-friendly as a small town could get. The liberal tourists helped a lot with that. As did the accepting sheriff with the openly gay son who just happened to be married to a well-liked member of the community and in a triad relationship with the brand-new town manager.

Nick hadn't intended to look for a job right away, but when it was discovered that the water pipes that supplied the majority of downtown were past their usable life span and crumbling under the harsh winters they had up here, the previous guy up and quit—though there were rumors he was forced out—and the position was suddenly available. Nick had applied on the strength of his management skills and his financial knowledge. Being the nephew of one of the town's favorite residents and the sort-of son-in-law of the sheriff didn't hurt either. Nepotism at its finest, as Paul liked to say.

They settled around the table, Ryan at the head, with Micah and Nick on one side of him and Maggie on the other. The rest fanned out, not much caring where they ended up. Micah watched carefully, as he was still hoping that Keegan and Finn might hit it off. Nick didn't have the heart to tell him that, from what he'd observed, Finn had eyes for someone else entirely. And that that someone was rather interested in the slim young man with the striking eyes.

Nick hid a grin when Xavier ended up at the far end of the table with Finn next to him. His ex-husband had such a type. It would be hilarious if it weren't so cute watching him try to draw Finn out of his shell while Finn blushed and refused to look up from his plate.

Keegan, Micah's intended target, didn't seem at all concerned that his potential date was talking to someone else. He was engaged in a conversation with Archer about his upcoming art show. Izzy and Alice likewise had their heads together, probably brainstorming the next big change they wanted to make to the barn. Now that cash flow was easier, thanks to Xavier's help, and Maggie was expecting a large settlement from Phillip's conviction, they were coming up with ways for the ranch to expand. There was even talk of bringing back riding lessons for kids, now that Maggie was able to get around better, though Nick was staying away from that one for the moment.

The conversation flowed easily, as did the food and drinks. When they finished eating, they relaxed around the fire pit, telling jokes and stories of past gatherings.

After getting another drink, Micah settled in Nick's lap. Ryan dropped down next to them, and when Nick leaned into his space, he reached up with blunt nails to lightly scratch the back of Nick's neck.

Nick soaked it all in: the sounds of his family's voices mixed with the drone of crickets and the occasional croak of a bullfrog. He heard an unfamiliar laugh and saw Finn peeking shyly up at Xavier, a pretty blush on his cheeks.

He put his lips next to Micah's ear. "Don't look now, but I think your plans for Finn are about to fall through."

Micah did look but shrugged it off easily. "Hey, I just want my people to be happy."

Nick chuckled and glanced at Ryan, who was watching them warmly. "And Xavi is your people now?"

Micah scoffed and leaned back against Nick's chest, and Nick wrapped his arm around Micah's waist. Ryan took his free hand and laced their fingers together. "Of course he is. As soon as *you* became my people, your best friend was stuck with us too." Micah turned his head and pressed his lips to Nick's cheek. "And you, my sexy boyfriend, aren't going anywhere."

Nick laughed softly and relaxed further, giving Ryan's hand a squeeze and getting a smile in return. No, he definitely wasn't going anywhere. Not when he was finally home.

**Wondering what Nick, Ryan, and Micah got up to the first time they actually made it to a bed? Visit my website by scanning the QR code on the back cover for a spicy outtake!**

**Next is Something Unintended: A Split Rock Ranch Novella, followed by Xavier and Finn's book, Something Unforgettable.**

THANK YOU for reading Something Unexpected, the second book in the Split Rock Ranch series! I hope you enjoyed getting to know Nick, Micah, Ryan, and all the other characters that make up the Split Rock Ranch universe.

If you want to share your love for these guys, please leave a review on your platform of choice.

I love to hear what parts of my stories you liked and share sneak peaks of my upcoming releases over in my Facebook group, Rory's Renegades. You can find up by scanning the QR code on the back cover and following the links to Facebook.

And finally, thank you so much to my editor, Alicia Z. Ramos, who spent countless hours making sure my plot worked, my words flowed, and that the laws that were broken actually made sense! I don't know where I would have been without you! And to The Bunny Squad, especially Sarah Honey, who supported and encouraged me as I wrote this, alpha read, beta read, proofread, and kept me pointed in the right direction. I could not have done it without you!

Rory Maxwell discovered romance novels on her mom's bookshelf when she was probably too young to be reading them—the reward for being a nosy kid with great reading comprehension. The magic of a dial-up internet connection led her to the wonderful world of MM fanfiction a few years later and she fell in love with the genre. In 2019 she woke up with a plot bunny, opened a word doc, and started trying to figure out how this writing stuff worked.

Rory grew up outside of Washington, DC, moved away, and then came back for reasons she doesn't fully understand. An artist and writer, she always has too many exciting ideas and not nearly enough free time. One day, she hopes to escape to the mountains where she can work from home and write as much as she wants. In the meantime, she splits her time between her day job and writing MM romance with endearing characters, lots of feels, plenty of heat, and a dash of kink.

Come find me in all the places I'm social by scanning the QR code on the back cover!

## Also by Rory Maxwell:

**The Split Rock Ranch Series**

MM & MMM Small Town Romance

**Something Undeniable - A Prequel**

Micah/Ryan

**Something Unexpected**

Nick/Micah/Ryan

**Something Unintended: A Split Rock Ranch Novella**

Hunter/Eli

**Something Unforgettable (coming late 2023)**

Xavier/Finn

**and more to come...**